THE MOVE MENT

Byron Bay: A cult classic

THE MOVE MENT

Byron Bay: A cult classic

KATE HAMILTON

Book cover designed by Luke Harris, Working Type Book Design.

This is a work of fiction. All the characters are fictional with no connection to any real person. Like all works of fiction, it is set within the background of the real world, but any reference to an actual place or entity is purely for this purpose and readers must not assume that any part of this story has any basis in reality.

Paperback – 978-1-7637271-0-6
Digital ebook – 978-1-7637271-1-3

We acknowledge the Traditional Owners
of the Bunjalung country, Australia and recognise
their continuing connection to land, waters and culture.

*This book is dedicated
to my brother Roger Hamilton.*

ABOUT THE AUTHOR

Originally from Canberra, Kate Hamilton spent most of her adult life working in Sydney. Before she became a writer, she had a career in higher education and was a politician and a CEO for a while. After that she earned a Doctor of Philosophy at the University Technology Sydney, however she decided to embrace fiction rather than academia. As a member of Sisters in Crime, she is delighted by the recent surge of women crime writers in Australia.

Hamilton's debut novel, *An Unholy Alliance*, is a whodunnit with attitude while her second novel, *The Movement*, is fast-paced, funny and readable and written by someone with lived experience and a healthy scepticism. Her readers are all those people who love reading crime and mystery fiction to be entertained, stimulated and amused and to lose themselves.

Kate lives in the inner west of Sydney and is writing her third book, *Murder in Marrickville*.

CHAPTER 1

ucy Lush Box was agitated. The house meeting had not gone well. She felt tired and hadn't slept. Moreover, her argument that, since she worked in a café to pay the rent, she should do less washing up, was strenuously contested by her housemates.

The warm night was clinging to Lucy as she tossed and turned trying unsuccessfully, to fall asleep. Her fine hair stuck to her neck and neither meditation nor self-fulfilment welcomed slumber. As she lay in her bed listening to the sounds of the night, she became aware of the distant humming of a plane engine and glancing over at the hands on the Mickey Mouse alarm clock beside the bed she saw it was midnight.

The Movement's administrators, the Elders of Isis, rented the house to accommodate the overflow of seekers, not far from the main ashram on the outskirts of Byron Bay township, an idyllic coastal town reposing on the edge of the Pacific Ocean in Northern New South Wales. It embraced several industries including tourism and retail. However, a permanent contingent of hippies resided in or near the town either on the dole or self-employed in the healing economy. Jobs such as massage, yoga, chakra realignment and tantric sex-sessions designed to allow participants to shed their middle-class inhibitions, along with their money.

It was the night of Valentine's Day when Lucy heard the light plane flying low over her house and circling the landing strip sounding so close she felt afrai it may crash. Why was it flying at night, she wondered, it seemed late? The engine rumbled and prepared to land. Without hesitation, she leapt up from bed, pulled on her shorts, slipped her sneakers over her bare feet and grabbed a penlight. Pushing the flyscreen up, she ducked out of her bedroom window which was an easy drop into the garden and looked up at the moon waxing full in a starry sky. During her exploration of the ramshackle garden, she had discovered an overgrown path running through depleted flower beds and past lilies and taller plants until it petered out in a deep grove of exotic trees, ferns and violets. It was enchanting. Beyond the fence the flat spaces of sandy soil grasped low clumps of banksias and saltbushes interspersed with scrubby trees and grass tussocks battered by salty winds. She flicked her torch on briefly when she reached the path leading to the bottom of the garden. The thunk as the plane's wheels hit the hard surface of the airstrip was echoed by another sound that caught her attention – the low burr of diesel motors moving towards the plane.

Her nerves fluttering she tip-toed further along the path before slipping into a secret hiding hole beneath the low branches of a tree stand whose glossy leaves folded about her. The foliage prickled her bare arms a little as she was only wearing a cotton T-shirt and shorts. Crouching low, close to a wire fence entwined by soft weeds and clumps of grasses that formed the border between the garden and the airstrip, she studied the light plane arriving on the runway. Lucy possessed enough common sense to realise that whatever was about to take place probably wasn't legal, but curiosity got the better of her.

In the distance, two four-wheel drive vehicles were cruising slowly towards the twin-engine plane that had taxied down the strip, turned around and motored back toward them before coming to a standstill about half-way along. The Land Cruisers moved forward to one side of the plane lining up end to end and a gang of four shadowy and muscular men climbed out of their vehicles only a hundred metres from where Lucy was hiding in the bushes. A sweet, salty breeze blew across the landing strip taunting an ancient wind socket as it tugged and flapped on the roof of the dilapidated hangar. She dared not move away for fear of attracting their attention. Slowing her breathing down, the way she had been taught in meditation, she managed to overcome a powerful urge to flee. One of the men walked away from the vehicles and stood looking about the airstrip and surrounding bush. He was alert and tense like an animal looking out for danger as he scanned the landscape his eyes resting on the foliage at the bottom of the garden. Lucy froze as she watched the man sniffing the air to identify any strange scents. Instinctively, she raised her fingers to her nose. Oh no! She whispered, jamming them between her legs and squeezing her eyes shut.

The plane's engine was switched off prompting the watcher to stride back to join the others.

Swinging his legs out of the cockpit, the pilot climbed onto the wing in one smooth motion. He was wearing faded cut-off jeans with a dark sleeveless T-shirt and rubber-soled lace-up boots. He waved a hand to the convoy waiting below and crossed the wing to the side door of the plane before heaving it open. From inside, he pulled out an aluminium ladder hooking it onto a couple of notches on the door opening and dropping it to the ground. Expertly he descended and walked towards the waiting gang. After conferring in low voices, they went to work unloading the cargo from the Land Cruisers onto the plane. Canvas tray covers came off and one man per vehicle leapt into the back and began lifting large bales wrapped in black plastic over the edge of each tray onto the backs of the other guys on the ground. The bales were awkward and bulky, and the men grabbed the twine tied around them for the short distance to the waiting pilot.

Scaling the ladder, the pilot adroitly moved back over to the open side door ready to receive each bale with a metal hook to hoist it into the belly of the plane. With a nod the older man signalled commencement. It was a smooth and efficient operation; after five minutes the pilot held up his hand in a stop sign, so the four men paused as he shoved the bales further into the plane's body then gave the come-on beckoning signal with one arm. The men responded and brought the rest over until all twenty bales were loaded into the plane. The door shut with a thump when the pilot locked it while the others sealed up the canvas covers of their vehicle trays.

Time became slower for Lucy waiting in the bushes,

shivering a little as an almost full moon cast an eery light on the people below. Growing up on a hippy commune had taught her that the black plastic bales were almost certainly a marijuana crop, and the men, most likely were growers and dealers. The gang of men now gathered around the pilot talking in a rumble of low voices. An older man was clearly the leader, and they were all earthy, physically capable people who had worked hard and now smelled of sweat.

Without warning, a woman stuck her head out the cockpit door startling the gang members. Her caramel skin and a tangle of hair illuminated by moonlight.

'Brendon!' She hissed urgently. 'Hurry up!' It was an order.

Automatically, two of the gang stepped back and pulled guns out, one trained on the pilot and the other on the woman co-pilot.

'Who the fuck is she?' The older guy growled.

Lucy emitted a tiny peep.

'Oh God! Oh God!' She gasped into the bushes willing the men to go away and not shoot each other. Brendon, the pilot, responded in a savage, hoarse voice.

'Keep your friggin' shirts on will ya! Call the boys off. That's my co-pilot. She's staunch.'

The older man's stance changed slightly, and he muttered to the men who pocketed their guns but remained edgy. Having delivered the order, the woman co-pilot disappeared into the cockpit again. The older man shoved a bag of money at Brendon which he stashed in a backpack as the co-pilot started the plane's motor. Abruptly, the leader and gang turned and stalked toward their vehicles driving off slowly without looking back. The pilot hoisted himself quickly back onto the wing of the plane, dropped into the cockpit and soon was taxiing down the runway before boosting the engines to lift its nose, and soaring off into the night sky. The whole thing had taken less than twenty minutes. Twenty minutes that would ultimately, change the course of Lucy's life.

Once she was sure all the men had gone, Lucy scampered back to the house with her breathing ragged and her heart in turmoil. All was quiet as she climbed through her window shutting and locking the flyscreen and the window behind her. Diving into bed and pulling the sheets over her head she scrunched down and hugged her knees to her body. When her breathing and heart rate had returned to normal, she got out of bed again and snuck around the house locking windows and doors. Meanwhile, her housemates slumbered and, not for the first time, Lucy wished Gil was here to hold her in his arms and comfort her. Instead, she hugged her pillow hard. Alone in her bed the night of the drug deal, Lucy gave in to fatigue. She felt small and confused. Confused because she didn't know what the Movement's position was on witnessing criminal drug transactions. Would the Elders advise that she ignore it? What if someone had been shot? Surely murder was illegal and wrong.

* * *

Looking back, Lucy recognised that her migration to the Seraphic Throng of Heavenly Light or The Movement, appeared counterintuitive. She thought they had a more realistic idea of what was going on for humans for example, they celebrated the physical and sensual life on earth, they had a leader or guru and most of all, they had a following of young people who lived together, worked, fell in love, laughed, and enjoyed themselves. Lucy was raised at Paradise Falls, a hippy commune, while her parents belonged to an Indian religious sect, the Sanyasin, informally called the Orange People by Lucy and her friends.

Despite her youthful appearance Lucy was insightful about human nature but she understood she needed to grow up, not least because she was still young and didn't have much life experience yet. The group house on Callistemon Street in Tyagarah was occupied by Lucy and three other members of the Movement. The weatherboards were faded and peeling adding to the sense of emptiness on the street, as though a whole community of people had left the area. Most of the other houses stood vacant with their gardens dried out and shrivelled over years of neglect. The group moved into the house for a variety of reasons: some personal like Gilgamesh Soul Poet, who was escaping his women wanting more. Lucy put her hand up to live in the Tyagarah house when her friend Hilary Hargreaves said she would join her. Hilly had a car and the two young women formed a close relationship. Hilly drove Lucy to work in Byron Bay terrifying her with her dangerous driving. Gil was a member of the Movement before Lucy joined and his thick dark hair tied in a Shogun knot on his head pierced by two chopsticks added to his appearance of being arrogant and emotionally inaccessible, coasting through life, pleasant but uncommitted. He expressed a philosophical interest in saving the world through spiritual transformation though Lucy thought he was a warrior who hadn't found a cause.

Unlike Seth, the guru of the Movement, who was wholly immersed in what it offered him and what he could get out of it.

Lucy had just turned eighteen when she joined the Movement and understood the importance of becoming a noviciate by undergoing the Sacred Naming Ritual. This ritual was an important part of becoming one of this group by giving up her birth name, and receiving her Vibrational Name and the Blessing that accompanied it. All religions had spiritual names she reasoned, like the Hare Krishnas or the Divine Lighters. For the members, called seekers, religion was their life. Because they belonged to the Movement, they were connected via a worldwide net in tune with the vibrations of the universe. All the members were taught devotion to their guru, Seth, Lord High Alchemist, and to Lucy, they were not a cult, but a true religion, she was sure of this. After all, Seth was a follower of Hermes Trismegistus, the renowned Egyptian Magician and Alchemist and had studied his treatises and ancient texts!

The Movement's promise of prosperity and fulfilment, accompanied by a belief in perpetual happiness, proved deeply seductive. However, the attraction for younger seekers lay predominantly in being part of a like-minded group that shared the beliefs of an elite receiving privileged teaching about the nature of the universe and their part in it. They felt special. Lucy vividly remembered the naming ceremony as it was held only a few months ago. The members of the Movement had all gathered at a sacred place called Blue Knob and were sitting in a circle around Seth. He had a perspex purple ball on his lap with name labels inside the globe and an opening at the top. He chanted the Holy Song of Songs, and everyone joined in spontaneously.

'Om Mani Shanti. Om Mani Shanti,' they chanted whilst the drummers set the beat and the sun beat down on them. The seekers were dressed in blue and yellow robes designed to heighten awareness and unity at these significant rituals. The colours of Jesus, Seth informed them sagely. Naturally, he identified with the Son of Man, after all, he'd read 'The Coming of the New Age Christ'. Seth was nothing if not eclectic.

He raised two fingers, the chanting and drumming ceased as he gazed at each noviciate slated to accept their Vibrational Name at this ceremony. They were each given up to three names, Seth explained, to capture the Holy Trinity of Love, Enlightenment and Obedience.

His clear grey eyes rested on Lucy.

'What birth name are you relinquishing my child?' He asked solemnly.

'Cassandra Olivetti,' Lucy breathed.

Despite being just over forty years old, Seth was already losing hair on top of his head and to compensate he grew it long to his shoulders dying it golden blond. He also grew a long, thick beard as part of his deliberately crafted Christ-like persona, which rested softly on a thick mat of chest hair. As it happens, many con men and religious charlatans are good-looking and charismatic, and Seth was no exception. He had tanned skin and little smile crinkles around his eyes. Moreover, he exuded self-confidence and well, a transcendental vibe, as though he had a purpose here on earth. A greater purpose.

Seth stared into the Perspex orb transfixed, carefully he

put his hand into the opening and chose three labels which he took out and held in his hand.

'I henceforth release this noviciate of her birth name and bequeath and bless her with her Vibrational Name – Lucy Lush Box!' He read this out slowly savouring each word. Everyone in the circle gasped and instantly imagined a beautiful and glossy Mount of Venus. Lucy blushed. At least she wasn't named Perplexity. The young man seated next to her, whose spiritual name was, Smoochie Mandala, bore a striking resemblance to a quokka. He ran his tongue over his lips and wriggled it at her simulating oral sex. Eeyuu! Thought Lucy. How gross. Seth fixed Lucy with a look that held her spellbound and unable to move. She became aware that she wanted to give her whole self to him and sate his obvious desire for her, not to mention, achieve a wondrous climax. As luck would have it, Seth wanted the same thing and later that night they shared a rapturous coupling that transported her to a higher plane of being. Doubtless, Seth a narcissistic fabulist and sex fiend, had found the perfect vehicle for seducing teenage girls via the cult and making them adore him.

CHAPTER 2

Since joining the team at Legal Aid New South Wales, Frank and Diana frequently sat together in the window booth of their favourite café, Enzo's Place. The café was snuggled into the fabric of the street and had been there since the turn of the twentieth century. Originally, a mixed business grocery store below a family residence, it had broad bay windows, chipped paint, and wonderful aromas. With tables and chairs right up against the glass windows, the front door was faded green with inset panels and a large brass doorknob in the centre above a letter slot. An enticing smell of food cooked in garlic and garnished with basil wafted throughout accompanied by an earthy aroma of ground coffee served from behind a high counter. An array of photographic mementos of Italy hung on the walls, faded and specked in places, the largest of which was a movie poster of the 1960s film star, Gina Lollobrigida. An ancient cash register with silver embossed swirls and curlicues sat proudly on the counter reminiscent of a steam train engine. The tiny kitchen behind the counter only fitted one person at a time. The two lawyers tacitly acknowledged a shared sense of place when they met at Enzo's café for lunch, as colleagues and friends and more. Diana Gianiovellis was the beautiful, sexy solicitor Frank flirted with the day he was hired by Legal Aid. At the time they first met, he assumed she was Claudia Karvan, the actor, doing a film shoot as she was standing on the street outside the Legal Aid office, a converted Edwardian terrace near Central Station. He struck up a conversation and invited her to join him for lunch down the street. To his surprise and her bemusement, she accepted his invitation.

This Wednesday, they walked down the street together to Enzo's Café, talking as they moved past people when Diana stopped and hung onto Frank's arm for balance. Lifting a foot behind her she scrutinised her heel, once satisfied she hadn't lost it, she let go and continued walking. She was wearing a patterned dark red skirt with a black, fine knit top and her glossy dark hair was scooped up into a sophisticated chignon. From time to time, he stepped behind where the footpath narrowed noticing she was taller and shapelier than Claudia Karvan. They fitted together. At nearly six feet three, Frank kept his hair short and, though he hadn't been running lately, he was still fit for a guy about to turn forty. For his part, Frank had left the immaculately tailored suits behind, opting for slacks and a smart jacket in the office, however, he would habitually don a suit and tie when he was in court.

He felt comfortable with power, derived from working in politics and now, after a series of adventures, he had moved on with a new life. What better way to start, he asked himself in the mirror that morning, affecting a rakish stance? Back on the street, Frank gazed at Diana for a moment before complimenting her.

'Nice outfit,' he commented appreciatively stepping back beside her, 'you look lovely in it, Diana.'

'Thank you, Frank. I borrowed the skirt from my sister. She hasn't found her pre-baby body yet.' She flashed him a mischievous smile.

The couple wriggled sideways into a window table and ordered focaccias, mineral water and strong coffee from Enzo Bellucci, the plump proprietor, since nineteen eighty-three. Enzo's tufty pale hair stuck out in clumps reminding one of an unclipped terrier dog, his eyes sat above pasty bags on an unshaved face. Today, as always, his long black apron was bedecked with flour, bits of cheese and tomato paste hanging like a pastiche over his voluminous belly. Outside, the sun shone on people bustling about their daily business while the two lawyers resumed talking until their food and drinks arrived. They rearranged papers, thanked Enzo, and settled in to eat food and compare notes.

'Let's go through the Mulligan matter first?' Frank popped a piece of bread in his mouth and chewed waiting for Diana to leaf through her case files and juggle her lunch into an accessible place. Once she cut her focaccia into four neat pieces, she put her plate to one side.

'Sure. Natalie Mulligan was last seen coming out of the Nimbin Post Office where she met someone in a four-wheel drive. Purportedly. This is according to a passer-by who vaguely claimed he knew her face. There's been no word from her since then. Her family have been looking for her and lodged a missing person report as well as posting notices on community billboards, and even making community radio messages.' She chewed for a moment and swallowed continuing the briefing.

'The Mulligans are a close family and argue Natalie would never just disappear without contact. They claim that police are disinterested and racist.'

'She's Indigenous? Frank raised his eyebrows.

Diana chewed a mouthful of focaccia and nodded assent.

'Why doesn't the family go through Aboriginal Legal Aid?' Frank puzzled.

'They believe the Aboriginal Legal Aid people aren't interested in missing women and their focus is land claims. The family wants to sue the New South Wales Police for negligence.' Diana resumed her explanation. 'The police said that Natalie had only been missing for a while and had probably gone 'walk about' and that there wasn't a case to pursue unless a body turned up.'

'Hmm. I see.'

The couple continued eating in comfortable silence for several minutes and Frank topped up their glasses of water before wiping his mouth with a napkin and stretching out his legs.

Diana absently tucked a stray lock of hair behind one ear which Frank noticed had a diamond stud. She drained her glass of water.

'I don't know, Frank!' Her frustration evident. 'Can one publicly funded entity sue another public service for not doing their job properly?'

'Probably. However, it is the family acting to sue the police and us representing them. However, my guess, it is a stoush that Brenda wouldn't like us to take forward.'

Their boss, Brenda Schwartz, Director of Legal Aid, was a force of nature. Frank had met women like her, now fully fledged Senators, heads of companies or Members of Parliament. They carried authority, were driven, competitive and often had a ready sense of humour. He looked across the café catching Enzo's eye indicating they were ready for coffee. The café buzzed with lunchtime customers from all walks of life including, tradesmen, Legal Aid clients and lawyers as well as an assortment of locals.

'The Mulligans want to draw attention to the fact that if Natalie was white, people would care more, and the police would be proactive and engaged, not dismissing the case as another Aboriginal woman, walking off into the sunset and wasting their time and resources. I can see the family's point of view,' Diana shrugged, knowing that Aboriginal women were the lowest on the social pecking order for police attention in these cases. She wanted to do something about it.

'It's just not fair or right!' She added fiercely.

Frank put his hand over hers with a quick, reassuring squeeze.

'No, it's not fair or right.'

Enzo appeared with coffee giving Frank a conspiratorial wink. He put Diana's cup in front of her with a flourish.

'For you, Bella!'

'Grazia, Enzo,' absently she put a spoon of sugar into the cup.

'Perhaps we can keep the New South Wales Police interested by letting them know we are thinking about accepting the

Mulligan case prima facie?'

'What good would that do, Frank?' Her eyes searched for an answer.

'Suppose Natalie has met foul play, and she does turn up dead, there will be a public record for the Coroner pointing to police apathy which might make them lift their game. Just having the pressure of being asked to account for themselves may elicit more cooperation.'

'Or it might make the police more hostile and averse to us.'

'Yes, there is that. Notwithstanding, there will still be a record.' Frank resisted the desire to call in Labor party favours.

'True,' she liked the idea.

'What have you got on now?' As Legal Aid lawyers they both had punishing workloads and not enough administrative support.

'Oh, the usual – crime, deception, domestic violence, ordinary violence and drugs.' Frank chuckled.

'No! All that and no respite?' She mocked him sharing the comic relief of trivialising the grim, diurnal rhythm of their jobs.

'Yep. Oh, damn!' Frank looked at his watch, 'I gotta go. I'm at the Downing Centre Courts in ten minutes, I briefed Anthony on the Villanova matter. See you later.'

Frank extracted himself from the café booth as Diana sorted and packed her papers into her black leather briefcase.

'I'll get this,' Frank was already On his feet leaving cash and Diana wishing they could spend more time together.

* * *

Built in 1901, the Downing Centre Court, formerly the magnificent colonial edifice of Mark Foys Department Store, retained its heritage features including the various departments and goods advertised in large gold letters in a band wrapping the second floor. Labels such as Hosiery, Fashion, Gloves, Coats, Wigs and Millinery festooned the building façade.

Stereo Villanova gained his nickname because he would carry a ghetto blaster on his shoulder when dealing drugs. He *excelled* as an Elvis Impersonator. It was a carefully contrived image that must have taken significant time each morning before the mirror. His dyed-black hair was sculpted into a perfect shape, a mantle slicked back at the sides and curving in a wave at the front with long chiselled sideburns that bisected his cheeks. All his lines were angular, thin and a little disjointed, starting with his hair. His sunglasses comprised a single, thin wrap-around band with shiny white frames and black lenses, a strip of techno mystery intersecting his face. His disconcerted barrister, Anthony Horlicks, insisted he take them off in court because the judge hearing the matter would be unimpressed. Stereo's white spandex jumpsuit with a lurid yellow shirt collar poking out and long pointy peaks clung to his thin body all the way to his knees where it flared out stylishly into enormous bellbottoms over a pair of silver boots with a chiselled heel. The ensemble was elaborately accessorised with multiple chains of fake gold and silver, matching chain bracelets and massive rings as big as knuckle dusters. The metal detector at the court's entrance had melted down and wouldn't stop blaring a raucous warning until Stereo took off his boots and metalware and put them through separately. The guards examined them concerned he might be concealing a stiletto knife.

Stereo, a pimp and a drug dealer and a self-styled entrepreneur was busted for dealing speed when copious amounts of pills and packets of powder were uncovered at his mother's house in Earlwood, where he lived. Unsurprisingly, his bedroom was a temple to The King. Bedecked with posters, photos, and memorabilia covering the walls it reflected all the stages of fame inhabited by Elvis until his death. Elvis' publicity machine had confirmed the story he died of a heart attack. Seemed less sordid. Stereo owned vinyl albums and videos of every performance, not to mention every film the great man made in his tragically truncated life. Every year, Stereo attended the Elvis Presley Festival, held in the rural township of Parkes in New South Wales. It is like a religious pilgrimage for many fans. There, surrounded by a tribe of fellow devotees of Elvis, all dressed up to look like The King and his entourage, Stereo was in sheer heaven.

The court was already sitting when Frank raced in, he bowed to the judge casting his eyes across the seats at Anthony. Their client, Stereo Villanova, was behaving like an unmedicated man with bipolar disease. He was manic. Febrile. Tapping his foot, twitching uncontrollably while holding a rambling conversation with himself; his nervous system was running amok, and he appeared doped off his face at two in the afternoon. Not a good look, Frank concluded, grimacing. If Stereo didn't calm down right now, everything would go South very quickly. Frank dug Anthony in the ribs and he jumped up to represent Stereo as best he could.

'The defence would like to be granted bail for our client, Mr Villanova, and the bail amount once set, will be covered by his mother, with whom he will reside, until the next court hearing, at a time set by Your Honour.' The Judge adjusted her glasses as she read the charge sheet and pertinent notes on Stereo's colourful and pointless life.

'Be calm!' Frank stage whispered an order to Stereo, who by now was humming and tapping Elvis tunes under his breath appearing to be in a trance. He began building to a crescendo.

'What have you to say for yourself, young man?' Judge Alstock looked up at Stereo, whose mother, a devoutly religious woman seated in the back row, hadn't stopped crossing herself since they arrived.

Stereo shot to his feet oblivious to the seriousness of the situation and burst into song arms thrusting outward, hips gyrating he sang to the whole court, *'I'm just a hunka, hunka burnin' lurve,'* in a rich baritone, that quite surprised Frank.

'Bail denied!' The Judge banged the gavel.

Stereo had reached a crisis point in his life, he put one hand on the burnished wooden railing enclosing the courtroom seats and vaulted smoothly over it. Hitting the ground at a run, he covered the distance to the doors of the courtroom in seconds pushing them both wide open before anyone could move. Galloping full tilt, he shot across the tessellated green and white tiles of the Downing Centre foyer towards the front doors and freedom. Regrettably for him, someone had the presence of mind to put out their foot on which Stereo tripped over, landing hard on his jewellery, skidding the remaining length of the foyer on his stomach, arms and legs akimbo looking for all the world like a cockatoo. He slowed to a halt at the feet of Judge Marcus Guthrie, an eminent jurist, with a wicked sense of humour.

As Marcus looked down on Stereo, a huge smirk carved his craggy face.

'Gotcha!' he barked with gusto as he made a gun sign with two of his fingers for the barrel aimed at Stereo.

Two burly guards bustled up either side of Stereo, while the gravity of the Courts dissolved into hilarity and people witnessing the theatrics in the foyer, shook with laughter. A great many of the legal fraternity dined out on Stereo Villanova's bold attempt to leave the building.

CHAPTER 3

For most of his adult life, Frank worked for one employer, the Australian Labor Party, culminating in his role as Deputy Chief of Staff, for the Honourable Bill Falco, Australia's longest-serving Labor Prime Minister. When he lost his job, shortly before Bill stepped down, he spent his payout on a house in the suburb of Downer, in Canberra. His adventures of the last few months, before joining Legal Aid NSW, involved looking for Bill's daughter, Stella, on the North Coast of NSW, with his former partner, April Moreland. April had since taken a job as a journalist in Lebanon, and mercifully, he liberated himself from the existential rut of living in Canberra in a dead-end job without a purpose. He felt relieved the turmoil of his adventures catapulted him into a new life in Sydney. It proved easy to find a buyer for his house among his contacts and colleagues in Canberra, mostly political staffers, who needed a base near Parliament

House. Having cleaned his place out in one weekend he waved goodbye to Mrs Fratelli, his next-door neighbour, pleased this chapter of his life was well and truly over. He drove back to Sydney with a happy heart.

'Thank God!' He declared when he reached Lake George, a mysterious body of water fifty kilometres from Canberra, and he turned up the volume on the radio singing along to the Sultans of Swing by Dire Straits. He was going home.

He bought himself an apartment off the plan on the third floor of a converted warehouse on Buckingham Street in Chippendale, an inner-city suburb. The suburb was an eclectic mix of buildings from different eras with a distinguishable manufacturing footprint and while the highest buildings were only three stories, they were surrounded by semi-detached homes. The streets were narrow and tree-lined each corner occupied by grocery stores, cafes and a collection of old-world pubs. On either side of the street, paperbarks and gums interspersed with bottle brush shrubs would shed bark, leaves, and flowers around themselves. Some trade tenants still occupied the other two floors of the factory including a picture framer and a security services company. His place had high ceilings and brick walls with windows made up of myriads of smaller panes through which light poured into the space. The developers had splurged on a stainless-steel kitchen with a gourmet, island food preparation bench in teak and a couple of matching stools. When Frank picked up the keys and let himself in, he immediately pictured a romantic notion of himself cooking there for family and friends.

His bedroom occupied a mezzanine level at one end of the

vast factory floor with broad wooden stairs leading to it. In the middle of the main room stood a gas heater, black cast iron box on legs, reminding Frank of a Ned Kelly helmet and through the oblong of glass on one side was a fake fire that twinkled when it was running.

'Holy hell!' Frank looked around his spacious apartment. 'I better learn to cook and get some furniture.' He experienced a thrill of a new life and wanted to ask his sister, Genie and her family to see the place. And Diana, of course.

Not this weekend coming though as he promised Genie, he would hand out How to Vote leaflets for her as she was running for a safe seat in New South Wales State Parliament. A few years had passed since he'd handed out leaflets for a Labor candidate and he was looking forward to the familiar ritual. Frank missed his family while he was based in Canberra, not to mention, working such long hours. His dad, Frank Senior, lived in a retirement village now and confessed his memory was patchy at times. Father and son spent Saturday afternoons either at the local pub or playing chequers.

Later that morning, Frank stuck his head around the door of the office Diana shared with two other colleagues. Both Vic Barraclough and Michelle Summers were employed with Legal Aid longer than Diana and welcomed her and Frank.

'Hey Frank!' Vic called out, 'Has Elvis left the building again or is he safely in custody coming off speed?' News of the spectacular attempt to escape by Frank's client, Mr. Stereo 'Elvis' Villanova, was all over the legal fraternity. In fact, Channel 9 News lodged the story by their court reporter, as the action occurred, including a shot of the escapee spreadeagled while sliding over the tessellated tiles in the grand foyer.

Frank's face broke into a wide smile while the others heckled and begged for all the juicy details. Vic, now in his fifties was functionally bald, of medium build and super fit, his black belt in karate gave him an aura of power. Michelle, a former trade union lawyer, claimed she needed more work 'flexibility' which everyone read as less politics. Her mess of greying blonde hair threatened to escape the bonds she applied each morning. A valiant attempt to look more professional and less 'blowsy', she explained, with an infectious laugh. Shapely and rounded she wore a black skirt, a white blouse showing cleavage and high heels considered as the uniform of legal professionals.

Into this boisterous recounting and noisy hilarity, Brenda Schwartz strolled, looking a little hung over and clutching a coffee. Diana was laughing with her head thrown back, as Frank detailed the postscript of the Elvis Impersonator, and his bolt for freedom.

Frank jogged up and relieved the guards, lifting Stereo's skinny carcass upright by the neck and pants of his white jumpsuit before frog marching him back into the courtroom to face the music. Following a brief consultation with Anthony, they argued that Stereo hadn't breached bail yet as he didn't leave the jurisdictional grounds. The Judge conceded the legal point and no further charges accrued and, highly amused by the whole fiasco commented with dry wit, that her estimation of Stereo, as a flight risk, was vindicated by his subsequent behaviour.

She banged her gavel pronouncing irrevocably, 'Bail denied. The prisoner is to be taken down until his court case on a date to be set. Dismissed.'

Brenda slapped Frank on the back and joined in the laughter and bonhomie.

'Well done mate! That's the funniest bail hearing I've ever heard. I drank a bottle of red with Marcus last night and he regaled me with your brilliant save.'

The director was renowned for her ribald sense of humour. Essential to work in Legal Aid, she argued persuasively. The team felt a warm camaraderie born of shared respect, a commitment to fairness and punishing workloads and, not enough time or energy to have ego-driven standoffs.

Brenda jerked her head sideways to her office up the hall and picking up her coffee she hoisted her bag over her shoulder ready for the day ahead.

'Diana, Frank, we need a case meeting in my office now. There's been a call.'

Frank unsure what the call was about, followed her out the door.

Diana stood and brushed down her skirt, grabbed the Mulligan file and her case book and walked after them. Vic and Michelle exchanged a knowing look.

'Brenda,' Michelle called after her, 'before you go, the toilet is blocked up again and it's become an occupational health and safety problem.'

'Shit.' Brenda took a sip of her cooling coffee, 'no pun intended. Call the building plumber, will you? We'll pay out of petty cash. The number is on the wall in the hallway.'

'Will do.'

Brenda led the way into her office which looked as though a bomb had gone off: there were piles of paper files in stacks on the floor, on shelves, all over her desk and on every available chair. Each one sported dozens of yellow paper stickies protruding out highlighting pages that needed her attention. She put her bag and coffee in the middle of her desk and scooped up all the chair files, opened a filing cabinet drawer and piled them in.

'Sit down, sit down.' All the lawyers regularly met as a group or individually with Brenda to discuss their cases and workloads. The office manager and administrator, Madelaine Perroux, who was everything to everyone and the lynchpin of the service, was at the dentist that morning.

Brenda, a short, auburn-haired woman of the 'don't mess with me' variety, was tough with a heart of gold. Today she was wearing an expensive tailored black suit, the skirt above her knees and a blue and white fitted pinstripe shirt underneath her jacket.She was fifty with an inverted A shaped body, her large bosum and narrow hips sitting on top of killer legs. She threw her jacket over her chair and rolled up her sleeves.

'Shut the door behind you!' She instructed as she moved around to her chair and pulled open a desk drawer. Diana stepped into the office and pulled the door closed with difficulty moving another pile of files out of the way.

Brenda's head was in the draw rifling around looking for something. She lifted a few items out like a notebook, a stapler, and a gun.

'Brenda!' Frank was sharper than he meant to be. 'Is that gun licensed?'

'Yes, Frank, of course it is.' Diana didn't bat an eyelid.

Eventually, Brenda found some Nicobates, the anti-smoking gum of choice, popping one into her mouth and chewing vigorously.

'I've received a call from the New South Wales Crime Commission,' she declared, putting the contents of the drawer back where they belonged. 'They want to know if we're working on any mafia connected cases.'

'The only one that's got loose threads is the Mulligan matter. Though there's no direct connection to mafia, that we know of.' Diana responded while cataloguing in her mind the other cases she was running.

'Okay. You, Frank?'

'I've seen a guy hanging around on the other side of the street. He looks like someone out of Central Casting.' Frank recalled the weasel-faced guy with the bad suit outside the building.

Both women looked at him blankly.

'You know, black sunnies leaning against a wall with a newspaper,' he felt pleased as the man puzzled him.

'I didn't notice him,' Diana commented, 'probably because I'm always looking at the pavement which is treacherous in high heels.' Perfectly reasonable, Frank agreed.

'Talk to me about the Mulligan case,' Brenda masticated her Nicobate vigorously.

'Daughter Natalie, disappeared. She didn't come home or turn up to work. Hasn't contacted the family. Police have been dismissive and uncooperative according to her mother and other family members. The family lodged a missing person report and advertised for information, pestered the local cops, and even got a piece on the local radio asking if anyone remembers seeing her.' Diana glanced down, 'Apparently, she spent some of the time in Lismore, with her mum, Elizabeth, and some of the time in a shared house at a village called Coffee Camp, on Nimbin Road.'

'I know the area,' Frank interjected, 'I was there last year.'

'Go on.' Brenda spat the gum into a tissue and put it in an overflowing bin beneath her desk. Frank watched Diana with a serious expression as she continued.

'The case came to us because the family want Legal Aid to represent them to sue the NSW Police for negligence and racism. They claim if she was a white woman there would be a concerted effort to find her and they wouldn't be fobbed off.'

'True!' Brenda snorted with disgust. 'Do you know how many Aboriginal women go missing or disappear without anyone caring?'

'Without a body it's a difficult case to bring,' Frank interjected. 'Not to mention running a case against a State department. The police would hate us, and we need their support.'

'We can look at it,' Brenda conceded, 'be better if the family could lodge a complaint with the Police Integrity Unit and try that angle.'

They all acknowledged that, even with a body and political will, it would be hard to prove a lack of police action resulted in a death, even with the Aboriginal Deaths in Custody Commission Report ongoing.

'Has Natalie had anything to do with organised crime then?' Brenda drilled down. 'Maybe the cops are closing it down for other reasons. Not just random acts of racism? I mean we're doing something that has attracted mafia surveillance it seems.'

'We just don't have enough information really,' Diana replied. 'However, Frank and I did discuss the matter.'

'I suggested that we talk to the police department's legal

team to see if we can elicit some more cooperation before recommending the family lodge a complaint with Police Integrity.'

'Nice move Frank.'

'What is the Crime Commission doing staking out our office?' He wondered.

'They didn't say exactly. They never do.' Brenda popped another piece of gum in her mouth. 'I surmise they're keeping tabs on some 'usual suspects' connected with their pursuit of organised crime gangs and spotted one hanging around outside our office.' As she chewed gum, her mind chewed the case over.

'Nevertheless, my spidery sense says these two incidences are connected,' she suggested. 'I don't know how, but if everything else is your bog-standard drugs, violence, and villainy then we look at the case we know least about. What does Natalie do for a living?' Addressing Diana.

'She is a crop duster. A pilot.'

'Bingo!' Brenda slapped the desk with her palm, delighted. Both Frank and Diana regarded her mildly surprised.

'What do pilots do when they are not crop dusting?' It was a rhetorical question. 'Why, they transport drugs around the country for growers and dealers – like the mafia!'

'Surely not all of them?' Diana countered.

Unbeknownst to any of them, the Crime Commission, responsible for bringing organised crime to justice, was erecting a camera overlooking the Legal Aid Office. Two operators, wearing grey overalls and posing as electricians were busy installing a surveillance camera into the 'Bellamy and Sons Shopfitters' sign on the building opposite the office.

The camera was screwed in behind the 'O' in 'Sons' and the fisheye lens was directed at the street.

'The mob may believe we know something about Natalie. Her family's quite open in broadcasting their need for more information as to her whereabouts,' Diana summed up.

'Presumably, they tracked the case to her aunt and uncle in Sydney and hence to us?' Frank added. 'Perhaps Natalie has something on the mafia and, she's been threatened by them, so they are cleaning up?' He reasoned looking grimly at Diana.

Diana closed the case file on her lap, 'what do you want to do, Brenda?'

'Take the case. Approach the Legal and Police Integrity people making it seem you're very reluctant, and argue we have a responsibility to the family to refer them. Address their grievance etc., then organise a conference with the family.' There was a reason Brenda was boss. 'Meanwhile Frank, you are now the investigator on the case. We need to follow up on Natalie, where she works and lives and find out as much as we can. That will flush the mob out into the game, I suspect, and we might even get a bit of justice for the family.'

'I'll ring the Attorney General and let her know this could be a headland case demonstrating that we are acting on Aboriginal issues by lodging a formal complaint of racism with the Police Integrity Unit. It's a hot political potato.' Brenda strategized.

Frank and Diana shared a look of agreement. They had their marching orders.

'We'll have to meet tomorrow, map it out and give you the outline,' Diana rose.

'Good.' Brenda moved on by then, she momentarily cleared her throat. They both looked back at her expectantly.

'Be careful. That's an order.' Brenda picked up the phone then put it down again. She reflected on her conversation with a former minister in the Falco government and mutual friend, about offering Frank Phelan a job. She liked Frank because he was forthright and humorous.

'I just need a desk and a phone,' he said when she asked, 'and somewhere to belong.'

* * *

That evening, Frank was slumped in front of the television in his bachelor pad, his mind ticking over recapping the meeting with Brenda about the Mulligan case. Both he and Diana were too busy that day to dedicate time to the case but cleared their diaries to make time to go through it the next day. He found a sweatshirt in the laundry basket he'd picked up on the way home and looking around his spacious warehouse pulled it on before wandering to his kitchen where he got a bottle of single malt whiskey and a glass out of a cupboard. Holding the bottle to the light he briefly considered the liquid inside before pouring it in the glass and adding some water from the tap. He returned to the couch and sat down flicking through a few television channels and settling on a British police drama. He took a sip of his drink which didn't taste too bad and thought about the past few years from Canberra to Nimbin and back to Sydney. He didn't regret leaving politics. It was his life for two decades though admittedly, the circumstances of his departure hadn't gone as planned. Nonetheless, he felt philosophical, knowing very few political exits are ideal, more often they were messy, unexpected, scandalous or humiliating. The euphemism about 'leaving to spend more time with the family', frequently trotted out by politicians, glossed over a multitude of hidden meanings. Meanings rephrased as, 'I hope to patch up my relationship with my wife and children, now my affair has been made public.'

In Frank's case, as Deputy Chief of Staff to the Prime Minister of the day, he fell on his sword after leaking sensitive information and was sent into political and career purgatory. He shook his head, bemused. From the grand narrative of the nation, shaping policy, and crafting responses in the crucible of Parliament House, now he was deep in the woods of individual human lives. One thing was certain, things change. Labor had been in power for eleven years and they were having a great run. However, Frank observed that Australians were basically conservative despite outbreaks of progressivism.

He took another sip of his drink, put a Miles Davis CD into his player and lost himself in the mellow saxophone while he ate his dinner. By the time he had eaten and cleaned up it was eight o'clock. He took a long hot shower and when he'd towelled off and changed into a T-shirt and light pants he walked into the living room, picked up the phone and dialled Beirut. April answered after three rings her voice somehow dislocated.

'Hi there, it's Frank. Is this a bad time?'

'Yes. It's early in the morning Frank!' Then, 'no it's okay. Nice to hear a familiar voice.'

'I have been meaning to ring for weeks. How are you going over there?'

'Honestly, it is intense!' She blew air out, 'the culture is vastly different from ours.'

'How so?'

'Women are completely subservient for starters.'

'That would be tough for you, April.'

'And it is a war zone of complex, deeply embedded hostilities, virulent hatreds, decades of vendettas and ...,' she trailed off aware that the hundreds of years of historical battles between families, nations and tribes couldn't be summed up in a few sentences.

'What are you doing now, Frank?' April asked.

'I'm working with Legal Aid NSW. Got the job through a Labor mate.' There was clicking and crackling on the line. 'What's that?' He asked.

'All the lines are tapped even the home lines. What were you saying, sorry.'

'I'm working in public law. Somehow, it's more real you know? Ordinary lives?'

'I feel the opposite. Like a speck of dust in an international battle for ideas.'

The line crackled and they paused waiting for it to clear.

'I met someone special, April.'

'That's great, mate! Look, I have to go.'

'Good to talk again. Take care of yourself.' He meant it.

'You too Frank and thanks. I'll call you when I get a break.'

When they hung up the phone he felt a mixture of affection, loyalty and separateness.

CHAPTER 4

Rover Mulligan, Natalie's dad, taught her to fly when she was a teenager, much to the chagrin of her mum who never trusted the idea of a light metal frame carrying a couple of motors and people she loved in the air. Rover flew twin-engine planes around New South Wales as a crop duster in the wheat belt and later, for large agricultural crops, further towards the coast. Rover died of cancer from the pesticides and the company paid the family a lump sum and made him sign a confidentiality agreement before he passed. It was enough money to buy their house in Lismore, where Elizabeth, his wife of thirty years, had grown up. Natalie's two brothers Nathan and Jason had joined the Army as soon as they left school and Natalie kept flying for a living.

When her dad died, he left Natalie his vintage 1949 Beechcraft DL 8S, a twin-engine plane, which he was rebuilding as a hobby project in his spare time. The plane enjoyed an honorary residence at the Tyagarah airstrip hangar, leased by the North Coast Light Planes and Gliders Association. It was the plane she'd first flown, and she knew it like the back of her hand. To Natalie, she was utterly beautiful, with a glossy, creamy body and deep maroon stripes and tortoiseshell dashboard and real leather seats. Natalie would go to the airstrip on her days off to tinker with and polish the Beechcraft and take it out for a spin.

As she wheeled high over the glimmering coastline with the hazy, blue backdrop of the mountain range and the white sands below, she felt a deep connection to her dad. These lands constituted the ancestral homelands as Rover was a Bundjalong man. When they went for a trip together, he'd point out all the symbols and spiritual signifiers of the geography beneath them.

'See those shapes bub, like a giant man lying down on the land? It's ancient when Australia was called Gondwana and the back runs along the Nightcap Range. And there at Blue Knob?' He'd point down to the volcanic outcrop, 'that's like the fella's head. His feet are way down near Grafton.'

Like most aircraft adapted for crop dusting, the Beechcraft had ground sensors in the wing tips which fed visual data back to the cockpit so the pilot could see on a small screen the boundaries of the land they were dusting. It was no longer acceptable to wide sweep crops dumping pesticides that drifted onto neighbours' lands. Natalie prided herself on being able to run along a dividing fence line and not get any dust from the pesticide on the other side of the fence, so accurate was her ability to judge distances.

Each year the Civil Aviation Safety and Security or C.A.S.S., as they were known, undertook a safety audit on the licences and conditions of private aircraft and companies. Usually, it just meant dropping by the office and showing the C.A.S.S. people her paperwork. This year was a full inspection of the insurance, logbooks, flight manifests, pilot licences and receipts on any repairs they had done as well as proof of the work they'd done whether joy flights, dusting or cargo flights. A Parliamentary Inquiry was underway because of two light aircraft crashes in the past year in which one person died according to the papers. The organisation was in the spotlight as the body that oversaw air safety and questions were asked.

'Damn!' Natalie muttered digging through her expander file to see if she'd kept any other copies of papers that might be useful. Her company, AgBlaster and its subsidiary, Bolt from the Blue, paid the insurance on the Cessna work plane and she knew, they had her insured. However, the Beechcraft was still registered in Rover's name for sentimental reasons. It made her feel connected to him.

It was the day after Australia Day, a typically hot January day and the tarmac at Lismore airport registered thirty-five degrees Celsius. Over beside the terminus arrivals and departures building, stood an aluminium and steel demountable with two boxy air conditioning units jutting out from each window. There were only two rooms therefore only two windows, in the demountable office and the overall effect made it look and feel like a refrigeration unit.

Natalie opened the office door and felt instantly cooler as the air conditioner thrummed noisily pumping out icy air.

The utilitarian space comprised of a reception room and counter and an office with a toilet. Behind the counter a young man in a light blue, short-sleeved shirt with an open collar and an open face smiled.

'Hi Steve,' Natalie had gone to school with Steve Perry.

'Gidday Nat.'

'What's going on? The usual?' Natalie spoke confidently knowing she had impeccable records. It was one of the many lessons her dad had taught her.

'Don't cut corners on the red tape, Nat,' Rover often advised her, 'you're an Aboriginal woman and one of the weapons the bureaucrats like to use against us is the paperwork,' he used the word as a pejorative.

'Yeah, I know it's a pain, but the big C.A.S.S. bosses are all over us,' Steve shrugged apologetically. 'They have sent Dave the Accountant, he's in the next room.'

'Dave the Accountant!' She remarked. 'Are you for real?'

'Shhoosh,' Steve hissed putting his upright finger up to his lips, 'you can go in Miss Mulligan.' He spoke up clearly over the noise of the air conditioners.

Natalie grabbed up her briefcase and walked into the second room where she found Dave the Accountant sitting behind a standard issue government desk. The only other furniture in the room was a filing cabinet and a straight-backed school chair on the opposite side of the desk to Dave.

'Natalie Mulligan, pilot.'

'Sit down Miss Mulligan.'

She opened her briefcase and unpacked a series of papers in cascading sleeves placing her pilot's licence and a photocopy of it to one side.

From his appearance, Dave was an uptight man who combed his hair over and parted it precisely. He wore his black rimmed glasses perched on the end of his nose creating a disconnect between the upper and lower parts of his face. He was earnest and pedantic, and she guessed, not open to chit-chat except, perhaps to the people in his church. She glanced at his exercise book spread out in front of him with red ruled columns. Yes, a church goer.

Dave went through the registration details and the manifest for the plane, and then gave them back to her.

'Your employer is still Agblaster, Miss Mulligan?' More a statement than a question.

'Yes, Dave,' she leaned over and pointed to the certificate of employment, 'it says that right there. I contract for Bolt from the Blue too, that's what this document is,' showing Dave another form.

'Right. Right, and the Beechcraft, you own that plane?'

'No, it's still my father's, I work on it as a hobby. You can see the registration papers in my father's name here,' pointing to another certificate. Dave drew a red line under the notes he had taken.

'That's it then?' Natalie queried.

'Yes. Thank you for your cooperation, Miss Mulligan,' he stood leaning over the desk slightly as Natalie picked up her papers and put them back in the briefcase then headed for the office door glad the meeting was over.

At that moment, another man stepped into the room slowing Natalie's momentum. Middle aged and crisply attired in a pilot's uniform with black slacks and shiny black shoes he wore a startlingly white shirt with gold epaulettes.

Evincing a bristly authority, the man's face was clean shaven, his sandy reddish hair cut short and close. The man held himself in a controlled military manner.

Natalie glanced past the uniformed man, and thinking he must be here to see Dave, stepped around him. Instead, the man stepped in front of her.

'I'm Trevor Cane, from C.A.S.S. head office.' He introduced himself officiously, 'may I have a word before you go, Miss Mulligan?'

Looking at the man she hitched her bundle up under her arm.

'Hi Trevor,' addressing the interlocutor, 'I know my paperwork is in order. Are you from security services or something?' Her eyes challenged him, the man apologised in a conciliatory tone, 'I'm sorry, it was impolite to step in front of you.'

'I'm listening.' Natalie stood at the open door between the two offices waiting for Trevor to explain himself.

'I've been authorised by C.A.S.S. to ask chosen commercial pilots to keep their eyes and ears open for any biosecurity or smuggling threats. Things like native animals, reptiles and the like.'

'What and spy on them for you?'

'Yes,' Trevor affirmed, adding, 'that would be helpful and the Australian thing to do, don't you agree?'

Seriously? She looked at him in a new light.

'No, Trevor,' she corrected, 'the Australian thing to do would be for you to say, 'if you spy for us, we will pay you handsomely and keep you safe. That would help everyone.'

Natalie figured she was the first pilot on the list to be

approached demonstrating that Trevor hadn't yet perfected the scenario for recruitment.

'Now please move out of my way. I've got work to do,' she stepped sideways in a deft dance move. Trevor didn't resist.

Once through the interior door, she looked over her shoulder and, as an afterthought, said, 'as you were!' She ordered Trevor, who was visibly shocked that anyone would have the temerity to tell him off and then to stand down!

Natalie crossed the outer room in two strides and stepped through the outer door almost falling on top of a man who was coming in from the outside. He caught her elbows as she hung onto the briefcase.

'Whoa babe, careful you don't fall!'

Until now, Natalie had never met this man and she knew most of the contract pilots. The heat washed over her as she gained her balance again. A jolt of electricity arced between them and a little flustered she pushed back from his body.

'I'm okay, thanks.' It was then she became aware of the guy who caught her. He had animal magnetism. Māori, she wondered. He was wearing a sleeveless dark T-shirt and faded cargo pants with many tattoos on display especially, on his muscled arms. Natalie fought the urge to take a deep draught of his scent and looked obliquely at his armpit where she could see black hair. He had smooth brown skin, close-cropped hair with a mullet pigtail and liquid brown eyes. Get a grip! She chastised herself. You do not need some human panther, ninja pilot in your life. Extreme danger!

Natalie crossed paths with the man whose name was Brendon, in the coming days. Perhaps he'd always been around and just now she noticed him, she had asked herself?

Yeah, sure. She went right on flirting with him. As always, animal magnetism and lust have a way of cutting through all the warnings, baggage, mental calculations and orthodoxies until you get down to the sex. Then it's satisfied.

CHAPTER 5

When Diana walked in the door of the Gianiovellis home in Sydney's Inner West her senses were assailed by the rich tomato and herby smells of pasta sauce and fresh basil still lying chopped on the bench top waiting to be added to the dish. They were aromas of her childhood, growing up in a migrant home full of people and cooking, with parents who were the centre of their community. Valentino was a dentist and people were always dropping by with vegetables they had grown or jam they had made in way of payment for his pro bono services and quiet advice.

The wall-mounted television in the family room was close enough for her mum to watch while she was cooking. Diana found her stirring the pasta sauce while adding the herbs the phone tucked between her ear and her shoulder speaking rapidly in Italian. Her dad rolled his eyes skyward and gave Diana a kiss murmuring a few words of greeting before making his way to the living room. Something caught Claudia's attention, she abruptly hung up the phone, eyes swivelling as she became riveted to a news story on the television.

'Look at that! What is that man wearing to a law court?' She was watching the denouement of the Stereo Villanova escape, aghast as he plunged forward and slid across the floor of the Downing Centre foyer on his stomach. A piece of slapstick the film crew could only dream of catching live for the six o'clock news on Chanel 9. It was a classic.

The item captured Diana's attention too and she laughed as Frank sprinted into sight chasing the escapee before swooping on him picking him up like a twig by his collar and the seat of his pants and guiding him back to court.

Her cheeks flushed and her eyes were watery from merriment – watching it on television was magnificent! Better than retelling the event in the office that day.

'Oh, that is so funny!' She sighed, took off her jacket and hung over the back of a chair.

'Who is this man, Diana? Do you know him? He is a lawyer too?'

In her mother's mind, all lawyers knew each other – therefore Diana knew Frank Phelan and his family, simply because he was a lawyer. Claudia fixed on Diana in the unnerving way she adopted when scheming a blind dinner date for her, waiting for an answer. Her daughter hesitated just a moment, composing an offhand response that didn't trigger her mother into a full-on inquiry, settling on a casual dismissive phrase.

'That's just Frank apprehending a client who tried to skip

bail today at the law courts,' tossed off lightly. Too late.

'How you know this man? Does he work with you?' Claudia questioned switching between Italian and English, a formidable interrogation tool.

Believing she had deflected her, Diana crossed to the sink and washed her hands then reached behind her to get a bottle of mineral water out of the refrigerator door before grabbing a glass from the dish rack.

'Yes. He's the new lawyer at Legal Aid,' she said walking back to the table and clearing a space. 'Mum, do you want a mineral water?' Claudia ignored the question. Diana picked up a *New Idea* magazine and took a sip from her glass.

'He is Italian!' Claudia exclaimed exultantly.

'No Mum, he not Italian,' Diana countered her, looking up from an article about Lindy Chamberlain she was pretending to read. 'If you must know, he's Australian Irish, I think. Phelan, that's an Irish name.'

Undeterred, Claudia was determined to get to the bottom of Frank's genetic and religious make-up. And his marital status!

'Catholic! I knew he was a good boy! Catching that criminal with his bare hands like that.' She proclaimed.

Diana turned her head back and continued to study how Lindy Chamberlain had *'stacked on the weight'* though she was still a woman *'not to be messed with'*.

Meanwhile, the sleuth had temporarily abandoned the pasta to get a better picture of her daughter's working conditions. Diana was famished.

'This man, Franco, he is married, yes?' Diana registered that he had gone from plain 'Frank' to a potential family member with an Italian name, 'Franco'.

Claudia, a statuesque woman in her late sixties, had her hair set and nails done each week and came from the generation of women who greeted their husbands in the evening, wearing a nice top and lipstick. In her worldview, everyone should be married.

Diana inwardly debated how much to tell her mother, knowing this would become a 'thing' in their lives. Before long, Claudia would be dropping by the office in the hope of inviting Frank to a family dinner. Diana often wished her mum had a full-time job so she would spend less time invested in her life, especially her love life,

'I'm not sure,' settling on, 'he was seeing someone.' Vague.

'But not married to that someone?' The television cameraman had shown a close-up of Frank leaning towards Stereo, lifting him effortlessly and zoomed in on his two-handed hold of the escapee. His left hand, gripping Stereo's collar, did not bear a wedding ring.

How on earth did her mother notice that tiny detail in the melee and movement as Frank prevented his client from escaping?

'Oh Mum!' Exasperated, Diana chided her, 'you have a one-track mind. Not all men wear wedding rings you know?'

'I want you to have a happy marriage. God wants you to use your old eggs before it's too late!' Claudia frequently referred to God's plans as authentication of her arguments.

'I will set the table,' Diana abandoned her magazine and applied herself to putting out plates and cutlery from the sideboard next to the dining table. She located a fresh white loaf of bread on the bench and placed it on the table.

'How many for dinner?' Her dad wandered back into the family room from the lounge where he too had seen the daring escape effort of the Elvis Impersonator.

'Good day at the office, darling?' He put an arm across her shoulders and gave her an affectionate squeeze.

The second born, Diana was a nerdy, serious girl who had always imagined she would have a profession first and after, get married and have kids. Her dad supported her ambitions and for much of her university years, she lived at home. She had boyfriends at university and then men in her life whilst working in a small law firm. Later she went travelling with a girlfriend to Italy for the Christmas holidays and when she came back and told her parents she wanted to do something more meaningful, she joined the Legal Aid Sydney team.

This didn't surprise her parents, both community minded people. For her dad, Australia truly was the lucky country. While growing up, their house was always full of people for whom Claudia would cook meals and take in troubled kids. Both daughters, Isabelle and Diana learnt to cook from their mother while Diana's big sister preceded her through the eighties with extravagant hair and boys in fast cars. Izzy married the accountant for the hairdressing salon she worked in, and then she and Flavio concentrated on having children. Izzy set up a home hairdressing business when the kids were little. Luca didn't come along until later.

By the time dinner was ready, Izzy and Flavio had arrived with their three kids and Luca turned up late with a mate in tow. The food plates were circulated while all the family caught up and heard Claudia's assessment of Frank's daring save in the name of justice. Diana laughed as much as everyone else and felt happy and loved by this noisy bunch. After they had finished eating, she stacked the dishwasher and put some coffee on, she and her dad sat talking about her work and his extra responsibility volunteering at the Migrant Resources Centre. Claudia kissed her husband on his head on her way to watch a video with their grandkids.

'You should meet a fine husband like this man, Diana.'

Diana and her father habitually discussed politics including world events. It was their special time together.

'I guess you like this man, Frank?

'Is it that obvious?'

'We know you well, darling.'

'True,' she acknowledged, 'he's a good man. I like him.'

'Then you had better warn him about your mother,' Val chuckled.

'You are so right.'

CHAPTER 6

Natalie parked her car, a 1988 Baby Blue Datsun 200, a few streets away from the Tyagarah airstrip where a collection of bungalows were only inhabited during the school holidays. With an attention to detail, informed by the degree of danger she knew could befall her, she wiped the car down inside and out for her fingerprints and cleaned out any scraps of food or receipts. She considered taking the plates off but decided to leave the car unlocked and the keys under the front seat certain some surfer would look in and take his board for a drive up the coast. She grabbed her backpack of equipment and set off to the airstrip walking in the back way through some scrub and wetlands as rain threatened. She counted on the meeting being in the hangar though knew she was taking a chance.

It was mid-week, and the airstrip remained completely deserted. It was close to two o'clock, and she felt too tense to be hungry, so decided to wait until her spying job was completed. She let herself into the hangar by a side door which creaked a little as she eased it open and took a deep breath of the smell of canvas and creosote and aviation fuel capturing the mustiness of history in the Nissan hut. It was like a cocoon to her. She looked lovingly at the Beechcraft-DS18 moored at the front end facing out to the doors which could be concertinaed open, leaving enough space for her to taxi out onto the airstrip.

There were three other planes housed in the hangar and the pilots knew Rover had left the Beechcraft with Natalie to care for its welfare. Many years ago, Rover and Norm, secretary of the club, leased the airstrip and the hangar for ninety-nine years from the local council for the North Coast Flying and Gliding Club. Rover paid a bigger part of the cost on the proviso he could use the hanger to park the Beechcraft and work on it for as long as the lease lasted.

Natalie often talked to her dad; for her people the soul of a person lived on in the land and through the memories and spirit world of their nation.

'I dunno, Dad,' she muttered under her breath, 'these blokes are dangerous people.'

Walking over to the plane she hoisted her backpack up on the wing first and jumped up behind it making the old plane tilt and groan as the cream wing dipped slightly supporting her weight. Unlocking the door of the cockpit she took out the equipment she needed plus her tool kit, swung her backpack in behind the seat and then sat in the pilot seat to begin work setting up the camera and listening system she had bought.

'Yes, yes. I know, Dad. That Brendon bloke is bad news.'

She was feeling shabby about the liaison with the smuggler. She wished her dad was alive to kkeep her safe, instead she talked out loud to him as though he was present in person.

Despite being able to fix the crop duster camera sensors she had never set up a surveillance system that she hoped would film and record the meeting between Brendon and the mafia henchmen. Natalie had noticed a thicket of shrubs and trees running along the fence line that would make a perfect hiding spot. Somewhere she could take her japara raincoat and food and watch proceedings from the cover of the bush.

It was sweaty and fiddly work and Natalie had to get inside the wing cavities of the Beechcraft and rewire the wing sensor lens to the small camera she'd purchased. The technology was designed to be put into bird observation posts in wild and remote places by nature conservationists and rangers to track the populations and the movements of birds. The film just rolled slowly and noiselessly filming their activities and recording them with the camera. It contained a highly sensitive sound pickup device to record their calls and responses.

Coming to Tyagarah to work on the Beechcraft between jobs was a hobby for Natalie, like a time when she felt calm and focused doing maintenance and polishing the plane. She was a competent mechanic, having watched her father fix planes, cars and lawnmowers. Rover would spread out an old sheet and explain to her that motors were all the same business.

'Just take 'em off and lay it out in the same order, Nat,' he'd point to the sheet where he had the components lined up.

'Then when you are finished start from where you put the last piece and work out replacing everything. Simple.'

Systematically, she unscrewed the wing plates and connected the wires up training them along until they reached the instrument board. The beauty of these old planes, her dad had explained to her, was that each component could be taken off and replaced. She was grateful that the infrastructure for filming field parameters When crop dusting was already there, though now, she felt like a spy engaged in a secretive espionage enterprise.

Finally, she gathered the wires and connected them to the back of the camera, next she would test the lens and film. After some fiddling and rearranging she turned the film on and hopping out of the cockpit walked around to the front of the wings inspecting the lenses embedded in the sensors on each wing tip. No one was around so Natalie made a few bird-like hoots before climbing back into the cockpit to complete the preparation.

Stopping the camera, she rewound the film And pressed the play button again. She watched herself intently on the small screen and checked that the picture was crystal clear. She relaxed a fraction and waited for her hoot – sure enough, the device picked up her bird hoot, so Natalie held down the 'reverse' button deleting the film of her testing the device.

'Right!' She whispered, 'wish me luck, Dad.' Steadily and slowly, she unscrewed the left-hand panel of the dashboard and inserted the camera behind the cover making sure the wires to both the wing lenses and the sound recorder wire were connected to the device. Satisfied she set the film rolling and screwed everything behind the cover so there was no evidence of cameras, films, wires, or recorders. The film had twenty hours of recording capacity on each little disc, and despite all her efforts, she knew getting the meeting and the people recorded was not guaranteed.

* * *

Fortunately, she had never mentioned having another plane to Brendon or anyone else for that matter. The Beechcraft was her secret. A feeling of regret for ever getting involved with him now flooded her. That morning when she decided to bug the Beechcraft, she had been lying awake in his bed thinking about how to get out of the situation. Her stomach in knots knowing that 'getting out' of drug smuggling, wasn't an easy task. Brendon was already awake making noises in the kitchen when his phone rang. When he picked it up, Natalie pulled back the sheet and tiptoed to the bedroom door which was ajar, to listen to the conversation.

'Alright, where d'you wanna to meet?' Older wooden houses amplified sound so as Natalie stood very still, she heard Brendon asked a question, 'Why Tyagarah? Thought we'd decided it was risky?' he waited while the person on the other end responded.

'Yeah. Nah. She won't be a problem.' Natalie stealthily moved back to the bed but not before the next chilling sentence stopped her in her tracks.

'Don't worry about the chick, Luigi. I'll get rid of her. See you tonight at seven o'clock.

Natalie weighed up what to do, knowing she needed to buy time and convince Brendon there was nothing wrong, that she didn't suspect he was planning to kill her. She climbed back into bed then got out again and grabbed her clothes, put them on and wandered into the kitchen where he was standing tense and distracted, drinking instant coffee. There was a hard and astute aspect to his gaze that frightened her. She put on her rumpled impersonation of a woman sated by her man but wanting more.

'You wanna come back to bed and do it before work?'

Brendon relaxed. No chick would be coming onto him if she had heard the conversation he had just had with his boss.

'Gotta go. Come back later tonight, eh?'

Natalie smiled seductively, 'See ya tonight.'

With that she fled through the flyscreen door, trying not to run, jumped in her car and kicked it over before pulling out. Natalie didn't look back as she drove out to the industrial part of Lismore where the commercial aircraft operated. She had a cash job that morning dropping feed to a local grazier, she had time to have a shower and get some breakfast at the passenger terminal like any normal workday.

A clear day transformed into an overcast mantle of clouds in the afternoon and Natalie, satisfied with her surveillance setup in the Beechcraft, tucked her cargo pants into her rubber-soled, lace-up boots and hoisted the backpack. Even if someone got up into the cockpit and had a look it was innocuous enough, just a spare set of clothes but no identification. She pulled out her japara raincoat and the food she'd made to keep her going and checked her backpack which held a water bottle and Maglite torch as well as her personal belongings.

The long lights of dusk sloped across the hangar as Natalie climbed out of the cockpit and locked the door behind her then she jumped off the wing holding her bag and landing on bent knees. She straightened up, shrugged into her japara and wrapped a cotton scarf around her neck. She felt nervous, like a reptile was crawling up her spine and the hair on her arms stood up. She took some deep breaths and checked her bag. Right, here we go, she thought.

Walking over to the wooden side door she had entered earlier that faced away from the main entrance to the airstrip, she stood for a moment looking back at the Beechworth. Natalie emptied her mind and waved her arm over the plane and the space saying softly, 'I was never here today. All traces vanished.'

Rover had repeatedly cautioned her that if she got into difficult situations and needed to back out, take a few moments to gather herself and then to imagine herself getting clear and not leaving a psychic imprint. Departing the hangar now, she opened the door and moved to the outside casting about cautiously before taking off across the few hundred metres of soggy grassland and over the fence and into the bushes.

It was now almost six thirty, when she crawled into the underbrush between the ferns and ground covers under a decent sized tree and sat down out of sight. Natalie needed to eat something. She had a direct line of sight to the hangar's side door and the front so could see any cars arriving and the occupants if they passed in front of the headlights. The night sensor light of the hangar was switched on but was unreliable. She opened her pack and pulled out her salami and tomato sandwiches. Suddenly she was ravenous and she wolfed down the first one realising she was too skittish to eat much that day. However, as a commercial pilot, she had access to the staff kitchen at the Lismore airport and kept four big sandwiches all wrapped individually in grease-proof paper in the freezer of a small fridge for emergencies.

Taking a swig of her water bottle she considered her precarious position as evening closed around the Tyagarah airstrip and the cool air touched her forehead. There was a mozzie buzzing around looking for a weakness in her defence shield, absently she waved it away and hunched down a bit more pulling her black japara coat around her and tightening the hood straps. As an afterthought she teased her cotton scarf out and covered some of her face, so her garlicky warm breath didn't attract more mozzies.

A rustle in the underbrush signalled she wasn't alone, and she waited without making a sound watching and listening until a small warm-blooded creature hopped forward. A potoroo's beady eyes glinted reflecting what little light there was while its long nose twitched constantly.

'Hi buddy,' she murmured softly. Just as abruptly, the creature swivelled sharply in the opposite direction and bounded off.

'They are here!' Adrenaline surged in Natalie. Sure enough, there were dim headlights and the distant hum of motors moving towards the airstrip, she strained to make out how many vehicles were coming. She'd expected to see Brendon's four-wheel drive and one other driven by the mob. What she hadn't anticipated was the dark-coloured Commodore moving slowly beside Brendon while the other vehicle lead the way. All three vehicles drove deliberately up to the hangar parking their vehicles facing each other.

Shit! Natalie looked out from the bushes at the cars forming a circle. Interesting, she thought, the Commodore looked like an unmarked police car. Sure enough, two plain-clothed detectives emerged from their car holding their bodies stiffly from the waist up. Brendon got out of his vehicle whilst the detectives kept their eyes on the other Landcruiser. The two mobsters sat talking for a few moments leaning towards each other before pushing the doors open and getting out, they ambled toward the group gathered on the airstrip.

'Never trust a bloke who is on the take. The only thing important to them is money and they got a lot to lose if they get caught.' Natalie remembered her dad's words.

Sound travelled on the airstrip: maybe not word for word but snatches of sentences and wavelets of sound. The wind redolent with moisture, blew in damp gusts slanting this way and that as though captured by a spirit from the land as it began to drizzle.

'Let's go to the shed,' one of the detectives motioned toward the hangar.

The group met for criminal purposes. Detectives Peter Mangan and Paul Condon were bent drug cops known to be duplicitous, conniving and greedy. Stationed at Byron Bay, they were assigned to locate and provide intelligence on local dope growers. Similar in appearance and deportment from many years of poor posture, their bodies were the shape of question marks with heads pushed forward and their arms hanging loosely. Both men were dressed in cheap suits with ties pulled open and jackets unbuttoned not bothering to hide their gun holsters. The mobsters evinced the relaxed confidence of the amoral: violence was a way of life for them.

Luigi Grollo and his son Con, were the men loading the drugs onto Brendon's plane on the Tyagarah airstrip. Brendon was the only person not carrying a gun. Nevertheless, he was an unprincipled survivor with a pilot's licence and thus was of value to the stakeholders of this meeting. There would be mutual checking for body wires, blackmail a powerful tool in their business.

Moreover, there would be bargaining for who gets what out of the meeting and Natalie wished she could hear what was being said. As a rule, the mafia gang paid off the cops as part of doing business, usually, these cops didn't traffic in drugs and only kept a stash in case they needed to frame someone. The cops kept a watchful eye on people coming and going in the area, always taking a cut from local dealers to keep the wheels greased and they had a pre-existing relationship with the Grollos that went back many years.

Con, stood half inside the doorway where he could see the airstrip, every now and then ducking his head inside the hangar. Both cops smoked Benson and Hedges cigarettes while the negotiation was going on. Paul Condon had a face of resentment; in his mid-forties, he was tall with hooded eyes and spoke from the corner of his mouth.

'Who is the woman?' He took a drag of his cigarette, 'Luigi reckons she's a ball buster. We don't like you bringing on people and not telling us.'

'Piss off. I don't work for you mate,' Brendon spat on the ground.

'She going to be a problem later?'

Brendon ignored the question.

The men moved around while talking, sizing each other up.

'Who's growing the crops for you guys up in Nimbin and Nardi?' Mangan walked over and touched the Beechcraft plane looking up at the wings in admiration.

'Why do you want to know, Peter?' Luigi asked.

'We are under pressure to deliver results and need to deflect attention. Figure Nimbin is a good place to do that. Send in the helicopters.'

'Yeah, alright,' Luigi inclined his leonine head. 'Look on the left side of Mount Nardi about halfway up. Follow the fire trail you'll find a crop.' He accepted some losses.

'Don't fuck with us or your lives won't be worth living.' His face impassive, his eyes cold, Luigi made it perfectly clear who was calling the shots.

Luigi Grollo's face was like a Roman Senator, leathery brown skin and deep creases around his forehead and either side of his mouth, he sported a mane of steely grey hair combed straight back off his face. Despite being of average height he gave the impression of being taller because of the way he handled himself. There was an accommodation with power and unpredictable violence: on the one hand, he seemed unconcerned, on the other watchful and prepared.

Brendon observed the power dynamics impassively.

'What do you reckon, Brendon?' Luigi asked him without taking his eyes off Condon.

'The woman is a gun pilot. She fies crop dusters and knows all the landing strips here to Queensland. She can land a Cessna anywhere.'

'You are doin' her?' Condon leered, sliding a knowing look at Mangan, who snickered.

'Yeah, of course. Hot chick.' Men like Brendon were not

easily scared. He assessed the inherent threat level knowing he could move on one of the guys and lift his gun. No problem.

Back and forward the conversation went incriminating everyone involved.

'We can't take a load to Bankstown. It will be a problem,' Brendon continued. 'Unless it's disguised as machinery parts of something.' Luigi listened, his head forward as he excavated between his teeth with a toothpick.

'What about the Campbelltown airstrip again?'

'Too many people around, Luigi,' Brendon said.

'Yeah well, we gotta get the crop out of the barn.' The toothpick between his teeth moved as Luigi spoke.

Over in the bushes, Natalie was praying. Praying the camera had worked and recorded the whole transaction. It was her ultimate insurance policy. She knew the mafia would kill her without hesitation. She hadn't expected the cops to show up making this meeting more dangerous as it meant she couldn't turn the tape over to local police. If there were two bent police in the Byron station, you can bet your bottom dollar there were more in the region.

A fleeting shadow crossed in the front of the hangar triggering the sensor lights to come on momentarily. From where she was hiding, she could see a shape move stealthily past the hangar's front door and off to the right deep into the shadows. Con stepped out of the side door with his arm raised holding a gun. She watched him creep carefully down the wall to the corner of the building where he halted searching around systematically tense and poised.

There, she spotted it! A pair of yellow eyes flashed in the darkness on the other side of the hangar. God, she thought,

I hope it doesn't come over here. It was probably a wild dog though not a dingo. Still, she had two salamis sandwiches left if things got tricky.

The henchman with the gun spotted the dog too and pocketed his gun moving away from the front of the shed and back to the door which was standing ajar.

Luigi glanced at his offsider.

'Wild dog,' Con resumed his guardianship of the portal.

After a short time, the side door opened, and a shaft of light flickered in the gap as the cops left walking out together heading towards the Commodore, they climbed in and drove up the airstrip towards the gates with their lights off. She watched them go and when they reached the gates saw they turned their lights on and hauled a left onto the road in the direction of Byron Bay. She wished she hadn't drunk so much water as her bladder was full. Minutes later the other three men made their way out of the hangar, Brendon came last switching off the fluoro light and pulling the bolt across the side door. They all got in their cars and drove up the airstrip with Brendon leading. He held the gate for Luigi and Con who peeled right turning their headlights on. Brendon closed the gate after he'd driven through. It scraped the dome of the tarmac entrance, and he slipped the metal clamp over both gate and post and loosely wrapped the chain around. Natalie spied his silhouetted figure walking back over to his vehicle whose motor was running and the lights low. He jumped in and turned right. Not yet, she cautioned herself and she stood up in the bushes, feeling stiff from the tension, she stretched. Bits of undergrowth were stuck to her raincoat although it was still dry in the undercover foliage of the camellias their glossy leaves forming an impervious cover. She shook herself out a little and looked around. The drizzle fell quietly stroking the trees and the world. It was only then she became aware that in the distance there was a dim light of a house. There were no other noises other than the cicadas and occasional night birds.

Natalie wondered how much of the airfield noise they heard from the house. Did they hear light planes come and go? Crop dusters and other planes used the airfield as there was an aviation fuel tanker and pump to refuel. But at night? It was now almost eight o'clock.

She squatted down again. 'I wish I'd brought the binoculars with me,' annoyed with herself for not having anticipated residents. She planned to hide in the plane and sleep until just before dawn and then fly away.

Stiffly she moved out of her position and took in the lay of the land before climbing through a fence between some scrubby bush and the garden she was hiding in and hunched over walked across the space until she was directly opposite the side door of the hangar when she heard a low growl. A dog was crouched in the lee of the building. Natalie began singing a low soothing song the way her dad had taught her to do. With the backpack in from of her protecting her chest and neck, she kept talking and singing as she groped for a sandwich out of her bag.

'Come on buddy,' she crooned reassuringly. The growling got deeper. Natalie stood still and reached into her bag and pulled out the sandwich pack. The dog looked hungry and scrappy, as though he had been a stray for some time his coat was dirty and he was thin. Once, this black and tan dog would have been a handsome specimen he stood knee high with a broad forehead and long tail, while his eyes were big and black with two tan eyebrows. He was cautious from a tough life at the same time hopeful this human being would help him out with a feed. Neither of them had a real best friend until they met each other, and their hearts were bonded over salami sandwiches.

The dog stopped growling not letting down his defences Natalie threw the sandwich in the air and the dog lunged for it as she jumped to the door yanking it open. The dog swallowed the sandwich then scratched and barked at the door. She relented and did a deal through the door, 'I'll give you food, but you've got to be quiet.' She opened the door a crack. The dog pushed his wet nose against the door. She could see his fur damp and tattered, 'Come with me.' Going over to a beer fridge she took out a packet of biscuits and poured milk on top of them. The dog gulped the meal down before shaking himself all over and wagging his tail. Natalie got her penlight out to look at her hanger-on and saw he was part cattle dog around knee high with some white fur on his chest and ears that flopped forward at the tips.

'You're lost and hungry, aren't you?' Shaking out some old hessian bags and cleaning rags for a bed she put them in a corner next to car tyres.

Natalie and the dog looked at each other, he tilted his head, 'You sleep here. Okay?'

The dog walked over sniffed the door and returned to Natalie sitting on a tyre with an oily T-shirt next to his bed.

'Come here buddy,' eventually the dog submitted to being rubbed down and scratched behind the ears. 'Now I must sleep. You stay down here,' she patted the bed beside the tyre.

Retrieving her night kit, she cleaned her teeth at the sink while the dog lay down on the bed with his head on both paws looking ruefully at Natalie. Even amid danger, the small rituals of life are somewhat reassuring.

She climbed up the ladder to the plane where she kept a bedroll behind the cockpit, curling up and eventually falling asleep, albeit fitfully. The door to the Nissan hut was ajar and Natalie was sure the dog would bark if anyone approached. She thought about her mum and felt remorseful as today was her birthday, the twenty first of February, and every year Natalie had dinner with her. It was their special time. She knew her mum would wait up for her confused as to why she hadn't phoned.

'I'm so sorry Mum,' she whispered the words, 'I need to keep you safe.'

Dawn had not yet arrived when Natalie woke sore from the previous night. Quickly, she got up and splashed her face with water. The dog was sitting his head cocked to one side watching as she slid the front doors open and pulled the Beechcraft out before closing them behind her. She climbed into the cockpit, checked her dials and prepared to taxi out along the airstrip in the dark. The dog barked and she looked out the window, there he was on the ground waiting to climb aboard. She relented, got out of the plane and the dog bounded around her, wagging it's tail.

'Come on then,' she coaxed the dog, 'but you've got to help me.'

Low on the horizon a sun sliver pulsed while Natalie pulled down the aluminium ladder and, with the side door open and her tension level high, she climbed up one rung hoisting the dog onto the ladder. When he slipped, she heaved his haunches until he was in the back of the plane. She followed up the ladder, pulled it up and slid the door shut and dropped into the cockpit, pushing the dog off as he tried to lick her neck. She pressed the starter button, the engines softly purring to life, Natalie and the dog taxied down the airstrip, gunned the motor and lifted the nose of the Beechcraft into the infinite ineluctable expanse of dark blue sky. The first light shimmering across the horizon, Natalie allowed herself a moment of relief climbing higher and leaving the earth behind them. The dog had settled in the back. 'We need to fly under thirty thousand feet,' she pointed out, 'that way air traffic control won't ask me difficult questions.' She rechecked her dials before adding, 'I reckon you'll like Alice Springs, Buddy.'

CHAPTER 7

Lucy loved being part of the group of young people that formed the Movement. It felt like a big family. Their leader, Seth Lord High Alchemist, pointed out to them, that they were a worldwide network of Enlightened Beings, committed to serving him as their guru. Seth was the self-appointed prophet of Hermes Trismegistus, the famous Egyptian Alchemist, he had even studied his treatises and ancient texts. Seth paraded the accoutrements of ecclesiastical power: The Eye of Ra, a plaster of Paris bust painted gold and black to look like Queen Nefertiti, with staring eyes lined in black kohl. Even more powerful, according to Seth, was the Rod of God, a burled walking stick with a thick pewter claw clutching the top on one end. He claimed to channel the esoteric spirits through the wooden staff and communicate Hermes' thoughts and wishes to his followers. He called it 'energetic channelling'.

As the only member of the shared house who worked in a job in town, Lucy spent her shifts serving on tables and making coffee at one of the numerous coffee shops in the local township of Byron Bay. The Bean Bar, a small operation on the main street was squeezed between a bespoke fashion outlet for very tiny females and a juice shop, with a dubious hygiene record.

The Movement made clear the division of labour and Lucy had attended the compulsory seminar on the roles that each member played within the organisation. Most of the seekers worked long hours, for no pay, at the industrial estate outside Byron Bay, constructing imported merchandise to be blessed by Seth.

Workers, he elucidated, were like the blood of the Movement, their work kept the body thriving and healthy. Everyone had to play their role by dedicating themselves to the well-being of the whole. He had the most important job as the cerebral cortex or seat of the psyche and soul, receiving cosmic vibrations from Hermes. There were others in the Movement who were recruiters and proselytisers, their jobs were to recruit more and more seekers to the fold, especially young people and tourists, who attended festivals and events in the main cities and on the North Coast. For example, the Mind Body Spirit Festival held annually in Sydney, proved a particularly fruitful ground for recruiters.

The organisational nerve centre of the group was made up of two men and a woman called the Elders of Isis, who organised the accounts and logistics. Paying wages wasn't an issue as work, called 'voluntary service', included getting unemployment benefits, some of which they were expected to donate toward the upkeep of the ashram.

The previous day, the members of the Movement gathered around Seth to share in his exciting news that all their sales, donations and hard work were going towards buying their ashram. At last, he rejoiced, we'll have a permanent home base.

The Elders of Isis were an inscrutable trio, although friendly on the surface, Lucy felt nervous being around them and twitchy if one of them spoke directly to her. She wasn't alone in her feelings of creepiness towards the engine of the cult, for that's what the Elders were, as they ran everything from work shifts to food shopping and the accounts. Many others felt uncomfortable about them too and gossiped. Lucy didn't really believe the Elders had the same spiritual powers Seth that obviously possessed.

This week was also notable because Seth and his followers, were taking possession of a big shipment of plastic paraphernalia imported from Asia. He would be spending time invoking the spirits and imbuing the artefacts with 'Spiritual Energies'. The blessing of the pallets meant the workers could begin the work of unpacking them and putting them together in preparation for sales.

The most expensive object for sale was a radiant blue plastic tube, called a 'Blessed Booblay' (pronounced boob-lay, like the crooner Michael Bublé) which took batteries and vibrated, looking suspiciously like a sex toy. The Karmic Talisman cards and Astral Charm bracelets were more mundane, resembling the stuff one wins at theme parks for banging the hammer or throwing a tennis ball straight. All seekers were informed the sacred artifacts contained powerful, magnetic charges of cosmic energy. Once assembled and ready for sale, the Movement would distribute them to other seekers and outlets in Brisbane, Sydney, and other cities. The Elders and Seth were always talking about 'virgin fields' which Lucy interpreted as other markets they hadn't penetrated yet.

* * *

Irrespective of the Movement's greater spiritual purpose, today was an ordinary workday for Lucy. She awoke early and put on her clean jeans and lace-up boots then combed her hair and put some lip gloss on. It was seven o'clock and quite cool outside, luckily, she was getting dropped off at work by Hilly, who would go over to the storage facility later and begin work on packaging the plastic artefacts once they had been blessed by Seth.

Hilly exhibited a disconcerting habit of looking at the person in the passenger seat and talking while driving, rather than watching the road. Lucy clutched her seat with both hands fearing a calamity.

'He can give me the Rod of God any day!' Hilly announced suggestively referring to Seth, of course.

'Hilly! Watch the road!' Lucy snapped as the car veered sideways to avoid a pothole.

'Keep your pants on,' Hilly didn't have a driver's license.

'You keep yours on and keep your mind off Seth's rod!' Lucy griped.

The wide streets of Byron were empty when they pulled over, Lucy got out relieved to be at work and not in a car accident. Rob, her boss, could be uncaring and bad tempered, not that Lucy blamed him, his was a thankless task trying out and employing countless international backpackers, many of whom were flaky or just didn't turn up. Lucy's shifts changed over time and now she had proved herself reliable and hardworking, Rob gave her more shifts. Plus, being a fast learner, she got the hang of the coffee machine, stepping in and making coffee whenever Rob needed time off. Her boss was waiting for her when she turned up for work leaving her with her six orders from tradesmen while he went outside and smoked.

It had been three weeks since she witnessed the illicit drug deal on the Tyagarah airstrip. Lucy remained cautiously circumspect about the incident, realising that talking to anyone at all, about what she's seen, would bring them into danger too. She hadn't heard any other deliveries by plane since that night either.

Later that morning, the café was bustling, and Lucy was juggling three coffees under the machine at once when Fleur leaned her sizeable bust on the counter and spoke in a staged whisper.

'That guy out there,' Fleur jerked her shoulder to the outside, 'has a crush on you.'

Fleur, a husky fair haired backpacker from Holland, was waitressing at the café before travelling to Queensland for the fruit picking season. Lucy met her eyes as she scooped up the three cups of coffee for the customers.

'Which one?'

'The one with the five o'clock shadow and the casual clothes that don't look casual,' Fleur giggled. Sitting next to a planter box on the footpath, framed by statice and marigold flowers, was a man who resembled the younger guy from the Tyagarah drug deal. Though it was more a sense of familiarity and dread as he emitted an unmistakable aura of danger. Lucy's heart did a backflip.

'Yuk, go and deliver those coffees, Fleur,' she managed to recover.

'Just saying,' Fleur giggled again and moved on to serve the customers.

Lucy continued making coffee, talking to the people, and thinking. Was there anything that connected her to the drug deal she witnessed that night? Proximity, she concluded. Or maybe something else had happened? She speculated the man had been sent out to gather information in the local area. There were dozens of houses and farms some close to the airstrip. Lucy just needed to keep her cool and not act guilty, she concluded.

Half an hour later Rob returned smelling of tobacco. Rob was average height with a powerful torso his muscular arms hinted at a life of surfing, berry brown from years in the sun. He was totally bald. Standing beside Lucy now with arms crossed over his chest looking out at the tables and people, he was mulling over the thin margins in the hospitality business and wondering if he could cut out after lunch and go surfing.

'I really don't like that guy out there,' Lucy complained, as she prepared yet another cappuccino, 'he's been staring at me for ages and hasn't ordered more coffee.'

Rob cut his eyes sideways. Jeez, this chick is like a baby lamb, he thought. Of course, he's looking at her!

'Well, you're a nice-looking girl,' he spoke slowly as though to a child, 'what do you expect?'

She took another tack. 'He's bad for business, Rob. Look how many people are left at the outside tables? That guy has scared them off. He's menacing.' True, he shrugged and proceeded to pick up a tray and wander outside collecting cups and leftovers before moving over to the mob guy. They exchanged some words whereupon the mob guy got up and left.

Good! Lucy was not under the illusion that being moved on meant the mobster wouldn't hang around the town or stake out the café again.

* * *

Across town at a new industrial estate occupying a lush paddock that was previously a fragile wetland, Seth Lord High Alchemist, had just signed for the shipment of plastic paraphernalia delivered to the Colorbond corrugated sheet warehouse that the Movement leased as a storage facility and workshop. Pallets that held cardboard boxes were stacked waist deep on the floor all tightly sealed. He and his offsider, Shorn, oversaw the truck being unloaded before closing the doors of the vast shed to briefly talk about the details of The Blessing. Seth didn't pay attention to the faces of the two delivery guys, however, Shorn noted they were Asian in appearance.

Shorn joined the Movement a few months prior because he needed somewhere to live. Somewhere between thirty and forty in age he was rangy and dangerous with a buzzcut and tattoos on both arms including the traditional markers of time spent at Her Majesty's pleasure – 'Love' and 'Hate', crudely tattooed across his knuckles. He hailed from New

Zealand and had avoided police attention by posing as a security guard for the Movement.

'You don't want perverts and scumbags wandering onto the farm,' he pointed out the obvious to the Elders of Isis, who nodded sagely in unison. 'Or the cops rocking up without a warrant looking for underage girls.' They hired him on the spot for a small retainer, a place to sleep and meals, glad of his expertise in these matters.

Seth and Shorn looked at the boxes.

'This is a serious business, Shorn,' Seth declared in a deep, thespian voice conveying the gravitas and moment of the ritual. 'I will need a quiet space to commune with Hermes and to impregnate all the boxes with his holy spiritual essence. I want you to stand guard at the doors and not let anyone pass until I give you the signal.'

Privately, Seth feared Shorn's edgy and unpredictable vibe. For his part, Shorn thought Seth was a total fraud and a wanker but envied his ingenuity in capitalising on the existential fears and anxieties of seekers by persuading them to give him their money. Until then, Shorn had only known about shakedowns, scams, and protection rackets. No one *willingly* gave him money! Ever. Obviously, soul-saving was a lucrative business.

'Righto,' Shorn obeyed stepping outside the door and pulling it closed behind him. Despite being sceptical about the veracity of magic vibrations saturating pieces of plastic manufactured in Asia, he reasoned that, if someone was going to pay them ten grand for a Blessed Booblay, then what a fantastic scam! He wanted a piece of that action.

Seth stripped off his rainbow T-shirt leaving just his dirty white linen dhoti tied around his waist with its folded section, like a sporran, across the front covering his crotch. He rifled through his shoulder bag and took out his bong and a bag of grass heads that were so full of resin they glistened. He opened the plastic baggy and took a deep draught. 'Hummmmm,' he exhaled. Then, as an afterthought, 'Ommmmmm'.

Gingerly, with dope bag and bong in hand, he climbed onto of the nearest block of boxed plastic objects and settled down cross-legged to smoke a few cones and chant some incantations. He packed the cone and licked his fingers and from out of the folds of his sporran he produced a yellow Bic lighter and lit the cone of the bong, sucking in deeply. Soon he felt heavy as though gravity was dragging him down, down and further down. Strange visions floated past.

'Seth! Seth! Get up! Get your fuckin' shirt on. For Chrissakes, the cops are here!'

A voice was shouting at him. Seth could hear it in the distance. He couldn't move. He couldn't open his eyes. The voice faded away again.

'Fuckin' moron!' Shorn slipped back from the crack in the door where he could see two unmarked cop cars and a sporty hatchback in the middle-distance between the rows of buildings driving past the other warehouses. Shorn had a sixth sense for cops. He knew he was clean. True, he had a record in New Zealand. What if he ran now? Had they clocked him? Nah. Too far away.

He swore again and headed around the back of the warehouses where his white panel van was parked out of sight. Struggling into a grey short-sleeved shirt with an MSS Security logo on the pocket and sleeve, he tucked it into his trousers. Climbing into his van he drove off steadily passing the first cop car, a black Commodore, before the second driver wound down his window just as he pulled alongside. Shorn slowed to a crawl.

'What's your business here?' The driver, wearing a pale blue shirt with his tie loosened, sized up Shorn in a casual, business as usual way, his passenger wore a police uniform.

'Work,' Shorn replied flatly.

'What sort of work?'

'Looking for warehouse space to rebuild vintage motorbikes.'

It rolled off his tongue like warm Nutella on toast.

'Is that right? What's your name?'

'Kevin Bogan,' the detective nodded, 'what's the problem?'

The cop ignored his question.

Shorn's face was empty of emotion besides mild curiosity, nor did he feel a smidgen of guilt about leaving Seth in the lurch. The dickhead deserved it.

'Move on,' the detective dismissed him. Shorn drove off.

* * *

It was time to move on alright! He drove straight back to the ashram located on a tributary road off the main road between Byron and Tweed Heads. The farmhouse, that doubled as an ashram and home to Seth and the seekers, was nestled into the surrounding countryside and had outhouses converted for living in. It was modelled on houses popular in Queensland, with a corrugated roof and bull nosed iron embracing wide verandas on three sides. Clad in wooden chamfer boards, the house was surrounded by tall Norfolk pines and a variety of other established broad sweeping trees that gave shade in the hot summers and a perfect place for the numerous seekers to play. A wide enclosed sunroom ran along the back of the house and served as a shared dining area and social space. Somewhere people could eat, meet and pray. Of the senior members, only Seth lived in the farmhouse as the Elders of Isis claimed two converted cabins with spacious bedrooms, kitchens and bathrooms installed.

The ashram's main driveway curved in a turning circle outside the front porch and there was a wide paved path through the trees covered with native violets weeds and leaves. And the fields surrounding the house were so efflorescent and green it was hard to believe.

Shorn parked his van a few hundred metres up the road out of sight and walked hastily along a track toward the main homestead house. He knew that everyone was out that morning doing a chanting ritual in the back paddock in preparation for hours of unpaid work constructing plastic shit into overpriced 'spiritual' commodities.

He formulated a cover story that Seth needed more pot for the Blessing and had sent him back to get it from his office at the farm. As it happened, he also knew where the Movement kept the cash from their products. In Seth's office! Money, they didn't pay tax on. The Elders practised a circuitous method for laundering cash through credit union branches. Shorn didn't know the details, but as a lifelong player, he was alert to code words, knowing looks and secret meetings and was sure of dodgy deals going on. They were, after all, a secret society.

Now, no longer Shorn, Kevin tiptoed silently through the front door of the ashram and studied the hallway running end to end to be certain no one was around. He pushed the office door ajar and sidled in over to the filing cabinet where Seth and the Elders kept the petty cash tin. Without wasting time, he cast around for an instrument to force the lock and spotted a dagger shaped letter opener.

'Sweet,' he murmured. He was amused by people who left the tools needed to break and enter next to the object to be entered. Like chairs and shovels. They should just write a note for the villains – *'Take the chair and climb on it then smash the bathroom window with the shovel. Enter through the window headfirst being careful not to cut yourself.'*

He popped the lock, reached into the filing cabinet took out a small metal box with a key and lock in the top and a sign sellotaped to the side that read 'Petty Cash'. He used the end of his shirt to wipe down and close the cabinet, wipe his fingerprints off the letter opener and wiped clean the door handles on the way out. He tucked his shirt in and stashed the box under it. It felt hard and cold against his skin.

Like an animal crossing another's territory, Kevin waited, listening to the noise of people chattering happily as they approached the back of the house coming in to make vegetarian lunches and herbal tea ready for long hours of work at the warehouse. He slipped out the front door and trotted over the wide, shady veranda. Normally, he never entered Seth's office except for one Thursday afternoon when he dropped in and caught Seth counting bundles of cash which he clumsily covered with a book on digestive gut health. The filing cabinet drawer stood ajar, and it didn't take a genius to work out where Seth stashed the cash.

Kevin loped the distance to the road grateful for the tree cover the front yard afforded. Swinging into his van he drove up the road having decided to get onto the highway, fill up the tank and then investigate how much cash his hunting foray gave him. Moderately, he motored along the road before meeting the main road and taking a left at the sign which pointed to the Pacific Highway. The petty cash tin was under the seat. Accustomed to an itinerant lifestyle, he kept his worldly belongings in his van just taking a bedroll into the ashram some nights where he rolled it out and slept on the porch on top of a yoga mat.

Kevin saw a service station coming up on his left, so he put on a baseball cap and sunglasses, before checking where the closed-circuit cameras pointed, then using a prepaid debit card he filled the tank. Jumping back in the cab he wheeled the van into the traffic heading towards Surfers Paradise, looking for all the world like hundreds of delivery guys or air conditioning installers. He planned to find a mixed business shop and grab some food and drinks, first, he would make a comfort stop, take a leak, and look in the petty cash tin.

Admittedly, he felt curious but not overly optimistic. He had enough money to go somewhere over the border to Queensland, after that get some cash-in-hand work as a kitchen hand and a panel beater. A few kilometres along the Pacific Highway squatted a solid brick building and a stopover table and chairs accompanied by a thoughtful sign that read, 'Rest Revive Survive.' Kevin wholeheartedly agreed with the 'Survive' part of the motto. He slowed down and veered left into the rest area, parking the van alongside the table and seats before reaching under his seat and groping around for the petty cash tin. His fingers grasped it, and he wriggled it out with the little key still sticking out of the lock on top of the tin. Kevin opened it and stared at the contents. He was gobsmacked.

'Jesus Christ! A flash of adrenaline surged through him like a hit of speed. He closed the lid quickly and checked the rear-view mirror and the side mirrors. Traffic whizzed past.

Assured he was alone, he opened the lid again. Nestled in the box along with a few scrappy receipts was a huge roll of used bank notes mostly fifty and one hundred-dollar bills. The spiritual enlightenment business sure pays he surmised, there was nothing petty about the stash of cash.

He undid the screws holding down the centre storage compartment between the two front seats then lifted the whole unit back, revealing another secret little space. Carefully, he got the sharp end of his nail file into a corner and pressed until the lid clicked open, revealing just enough room to fit the whole cash tin, he pushed it in and closed the lid then closed the separator storage unit and screwed it down tight using the round end of the nail file.

Only then did he jump out and lock the van before he went to the toilet and washed his hands at the side tap before walking back to the van shaking them dry. Kevin took a big stretch swinging his arms from side to side making several of his vertebrae click. Having limbered up he headed North. Maybe he'd get work as an exotic dancer? Chicks loved his MSS security uniform.

* * *

Detective Chief Inspector Olaf Petersen and a uniformed policewoman next to him arrived first, followed by Detective Senior Sergeant Greg Forman and another constable. Olaf halted in front of the warehouse just as Greg swung his car in next to his boss and all four police gathered outside the warehouse looking at the woman in the hatchback who had parked and was joining them.

Wearing a tailored red skirt, and a gleaming white blouse her name label read, 'Katrina Delgado, Real Estate Agent'. She was immaculately made up and rattled a big key ring in her hand with a dozen keys attached.

'Who was the guy in the white van?' Olaf asked Greg under his breath.

'Kevin Bogan,' Greg recalled. He looked up as the real estate agent got closer.

'Plates checked out said he's looking for a warehouse for a client. Had an MSS Security shirt on like he was working.'

'Coincidence?' Olaf smiled at Katrina. 'Thanks for facilitating our visit, Miss Delgado,' he acknowledged the agent reaching to take her hand in a brief shake.

'You are welcome, Chief Inspector, I want to help the police.' The agent lowered her eyelashes. He took in her glossy, red lips, which were amazing. Katrina stepped in front of the police contingency and went to open one of the sliding doors, only to realise the doors weren't locked.

CHAPTER 8

The city of Brisbane was only a two-hour drive from the ashram and lay across the landscape on the mouth of the Brisbane River sprawling and brownish. Originally, a regional trade centre, it seemed to become a city before its residents realised notwithstanding becoming a ghost town each weekend.

Kevin's priority was to get his van rebirthed and create a new identity as his order of business. First, he had to get himself a locked box and stash his cash plus any other papers that identified him as Kevin Bogan. He took a turn off the highway before the first traffic lights and wound his way through the suburbs in the eastern outskirts of Brisbane. He knew this area like the back of his hand from being a stand-in taxi driver for an old cabbie who reckoned he was sick of driving nights. He didn't sleep much anyway, and the tips were good for escorting hookers home after a long night or dropping a courier off with a backpack of drugs. Entering the shopping centre of a suburb called Danklea Park, he followed the road around to the car park behind a supermarket out of sight of the main drag. He chose this suburban shopping centre for its ordinariness: with a burger bar, a newsagent, a chemist, a supermarket, and an assortment of other outlets such as a Totaliser Agency betting outfit and the local post office, which rented locked boxes. Reaching under the seat he groped around for his spare license and miners' card, claiming he was a Mick Spillane from Logan. Spreading his map of the city across the steering wheel he unlocked his hidden stash of cash secreting half the money back into the space. Carrying the money in his bag, he climbed out of the van and went around to the back door where he changed his shirt into a checked short-sleeved cotton one and put a cowboy hat on his head. The glasses were the final touch giving him the appearance of a short-sighted rancher or mine worker. Most people, Kevin discovered, noticed a few features of another person, 'he wore glasses', they would state. The woman at the counter of the post office was June, on the phone to her best friend, Shereen, she looked up at Kevin as he entered. In her fifties, June got her white-blonde, sculptured hair done every Friday before going to the Return Services League club to have dinner and a flutter with Norman, her husband.

I know,' she dragged out the syllable, 'and you know what she said? Hang on Shereen,' June put the phone down irritably. 'Can I help you?' She asked him as he stood at the counter.

'I want to rent a locked box,' he stated.

'I will need your driver's licence and sixty dollars,' June glanced at the phone lying on the counter. He produced a license for Mick Spillane and sixty dollars in notes while June wrote up a receipt and put the corresponding details in a school exercise book, she kept under the counter. She gave his license back and a plastic disc with the number 112 embossed on it. The beauty of this system is that once you close a locked box and put in a personal combination of numbers, it can't be opened by anyone else.

'Thank you,' Kevin turned noting that June and Shereen had resumed their phone conversation before he opened the door. Once he'd stashed the cash and secured the locked box, he got himself a burger and a coke from the takeaway place next door, comfortable in his anonymity, he went back to the van satisfied with his work.

He still had some contacts to buy like a fake licence and other forms of identification, not to mention a paint job for the van and new plates. The administration of covering his tracks and becoming another person was circular and time-sensitive, so he drove to the car rebirthing place. He needed a builder's licence, and another driver's licence and figured he had a few more hours should the coppers join some dots and factored him in as a person of interest.

He countered on not being named by the Elders or Seth as part of their grubby deals because he could grass them up. He hadn't engaged with the seekers while he was at the ashram ensuring security and was inherently cautious of sexually tempting young women. Trouble he thought. Instead, he would get up early and eat breakfast on the front veranda then carry out his various duties. The Elders gave him a surly induction that included keeping your hands out of the till and don't ask questions. One thing he'd learned: belonging to a religion, even a crazy cult like the Movement, gave him a certain insularity, even cachet, whereby he was considered by some to be deluded, but not dangerous. If he assumed the cloak of a Christian, he would appear innocuous, like the lamb of God, he smiled at the irony. Maybe, he'll go into a new profession as a man of the cloth once the heat is off.

Not even his own mother thought Kevin was a beautiful baby. As he grew into a teenager, he became less attractive, with a tall raw-boned frame, broad shoulders and beady black eyes set too close together. His nose was small and knobby. His ears stuck out from his head, a feature made predominant when he shaved his hair.

He loved punk rock, especially Johnny Rotten, the crashing punchy iconoclastic beat was destructively euphoric. Of course, the speed helped too. His father was an alcoholic stevedore who taught Kevin everything he knew, which was to climb and operate a forklift.

'Reaction time, mate,' his father, Barry, would slur, 'punch first then ask questions.' Having dispensed his wisdom, he would collapse sideways off the barstool, dead drunk.

He did a stint in juvenile detention following Barry's advice. Later, after a brief stay in jail for receiving stolen goods, he decided jail was for mugs and he would try to stay mostly on the right side of the law – which is why he felt pissed off about Seth being busted.

'Fucking wishy-washy hippies,' he remonstrated contemptuously, changing lanes when heading towards the Body Shop, a panel-beating shop owned by Ricky Spooner.

Renowned for his craftsmanship, Ricky, Sergeant at Arms for the Hyenas Motorcycle gang, was connected to criminal networks all along the eastern seaboard of Australia.

'What d'ya want,' Ricky asked abruptly, wiping his hands on his jeans, and tilting the visa of his welding helmet back revealing a heavy-set man with a two-day growth and shifty eyes above a wide scar clinging to his cheekbone, which should have been stitched at the time it was inflicted.

'Need some spray-painting work and new plates on the van,' Kevin didn't waste time with niceties.

'No problem. Leave it a couple of days. Cost you a grand.' They settled on racing stripes in blue and lettering on the back reading 'Pool Repairs" with a phone number that didn't exist. Kevin put five hundred dollars as a deposit on the side bench and set off further into Fortitude Valley, the sleazy end of town, where most things could be purchased including identity papers and false passports with a tattoo or two thrown in for good measure.

The tattoo parlour was tucked below an adult book outlet next door to a laundromat, on a road reminding him of shopping strips in small towns he'd seen at the movies. Both the window and door of the shop were covered with tattoo designs writ large, making the inside area feel as cloistered and colourful as stained-glass church windows. A silver-haired older gent greeted him wearing a leather sleeveless vest with long tassels, black jeans and neck to waist tattoos set off by chains. He slid his stool away from the work recliner chair revealing a pair of embossed cowboy boots with heels. He looked like Kenny Rogers, the country and western crooner, adding to the American atmosphere, a feeling reinforced by the country and western radio channel playing in the background.

'Help you?' Kenny Rogers casually looked him up and down.

'Yeah, I need some I.D. papers,' Kevin standing next to the counter, held his arms loosely folded. 'What happened to the other guy who owned this outfit?'

'Doing time.' The man waited for a few moments.

'Change of career,' he revealed his Love and Hate jail tatts, 'I want to get rid of these too.'

'That right?' The man hitched his silver eyebrows. 'Alright, you'll need a name. One grand for one hundred points. Come out here, I'll get a photo.' He stood Kevin against a white background and took some photos.

'Sean Wellington,' Kevin suggested, 'that's Sean with an 'ea',' he sounded it out.

'Let's have a look at the jail tatts,' Kenny Rogers inspected Kevin's knuckles, 'You got two options, mate. I can disguise them with white ink. Takes an hour each hand – two hundred bucks a hand. Or I can send you to see the dermatologist who does skin grafts. Gives us a kickback.'

'How long do the grafts take?' Kevin liked the second option.

'Dunno, he takes the skin off your arse first then grafts it over the tatts. Cost a bit. You need an anaesthetic.'

'I'll get them inked out. Haven't got time for an operation.'

'Fair enough. The papers will be ready when you come back tomorrow for the ink. Need a thirty per cent deposit on the paperwork.'

Next stop for him was to find a hotel, have a shower and get some clean threads and a decent feed. He looked forward to feeling clean.

Business organised, he stepped out onto the pavement to flag a cab and locate a quiet suburban pub to stay at for a few days. He gazed around and saw a creaky looking red and white cab approaching and he flagged it down. The driver chucked a cigarette butt out the window as he pulled into the kerb.

'Where do you wanna go?'

'Know a quiet pub I can get a room and a feed?'

'I'll take you to the Lord Byron, it's in Batley just a bit out from the city centre.'

'Thanks,' Kevin guessed the driver knew what he was talking about as he probably drank there, in addition to getting a kickback for dropping customers off.

After eight minutes, during which time the driver didn't bother with chit-chat, he hauled the cab into the kerb outside a pub typical of many Australian hotels. Built in the 1880s, the Lord Byron pub, sported a Victorian frontage with balustraded steps, small windows and doors on two sides. The second story lurched over the ground floor loosely embraced by a wooden veranda that looked untrustworthy. A blackboard A frame sat on the street advertising juicy steaks and pies.

'This will do,' Kevin gave the driver ten bucks and grabbed his bag.

Entering the front bar, he saw a smattering of locals nursing their beers and watching the racing on the big screen attached to a wall above them.

'You got a room for a few nights?'

'Cost you fifty bucks a night and no trouble.'

'No trouble,' he agreed, 'I'll have a steak and a middy.'

'That's ten bucks.'

'Go and see the missus when you've had the steak,' the

barman handed him a cold beer and a meal ticket jerking his thumb towards the dining room alcove.

'Thanks,' he found a table where a previous patron had left the Telegraph newspaper. He sipped his beer and contemplated his efforts for the day. From the swamp flat of industrial Byron Bay to the streets of Brisbane. A rebirthed car and a set of papers. Not bad. He didn't have to pick up his car and new identity until the next day giving him a couple of hours to kill. Having paid in advance, he went upstairs with his room key, and ditched his bag on the double bed before taking a long hot shower.

Feeling clean again, he sat on the bed leafing through the Yellow Pages telephone book and found a St Vincent de Paul charity shop located only a block away. The doorbell rang when he entered the second-hand shop, the assistant behind a counter, ignored him. He ran a hand over the clothes display divided into racks of shirts, pants and jackets which were all clean and in good condition. He picked out three shirts and tried them against himself before moving onto the suit rack.

Unaccustomed to wearing suits, he understood that clothes did maketh the man. When he returned to the front counter, he was carrying two suits, three shirts and a pair of smart leather shoes in his arms. He paused, studying the glass fronted cabinet containing jewellery, something caught his attention. Nestled in a white silk lined case he spied a gold crucifix on a chain.

'I'll have that too,' pointing to the crucifix.

The shop assistant ran the clothes and the crucifix through the cash register, removing their prices one at a time.

'That will be forty-six dollars altogether,' she chewed her

gum absently.

'You got a bag to put them in?' He asked.

'Do you want a suitcase? They are down the stairs there with the kitchenware.' The woman waved a hand vaguely to the middle of the shop. He hadn't taken much notice of the other people in the shop though he did see a woman go down the stairs.

'Yep, I'll go and get one,' he followed the woman.

On the lower level, there were shelves of plates and Tupperware while on the back wall bags, satchels, and backpacks were piled on two shelves opposite a wall of paperback books, DVDs and jigsaw puzzles.

'Cool,' he said. He found a lightweight navy suitcase with wheels and grabbed a James Patterson novel. He waited while the shop assistant served two people before him.

'That's another five dollars,' the woman piled his clothes into the bag with wheels handing him the crucifix in its case and eventually, he left the store with his new clothes and novel, wheeling the suitcase behind him.

Piece of cake, he thought, pleased with himself. Looking across the street as he approached the hotel, he noticed a red brick church with a spire and a sign urging repentance for sins. The billboard read that Mass at St. Ninians, was at six o'clock that evening. He deposited his things in his room, hung his suits and shirts in the cupboard and slipped his gold crucifix on. He planned to visit the church for mass and to begin his research. It was important, to look the part so he swapped his jeans and T-shirt for a clean white shirt with a pair of slacks from his new wardrobe together with his leather shoes. He tucked his shirt in and looked at himself in the bathroom mirror uncertainly, his crucifix lay on his chest framed by his open-necked shirt. He crossed the street and walked up the front stairs of the church and was greeted by a beaming priest with a black and white robe over his trousers his hand outstretched towards him, delighted to see a new face.

'Welcome. Welcome to our humble church. I am Father Conrad,' he extended his hand and shook Kevin's warmly with both of his. His hands were warm and dry. 'You are new to our parish, son. What's your name?'

'Sean Wellington. I'm passing through on my way to a job up North.' He tried out his rebirthed self. As a lapsed Catholic, Kevin knew the drill, despite not being in a church since he was nine years old. His recent experience running interference for the likes of Seth and the Elders in their spiritual adventurism had opened his mind to the opportunities for financial exploitation of people who needed to believe in a god.

'Please find a seat, we'll be taking the sacrament shortly. The hymn sheets and bibles are in the back of the pews.' Father Conrad waved in the direction of the pews down where he observed the parishioners as they filed in, genuflected, crossed themselves and kissed their crucifixes. The priest called the faithful with a sing-song voice full of hope and joy.

'Welcome all our parishioners, our regulars, the new and the old. Jesus welcomed everyone into his heart and his church,' Father Conrad looked down the aisle beaming love.

'Welcome to our brother Sean, this is his first Mass with us. Know that when we come to Jesus and ask his forgiveness, he enfolds us under his mantle with love.'

Brother Sean, thought Kevin, that sounds good. He sang

loudly and in tune, he prayed, petitioning God. He took the wafer from Father Conrad and, when the donation plate was passed around, he dropped a twenty dollar note in it and crossed himself boldly. The flock filed out after the service stopping to say a few words with the priest as they departed. After waiting his turn, he shook the priest's hand again and thanked him for such a moving service then he set off, standing at the kerb a few moments for a car to pass before crossing the road back to the pub which emitted warmth and welcome.

The Movement has nothing on the Catholic Church, he concluded, but for some people, Catholicism was too conservative. Back at the pub, he bought a cup of coffee and ordered a toasted cheese sandwich, taking them to his room on a tray. Once there, he turned on the television, picked up the Yellow Pages and sat on the bed thumbing through the 'Churches' section, aware he needed to represent a faith-based sect that didn't scare the punters nor make them feel guilty. The Catholics had cornered that market on guilt. Running his finger down the small writing he found an assortment of churches and groups advertised. From Jehovah's Witnesses to the Church of Christ the Shepherd, though what the difference was, he didn't know. Kevin took a bite of his sandwich and kept looking, 'Now we're talking,' he commented aloud, keeping his finger on a group advertising themselves as 'MYSTICS RUS'. They had a drop-in centre a few suburbs away in Glenmore. 'Searching for answers?' Their advertisement asked, 'Drop in and talk to us soon.'

'Maybe I will,' Kevin mused, 'maybe I will drop in. After I pick up the van tomorrow.'

CHAPTER 9

*I*t's open,' Katrina announced to the two detectives behind her before pushing the unlocked, sliding doors ajar and stepping into the warehouse. She was taken aback by the vision that greeted her though the smell was unmistakable. Lying prone across a bench of wrapped cartons was Seth, known to the real estate agent as John Owens, a 'businessman', who paid a year of rent in advance.

'Excuse me please, Miss Delgado,' Olaf Petersen gently moved Katrina to one side and stepped past her, followed by Greg Foreman and the two uniformed police officers who quickly closed the gap unsure as to what state of consciousness the prone man was in. The evidence of his soporific drug ingestion was vividly clear. What else may he have ingested? The group speculated whether Mr Owens had died rather than being blissfully comatose.

'Is this the man who signed the lease with you?' Olaf

pointed to the recumbent Seth.

'Yes, he's definitely John Owens, the man who signed the lease.' Katrina confirmed.

'Good,' Olaf went on, 'we can take it from here Miss Delgado,' adopting a professional and polite manner, 'thank you for your assistance. We will update you in the event we need to re-enter the premises.'

The fact that she really wanted to stay and see what happened was irrelevant, the police took over. Olaf's clear blue eyes revealed nothing of his thoughts about the poised woman who moved through life without a hair out of place, never smudging her lipstick or snagging her pantyhose.

'Oh,' she pouted, 'as you like, Chief Inspector,' her disappointment showing. 'If you need anything else don't hesitate to call me,' she suggested, adding emphasis, 'anything at all.' Batting her eyelids again, she turned on her heel and walked off to her car.

Olaf's partner barely disguised his amusement.

'What?' He challenged Greg.

'Anything at all?' Greg questioned. Olaf twitched his mouth, his eyes creased, he shrugged as if to say, 'I'm a sexy Dane that's all.'

Greg Foreman carried himself like a fast bowler with long, muscular arms loose at his side and a tan that spoke volumes about an outdoor life playing sports and presiding over endless fundraising barbecues for local kids' clubs. He was light on his feet despite being over six feet tall and Olaf enjoyed working with him particularly, because of his garrulous, down to earth Australian humour. The moment passed. Olaf gave some rapid instructions to the team to deploy them around the warehouse to fulfil the search warrant. His previous work with the International Crime Syndicates Unit, tracking down an Asian heroin smuggling ring exploiting existing networks in Australia, made Olaf a perfect fit for this project.

The Unit had picked up and interrogated a drug mule en route from Bali to Byron Bay, carrying a large quantity of acid tabs hidden in his surfboard. The threat of not surfing for ten years was more than the man could bear and he rolled over and took a deal naming people in a larger import group and their distributors. James, the mule, overshared in the hope he could gain enough quid pro quo to be let off with a warning. The goods also came into the country via importing businesses, they expanded and moved to various warehouses on the Eastern seaboard. They were delivered by people posing as legitimate manufacturers and distributors. This intel, gathered more by chance than clever planning proved invaluable.

'Let's wake up Mr Owens?' Olaf stepped up beside the palette where Seth slept oblivious, firmly shaking his shoulder.

'Wake up, Mr Owens. Wake up! It's the police. We have a search warrant.'

Seth's lips moved as he mumbled sweet nothings curling up in a foetal position.

Greg went over to a kitchen bench on the far wall and filled a kettle with cold water then returned and tipped the entire contents over Seth's head.

'Wake up! Police!' He barked the order.

Seth splurted and gasped then choked, before struggling

to a semi-standing position looking about in total confusion before his self-protective reflexes kicked in. What he saw was a big threat.

'Who are you? What do you want?' Spotting the police uniforms, he adopted a wheedling, conciliatory tone.

'It was just a bit of weed for my own use,' he bargained lamely. 'I fell asleep,' picking up his shirt and wiping his face, he put it on.

'Mr Owens, we have a search warrant for the building, its contents and any personal items,' Greg held the search warrant in front of Seth who squinted buying time, realising that they had information from the real estate agent including, his real name.

'My name is Detective Chief Inspector Petersen, and this is my colleague Detective Sergeant Greg Foreman. Detective Constables Damien Tudihope and Donna Costa are accompanying us,' Olaf gestured with his hand at the other police team members. 'We have a warrant to search the premises now. We will be taking you in for questioning about this matter however, your cooperation will be noted. Have you got that?' The cool and professional detective watched Seth's eyes and the inflections of his body language.

Seth's mind was racing. Why a search warrant? Was it the dope bag? Where the fuck is Shorn? His eyes gave him away.

'Mr Owens, one of my officers is going to take a statement from you and give you a cup of coffee which I want you to drink while we are looking through the boxes for contraband.'

'Contraband!' Seth squawked as the penny dropped. 'There is no contraband here. It's all legit.' His anxiety levels soared, while the contents of the kettle dripped from the ends of his blond beard making him look like a bedraggled family dog.

'We'll be the ones deciding that Mr Owens,' Greg replied firmly. 'Now go over there with the constable for me.' Damien stepped forward leading the way to the kitchenette, pointed to a chair. Seth obeyed.

Greg and Olaf set to work identifying the boxes on the palette and reading the labels while Donna stood by holding a Stanley knife.

'Don't rip up the plastic seal too much we'll need to rewrap some boxes.' Olaf was out of earshot from Seth, who wore the befuddled expression of someone whose fate had caught up with him. The contents of the boxes were written on their sides identifying items inside. Several boxes marked as 'Booblay' were filled with multicoloured, plastic tubes and judging by the picture on the side, came with some other contraption that fitted inside the tube like a plunger. The air was muggy in the warehouse and Olaf loosened his necktie and undid the top button of his shirt. He didn't like the humidity.

Over against the wall, next to the kitchenette seated on two white plastic chairs, Damien was writing down Seth's details, place of residence and occupation. They got stuck on the professional aspect of Seth's persona.

'You say you are the head of this movement that sells this plastic stuff to...' Damien looked down at the jottings on his notepad, 'to 'seekers of the truth'. Did I get that straight?'

'We are not a cult!' Seth protested emphatically. 'We are a Movement that follows the teachings of an ancient Egyptian alchemist and magician, Hermes Trismegistus. I am Seth, Lord High Alchemist, his prophet!' A proclamation of lofty hyperbole, as though his association with a dead 3000-year-old Egyptian, conferred authority on him. Writing his handle down painstakingly, Damien's eyes scrutinised Seth's face for insincerity, 'How do you spell 'Trismeg...' please?'

Seth spelled it out.

'According to our records and the lease with the real estate agency, you are John Owens of 20 Riverside Drive, Coffs Harbour. Any comment?'

'That was my previous life!' Seth hastily qualified waving his hands around. The cop tried not to laugh and thought to himself that he'd heard everything. Apparently not. He gave his head a small shake. Seth discovered how useful it was to airbrush out his previous life, a trick he picked up from Sir Raj, former guru and founder of the Seraphic Throng of Heavenly Light – the Movement.

Greg walked over to Damien and Seth, 'Take Mr Owens out to the car for the rest of the statement please.' They both left through the front doors and went outside the warehouse to the parked car. Seth knew he had no choice, and his protestations didn't make any difference.

'Greg, over here,' the tension apparent in his boss's voice.

Greg walked around the pallets of boxes to where Olaf and Donna were standing over a box with its contents of plastic paraphernalia spread on a trestle surrounded by shredded paper material and bubble wrapping.

'What does this look like to you?' He nodded at the box.

'Not sure,' Greg looked down at the wrapping still scattered across the bottom of the empty box and the stack of assorted smaller boxes beside it. He shrugged.

'Pick up the other side.' Together they both picked it up and realised that it felt heavier than they expected it. Olaf looked at him.

'False bottom. Moulded into it,' Greg concluded in seconds, 'very cleverly done.'

They flipped it over and put it down again. Donna picked up the Stanley knife and tried to slice along the side of the box close to the bottom. It was thick and tough.

'It has been reinforced.'

'Yep. They wouldn't want it getting wet,' Greg agreed.

'Wrong tool for the job,' she suggested.

'I'll get the toolbox out of the boot,' Donna disappeared outside and returned with a metal toolbox and a box cutter for good measure.

Soon the police were busily hacksawing their way through the bottom of a box until they discovered waterproof material wrapped around one kilo bags of tablets and sheets of blotting paper. Both senior police officers had been engaged in busting drugs and knew it was a substantial haul though how much more was enclosed in the shipment, they couldn't guess.

'I'm going to say we have speed and acid tabs,' Olaf straightened up.

'Greg, come with me and we'll have a talk to Mr Owens, get some details.'

'Donna, take out your gun and guard the boxes,' Greg ordered.

Olaf and Greg stepped through the warehouse doors and looked around for any signs of cars or people taking notice of them emerging from the warehouse, Damien had move the car. Walking around the side of the warehouse to their car they found Seth in the backseat of the unmarked police car handcuffed. He was whining to Damien and was overwrought and voluble, as he squirmed and struggled to get free of his cuffs.

'I demand to be released!' He demanded. 'I demand to call my lawyer!' He demanded. An unfounded claim as he hadn't been charged yet.

'Damien, join Donna, will you?'

'You can't treat me like this! I'm not the dog you know. You can't lock me in the car with the window down. I've got feelings. I've got rights!'

Greg leaned in and unlocked the cuffs, Seth, still indignant and outraged, rubbed his sore, chafed wrists and sulked.

'Relax, Mr Owens, the constable merely restrained you for a few minutes, so you didn't run for it,' Olaf's eyes showed little other than mild curiosity at Seth's temper tantrum.

'Are you here alone, Mr Owens?' He levelled his gaze at Seth.

'Yes. Yes, it's just me,' Seth bleated, 'the others will come in a couple of hours.' Where the fuck did Shorn go? He thought again. The quality of the air was crisp, and the morning light made the landscape glow and vibrate an emerald green. Most of the warehouses were new and looked utterly incongruous with the natural surroundings, adding a sense of surreal temporality to the scene playing out.

Olaf beckoned Greg aside having handcuffed Seth in the car again, 'We'll leave Damien and Donna to guard the place while we take Seth back to Tweed.'

'They'll need back up and cover in case the workers turn up.'

'Call in a couple of highway police and tell them to hide their car. We'll let Damian and Donna know.'

* * *

Tweed Heads police station, built in the 1960s for a quieter time in law enforcement, was basically a box set above the street overlooking the main boulevard of the township which ran as a concrete ribbon of boardwalk above the beach. The plate glass frontage of the station reflected the moods of the sky and white clouds floated across its face while the town grew and expanded around becoming the service centre for surrounding developments. Pulling into a carpark located at the rear of the station, Olaf and Greg led Seth into the back of the station and down a corridor to a soulless interview room to help with their enquiries. Setting him down at an equally featureless Formica table with three plastic chairs around it, Olaf switched on the tape deck to record their interview.

'For the benefit of the tape, it's Tuesday 8th March at the Tweed Heads police station, interview room two. Detective Chief Inspector Olaf Petersen and DSS Greg Foreman are interviewing Mr John Owens, whom we arrested in a warehouse in the Byron Bay industrial estate, in possession of a bag of marijuana.'

'In addition to finding Mr Owens asleep and under the influence of drugs we discovered a quantity of blotting sheets and LSD acid tabs and pills hidden in the boxes of spiritual paraphernalia in the warehouse,' Olaf looked into Seth's eyes coolly and continued.

'Mr Owens, I want the names and details of the Movement's

accountant and senior staff who organise the deliveries of merchandise and the repackaging and selling.'

Seth looked at him puzzled.

'Who runs the logistics?

'Who ordered the imports and who takes and receipts the money?' Olaf spelled it out.

'Ahh! The Elders!' A light went on and Seth threw them under the bus without hesitation. 'We live together in the ashram near Byron Bay. It's a sanctuary for the followers and believers in Hermes. The Elders have cabins and I have the main house.'

'Their names please, Mr Owens,' Greg asked again.

'They are Reuban, Max and Ruth Zelwag, known as the Elders of Isis, they do all the organising and bookwork,' Seth reiterated trying to concrete an escape route for himself.

Olaf patiently waited. He held all the cards and the destiny of this silly individual who now shrugged off the effects of the dope and was having a prolonged moment of clarity.

At this point, Seth decided again not to mention Shorn. He was afraid that if it came out and he went to jail, Shorn would pay someone inside to punish him for betraying him.

'The Zelwags were with the Movement before I joined,' he hastily explained.

* * *

The Zelwags first met Roger Skouder at a spirit festival in Darling Harbour in Sydney called Organs of Awakening in 1990. He was a used car salesman in Sacramento, before entering Australia, where he managed to escape prosecution for fraud. Roger used his marketing skills to establish a new career. 'Same shit,' he said to himself, 'different place.' He arrived in Australia on a temporary working visa in 1985 and, within four years, with the help of the Zelwags, he established a not-for-profit business in spiritual revelations based on a channelled book called 'Seth Speaks.' Roger was pleased with the cult's collection of religious ideas however, he decided to abbreviate the name, the Seraphic Throng of Heavenly Light, to the Movement, as the full name was such a mouthful. Occultism and theosophy provided a hotbed of philosophical and quasi-religious ideologies and people flocked to Roger's stall to find answers to the existential questions of humanity. Roger soon realised that he needed a more spiritual sounding moniker perhaps, with Eastern religious overtones, popular with seekers of truth. Places like Byron Bay on the North Coast of New South Wales, were a magnet for a panoply of gurus, yoga teachers, spiritual guides, healers and hippies in general. Many earnest young things, attracted to the coastal lifestyle and relaxed laissez-faire attitudes, created a side hustle in the healing arts regardless of any abilities or qualifications.

Max Zelwag had approached Roger at the Festival following a particularly moving séance where he channelled a powerful being from pre–Christian Egyptian civilization called, Hermes Trismegistus. Claiming to find his message uplifting, Max, joined by his brother and wife, suggested they could help Sir Raj establish a business to spread the word and make money. It was a management team made in heaven.

What Olaf and Greg didn't know, was whether the Movement was directly involved in importing the dope themselves or being used by an Asian syndicate greasing their international smuggling via wilful blindness.

'When did the Zelwags begin importing plastic merchandise, Mr Owens?'

'I don't know,' Seth shrugged his shoulders, 'they were do-

ing it when I joined the Movement, as a seeker.' Being an innocent bystander suited Seth's story.

'Explain to us what you did as a seeker when the shipment
of merchandise came in. Was there always a warehouse that
it came to and where the followers worked?'

The door opened and Sue Murray, put her head around the
door to indicate the sting had been set up at the warehouse. It
was time to put the next part of their plan into place.

'We need you to ring the Elders and tell them you have finished the blessing in case they rock up with a busload of seekers for a day's work.' Olaf grimaced and checked his watch.
Seth sat with his hands loose on his lap waiting for further
questions.

CHAPTER 10

Acutely aware of timing, Olaf sought to extract more information from Seth. He and Greg dispatched the forward team to the warehouse to support Donna and Damien, while the two uniforms were deployed to the area around the ashram awaiting orders.

'I want you to realise, Mr Owens, that life possibilities for you are diminishing, outside of jail,' Olaf waited a few seconds before finishing, 'unless you give us your full cooperation.' Seth and the two senior police officers were still sitting in the interview room facing each other.

Apart from doing a bit of weed and bonking chicks, Seth calculated the police were fishing. Sure, there were some misdemeanours with skipping fines and court appearances in his previous life. He wished they would call him by his assumed name, Seth, Lord High Alchemist. Deep down, he suspected they were holding something more over him, especially the ice-cold European cop. Seth racked his brain. Nothing. He decided to play for time and work out what they were threatening him with.

'Surely, officers,' he leaned back in his chair all bonhomie, 'a little pot smoking won't be more than a fine and a slap on the wrist?' The two detectives wryly watched the hirsute Lothario, anticipating the moment when he put two and two together and came up with the meaning of contraband. A salient point that escaped him thus far.

'Mr Owens,' Greg leaned forward with both hands on the table in front of him like a sphinx, 'you are facing serious charges of smuggling, tax evasion, and having sex with minors.' Feeling exercised by the denouncement, Seth stridently defended his record.

'I have not knowingly had sex with minors,' he argued, a fleck of spittle on his chin. 'I mean those women, they *wanted* me. They seduced me!' Only then did it dawn on Seth he was being set up for smuggling charges. So that's what they meant by contraband! He finally concluded.

'Smuggling? What do you mean smuggling?' He wailed, shocked and alarmed.

'Mr Owens,' Olaf resembled a headmaster, 'we mean smuggling contraband drugs hidden in the cartons of plastic paraphernalia sold on to seekers as spiritual tokens.'

Seth's protests became increasingly strangulated as he frantically pleaded his innocence.

'The importing has nothing to do with me! That's all the Elders! I told you that!' Seth felt no compunction whatsoever. 'I am just there to bless the artefacts, that's my job. The Elders have been importing the stuff from the same company for years.'

'What is the name of the company the Elders use, Mr Owens?'

'The Sunrise company or Sunset, something like that.'

Olaf and Greg believed him, not because he was a consummate con man. No, it was because he felt betrayed and indignant that the Elders conned him by not including him in a rich vein of revenue. To add insult to injury now he was being framed.

'We are pleased you understand the seriousness of the situation and I take it you agree to cooperate fully with us?' Olaf waited.

'I want a deal!' Seth spoke emphatically. 'I will cooperate and tell you everything I know. I can't go to jail.'

'You explain to us the whole process of importing the plastic articles, and, for the benefit of the tape, we will do our utmost to see you that is taken into consideration.' Olaf had manoeuvred Seth into a pliable position to help them and Seth was keen to press his advantage.

'The importing business is part of the spiritual movement's offerings to the seekers of truth,' Seth articulated. 'It was going on long before I took over as the guru of the Movement under Sir Raj.'

'Who is Sir Raj?' Greg asked.

'He was the founder of the Movement. When I became his disciple, he imparted the spiritual wisdom on eternal life by our prophet Hermes Trismegistus. Before he died of incurable cancer,' Seth was voluble, now the attention of the two detectives shifted.

'Talk to us about the Elders, Mr Owens. Clarify the relationship for us,' Greg spread his hands inviting Seth to expand on his blame shifting.

'The Elders run all the operations of our Movement including the business side of importing and selling artefacts, paying rents, and ordering food. The two brothers, Reuban, and Max Zelwag, run the ashram and the business and Ruth, is the accountant. They all live at the ashram in cottages attached to the main property.' Both detectives were taking notes occasionally indicating to Seth, to keep revealing the workings of the Movement.

'Outline for us the process the Elders use for ordering and receiving the boxes of plastic stuff, Mr Owens please.'

'I don't have anything to do with the ordering process, my role is to impart the blessing and to spiritualise the artefacts, so they are carrying the sacred essence of Hermes.' Seth was getting hungry he hadn't had breakfast that morning.

'The Elders have a standing arrangement with the import company. Every time we get low on the products they order more to be delivered and we have the seekers unpack all the goods from the boxes.'

Over the next period, Seth gave a detailed account of deliveries by the Rising Sun Imports Company, the blessing, the unpacking, and the retrieval of the boxes. He explained that the import company came and picked up the boxes still in a box shape, unflattened, so the workers could put the wrapping material back in the boxes. He knew the routine as it had not changed since he was a seeker, some years ago before being apprenticed to the founder guru, Sir Raj. However, he had no idea when the Elders had made a deal to smuggle drugs into the country.

'What happens then?' Olaf absently rubbed his chin.

'Can I have a sandwich and a cup of coffee?' Seth requested politely.

'Sure. Just a couple of things first, Mr Owens. After the blessing do you call the Elders and tell them you have finished?'

'Yes, I must call them now. That's the signal to bring the group of workers out to unpack the boxes for the rest of the day.'

Olaf and Greg exchanged a silent agreement then Greg spoke, 'For the benefit of the tape we're having a break,' he switched the tape off got up and walked to the door. After a minute he returned having requested refreshments be delivered by an officer.

'A sandwich and coffee are coming.' A few moments later, a uniformed cop popped his head around the door, with a pre-packed sandwich from the café and a disposable cup of coffee, Greg took them with thanks.

'Now Mr. Owens, we'll set up the call and you are to tell the Elders that the blessing is done and then you will say you are going for a swim. Then hang up. Is that clear?'

Seth had reached for a sandwich and was chewing and nodding. He swallowed and drank some lukewarm coffee provided. Greg switched the tape back on and confirmed they were recoding the conversation.

Olaf pushed the phone close to Seth while Greg moved his chair around and next to the hungry guru. 'What's the number?'

Seth placed the sandwich back on the plate his hand hovering over it reluctant to let go.

'It's 66 2020, that's the line to the main house.'

'Okay, when I give you the phone, Mr Owens, take a bite of the sandwich and talk with your mouth full. Say exactly what you always say and that you're going for a swim. They don't expect you to let them in do they?'

'We both have keys,' Seth said.

Greg dialled the number and gave the handset to Seth who picked up the sandwich and took a bite. The phone rang and after five or six rings a woman's voice answered.

'Hello,' she was a little out of breath.

'It's Theth, the bledding is done,' he spoke around the ball of food in his mouth then swallowed it with a noisy gulp.

'A sandwich. I'm going surfing now. See you later.' Greg put his finger on the phone cutting them off and moving back around the table.

Seth kept eating and drinking. He burped. He calculated his release was imminent as he'd performed his end of the bargain.

'How did you get to the warehouse this morning, Mr Owens?' Caught off guard momentarily, Seth reconsidered revealing Shorn to the interrogators. Seth walked a fine line of legality and public exposure in his work as a guru for the Movement. He was terrified of Shorn. There wasn't a skerrick of doubt in his mind that Shorn would find him if Seth dobbed him in. After all, Shorn operated outside the law when it suited him, and he lied smoothly.

'One of the seekers gave me a lift here from the ashram we have people coming and going all day.'

'Who was this person, Mr Owens?' Greg persisted.

'Honestly, I can't remember his name. I was pretty stoned,' Seth claimed. It was second nature to prevaricate, and he embellished the truth to make himself look good. Mercifully, no one had a mental crisis during his time as an all-knowing guru, truth seeker and soother of tortured souls. He didn't even know any First Aid.

'What happens now, Detectives?' Seth addressed Greg chattily.

'Mr Owens, we are not going to charge you at the moment We do have some more questions we would like to ask you later and, will keep you in custody for a few hours while we complete activities based on the information you have supplied so far.'

'For the benefit of the tape, Chief Inspector Petersen and Detective Sergeant Foreman have completed the interview with Mr John Owens,' Olaf concluded switching the machine off.

'We're going to ask you to wait in the family support room while we go and talk to the Elders. You will be detained and not allowed to leave yet but you can watch television and you'll be quite comfortable. The constable will take you to the toilet.'

Olaf gestured that Greg should leave and gather the team for the bust of the smugglers and the Elders. They had left Donna and Damien to tap the phone and relocate to the surveillance warehouse across the road. Greg called them advising them both to detain anyone letting themselves into the warehouse other than the Elders or seekers due to arrive en masse in a minibus shortly.

They put Seth in the family room feeling optimistic he was immune for the time being and watching a television show, The Price is Right, an irony not lost on Olaf.

The team, Greg and Olaf had picked were gathered waiting for the word to move. Sue Murray, a crack shot and an Army Reservist, had been tasked with maintaining contact with Donna and Damien and getting an update on the stakeout, when Olaf and Greg joined them.

'I'll have a word, Sue,' Olaf fitted the headset over his ears, 'talk to me, Damien what is going on? Where's Donna?' Damien and Donna had planted a bug in the phone successfully, locked up the warehouse then relocated to the stakeout site opposite.

'Donna's up the ladder with the binoculars. We haven't seen anyone go into the warehouse however there's been traffic back and forward.'

'We are on our way. Damien, you and Donna, good work.'

'Righto boss.'

CHAPTER 11

n the week leading up to the bust Greg and Olaf conferred about the logistics of deploying staff. They were worried that the details of the planned takedown would leak to the crooks and the press.

'You need to brief the team,' Greg said to Olaf, 'They're solid but they haven't been involved in this sort of operation before.'

'You're right. Call everyone together, Greg.'

'Okay. Listen up!' Olaf called the team together. The police officers and detectives were all standing around the training room, a bare soulless grey and white room with aluminium windows facing the road. On the walls, the standard inspirational posters proclaimed there was 'NO I in TEAM'. The nervous energy in the room was palpable as was the excitement of Sue, Damien, Nick and Donna and Vanessa at being chosen for a mission.

'Greg and I have chosen you all for your skills but also your ability to work as a close team,' Olaf began, 'Now before we brief you,' he lowered his voice, 'you are all now bound to complete secrecy on pain of being ejected from the team if there is a single leak on this case. Do you understand?' He studied the eyes of each one of his subordinates.

'There will be no talking among yourselves. No sharing with other detectives. No mention to family. No knowing looks between each other to intimate something other than a bust that may not yield anything much. Is that perfectly clear?' People nodded and shifted their weight. 'It may be all over by the end of the day, if not we'll do shifts around the clock.' The team murmured in agreement.'

* * *

On the morning of the bust, Greg had given everyone copies of maps showing the area and streets at the industrial estate and the warehouse they were targeting as well as the names of the surrounding businesses that occupied the estate.

'We'll all go in unmarked cars or our own vehicles at staged intervals and park them in car spaces or around the back of the surveillance ops warehouse.' Olaf explained.

'Alright, let's go. Greg and Sue, you drive in first and go around the back of the Ops warehouse. Nick, you drive your ute after them and head for the end of the street. I'm going to pull into the car body repair place.'

Sue and Greg got a radio call on the way out to the estate from Donna to report that a minibus of young workers turned up at the warehouse accompanied by the Elders, who she described as two men with bald heads wearing traditional Indian loose pants and tunics.

'The game is on,' Greg felt tense and excited, he looked at Sue as they sped down the highway together to the Ops warehouse to bust the smugglers.

'It's great Greg, real police work,' she backed him.

The police arrived at the industrial estate as planned with no one drawing attention to themselves, just ordinary people going about various business interests. As they drove past the target warehouse, Greg and Sue observed the last of the workers filing in followed by a person they assumed was an Elder who pulled the door across behind him. Sue studied a regional map to cover her face and Greg looked for all the world like a country cattleman with an Akubra hat tipped back and dark glasses. They made their way to the back entrance of the warehouse where their base was set up and parked the car out of sight.

Tracking the movements of the import business had alerted Olaf to the delivery deals they established with small, innocuous concerns such as a florist in Fortitude Valley, an Asian small goods company in Brisbane and to the Movement, at Byron Bay.

Drug dealers and smugglers were changing their business models by diversifying delivery points and enlisting local businesses and initially, Rising Sun Imports began delivering the Movement's plastic artefacts without drugs in their boxes. But over time, a key person in Australia, talked to the Elders about making some more money and they agreed on a system of deliveries, alert to the money-making possibilities of looking the other way.

Both Elders were busy with the workers in the warehouse unpacking boxes when Olaf drove and parked next to a line of cars awaiting bodywork outside a workshop advertised as 'Stan's Auto Repairs'. Stan's workshop doors were wide open and when Olaf strolled inside, he could see cars and pulleys, benches and panel beating equipment, oxyacetylene gas cylinders and all the Tools and equipment to run his business.

Stan was working on a car hoisted above him listening to a radio playing hits from the 1980s and further back a young bloke with a face mask was applying a torch to the body of a dinged car.

Olaf raised a hand and strolled into the mouth of the workshop. He was dressed casually in jeans and a polo shirt with a pair of sneakers. Stan turned; his face looked irritated.

'Yeah, what do you want?'

'Hi, I'm just looking about for a warehouse to set up my business.'

'What's your business?'

'Body building equipment for gyms.'

'Go and talk to Catriona, at Elders Real Estate.'

'Thanks for your help.'

Olaf crossed the street then glanced back to make sure neither Stan nor anyone else noticed him as he passed the Operations warehouse site where Greg had left the door ajar. He slipped inside.

'Gather around everyone,' Olaf directed. There were a couple of tables set up with the intercept transistor system for the telephone bug, police vests at one end and by now everyone slipped on a uniform and their pistols. Greg's sheet of paper was spread out on a table cross-referenced to a map of the street, the warehouses and parked cars.

'According to our informant,' Olaf opened, 'one of the Elders will phone the import company when the boxes are all emptied and stacked next to the doors at the end of the day. We are looking for a Tommy Tortoise moving truck or something of a similar size. Certainly, the sort of vehicle that would normally come and go from a warehouse storage estate.'

'How many people will come to pick up the boxes?' Sue was eager for more information.

'Here is what we know,' Greg outlined, 'at least two people will come to pick up the boxes and take them away. This will happen once the workers have left for the day. The Elders then call in the truck driver and a sidekick. But we can't be sure until we eyeball the truck, there may be three.'

'What about these guys, the Elders?' Damien interjected.

'We don't know if they will be dangerous,' Olaf elaborated.

'I think we can count on the smugglers doing a runner, we just don't know whether they'll be armed. The company is a Chinese Indonesian outfit but the people working in the country could be any nationality.' Olaf stressed.

Olaf and Greg marked out the places the team would hide themselves to execute the bust as a pincer movement.

'We will need two fast-running tacklers in case anyone legs it. Sue you'll shoot out a truck tyres if they try to drive off,' Greg directed.

'The most important part is to have the Elders sign over the receipt for the boxes and catch the smugglers red-handed loading the boxes. They could be desperate and possibly violent people however we have the advantage of surprise. Let's run through some mock arrests while we are waiting.' Olaf was big on practice moves as he'd learnt it primed the mind and body for action and this operation contained so many variables.

For the next few hours, the team of six people took turns watching the warehouse for movement and practising arresting. It was now a little after four o'clock in the afternoon and still quite warm and humid.

Greg was taking a turn at the window. 'Hang on guys,' he waved his hand. 'A couple of people are outside having a cigarette.' Olaf was on a walkie-talkie quietly giving orders to his counterparts over the border in Queensland, who were poised to sweep into an Asian Food Emporium which housed the Rising Sun Imports company. He and Greg organised a team of police to raid the ashram once they busted the Elders. Greg would drive over and supervise the search warrant with the other team of police.

The sun pulsed in the sky while the glistening green fields surrounding the oddly juxtaposed collection of corrugated warehouses gave a surreal two-dimensional impression. Before too long a clamour of tired chatter could be heard as groups of young people in colourful clothes with long hair and amulets left the warehouse ready to return to the ashram in the minibus. Two Elders hovered around making sure everyone got on the minibus and departed before returning to the warehouse and sliding the doors behind them. The police team were ready, excited and determined to bust their quarry.

'Here we go,' Olaf, headphones against one ear, heard their

bug picked up the call from the warehouse. 'This is Max, at Byron Bay, we're finished. Come and get the boxes.'

'Okay.' A person with an Asian accent replied.

'Time to deploy,' Olaf clenched his jaw. There was much riding on capturing the organised crime gang and the Movement simultaneously and there was always an element of mortal danger when dealing with drug smugglers.

The team stealthily deployed to places around the door of the target warehouse while Nick and Donna slid around the sides and covered escape routes to the back of the warehouse.

Meanwhile, the battered red and yellow Tommy Tortoise removal truck must have been close by because ten minutes later, it trundled along the estate road then braked and reversed the back to the door of the warehouse. Two wiry men of Asian appearance jumped out of the cabin and swung open the doors at the back of the truck. The Elders were waiting inside and slid the warehouse doors wide for the truck. The driver and his offsider put down a ramp then wheeled trolleys into the warehouse to collect the boxes. The two drug smugglers worked steadily loading the emptied boxes onto the truck. Once all the boxes were on board, the lead man walked back over to the Elders and handed Max a brown paper bag which disappeared into the folds of his tunic.

'Gotcha!' Whispered Olaf, from behind a car where he and Sue were hiding.

Olaf stood and waved the others, 'Go! Go!' He signalled. The police ran towards the smugglers guns drawn shouting to get down on the ground. The Elders dropped to the ground on their knees but one of the smugglers instantly ditched his trolly and made a run for it down the side of the warehouse. Damien chased him in hot pursuit as Donna and Nick moved towards the bust and grabbed the other smuggler who squirmed and lashed out and was handcuffed by Sue, disappointed she didn't get to shoot the truck's tyres out. Greg handcuffed the Elders, leaving them contemplating their options, before searching them and finding the bag of cash.

'Sue, you and your team read their rights to them. Handcuff the two foreign nationals together,' Greg ordered.

'Reuban and Max Zelwag, you are under arrest for smuggling drugs, for receiving and profiting from the act of smuggling drugs into Australia. You do not have to say anything that may harm your defence in court however what you do say will be taken down and may be held against you. Do you understand?'

'We want a phone call,' Max demanded.

'Certainly, Mr Zelwag,' Greg all business. 'Once we charge you formally you will be entitled to call a lawyer or to have one appointed.

Wordlessly, the Zelwags were marched out to a waiting unmarked police car while the smugglers were in a paddy van called in to take them away. Two other uniformed police on motorbikes arrived at the scene as an escort for the boxes in the Tommy Tortoise truck.

'Right, we need two of you to take the confiscated truck to the station and organise getting it unloaded and investigated and all the evidence bagged and recorded.' Damien and Nick stepped up.

The caravan of police and culprits set off behind Olaf with

the truck in the middle and the highway police forming a guard.

Greg had briefed the team waiting in hiding outside the ashram in Byron Bay. 'We'll be there soon wait for our arrival.'

'Let's go and pick up the third Zelwag,' Greg and Sue peeled off to meet more of the team waiting to bust the ashram and to bring Ruth Zelwag in for questioning.

CHAPTER 12

The Elders of Isis triggered a minor alert on the Australia Security Intelligence Organisation (ASIO) watch list, based on their unfortunate choice of name which resembled the name of an Egyptian terrorist organisation. Eventually, the researchers wrote them off as harmless cult followers, albeit ones that dressed as imams in white tunics and loose pants.

Seth could easily have set up his own movement, he decided. Basically, he was too lazy and self-serving and instead, he negotiated a split of the profits as his payment for being a charismatic guru replacement. He was approached by the Elders, shortly before the untimely death of their founding guru, Sir Raj, formerly Roger Skouder, a car salesman from California, America.

Having joined the Movement eighteen months prior, he'd assessed the power relationships within it, attached himself as a loyal lieutenant to Sir Raj, massaging his ego and procuring younger women for him. An arrangement that worked well for both the men. During the past decade, Seth floated around hippy alternative communities where accommodation was cheap, grass was available and the women plentiful. He spent some years cultivating and selling dope before selectively aligning himself with spiritual movements chosen for philosophies that allowed promiscuity and chanting over hard work. Seth undertook past lives work, clearing his chakras and meridians and, his favourite, energetic recharging. His followers longed for his spiritual bestowals as he became eloquent at trotting out self-discovery platitudes and professed self-love.

The fundamental doctrine of the Movement was a belief that, through dedicated spiritual practice and work, you could achieve weightlessness and communion with all the divine beings around the world, past and present. From the perspective of the Elders, Seth was pleasant and pliable, better still, he didn't have a shred of moral scruples. He played the game, which was all they needed to keep the business ticking over. The most lucrative elements of the cult business were the products that conveyed magical powers upon the purchasers via energetic transmission. Sir Raj, an astute entrepreneur, invented a line of business sourcing plastic merchandise from Asia at discount rates and showing Seth how to promote and sell the 'blessed' objects. Central to achieving this goal was a divine essence of Sir Raj, his wisdom and power bestowed upon the pieces of plastic, repackaged for consumption by gullible seekers. When Sir Raj was diagnosed with inoperable cancer, he and the Elders concocted the 'Surge of Power' whereby he anointed his chosen follower, Seth, with his transcendental holiness, thus making him the successor guru of the Movement. There was a lot of chanting and dancing, spumes of incense and mind-altering drugs as the whole Movement swirled, swayed and swooned around the two men communing on a higher plane of being. Sir Raj named Seth after the Egyptian god of chaos and war.

As a cult, the Movement took an eclectic approach. They appropriated much from Hindu traditions and other mythologies such as, karma, auras, nirvana, yoga and the sutras. The Kama Sutra was Seth's favourite. Sir Raj founded his cult of seekers based on his connection to and channelling of the ancient Egyptian magician known as Hermes Trismegistus. However, as a guru, Sir Raj soon realised that Hindu and Buddhist ideas held more sway over the seekers, so he simply absorbed elements of different religions and belief systems in addition to a mish mash of cosmic mythologies.

The Elders, instinctively realised Seth was a fellow con man who would embrace their cult practices including encouraging the followers to work in the warehouse and to spread the word of the Movement. These seekers were rewarded by special sessions with Seth where they would sit in a close circle, sometimes holding hands and chanting in time to the meditation tapes being played in the background. Of course, Seth was open to propositions and enjoyed shampooing – a term he found in the Kama Sutra meaning having sex. While Hindu and Buddhist treatise emphasised the liberation from the cycle of life and death, the Movement preached prolonging life and enjoying it. Seth and his followers embraced a life that promised riches and wellbeing moreover, happiness was a birthright, they claimed.

Petty problems would arise from time to time, the Elders and Seth became adept at resolving them with group work interspersed with the lectures about the body being a sacred vessel for the expression of vital energy channelled into work and self-realisation.

The subtext was the followers were meant to share their bodies and beds without pair bonding and being possessive. People coupled and some stayed while others went off to form households and be temporarily monogamous. The Movement accommodated it all with a ritual or a session sitting in a circle singing.

Children weren't encouraged as it made the Movement answerable to a range of society's guardians such as the education systems and child protection.

As the cult developed and the stock of capital increased through the clever manipulation by the Elders, they resolved to assist followers to rent shared houses near the main ashram and attend the evening meal and the group prayers or Satsang together with those who were staying at the ashram.

The Elders had followed Sir Raj into the business of spiritual enlightenment without missing a beat having recognised early on the zeitgeist of young idealist people searching for a purpose for their existence and willing to dedicate a period of their lives to self-discovery. They were the forerunners of a wave of middle-aged seekers looking for enlightenment through psycho-emotional transformation, but with less money to spend getting there.

Unburdened by Christian notions of parsimony and prudence and that whole thing about the rich man, the camel, and the eye of a needle, they established the infrastructure of the organisation and, in time honoured tradition, ran two accounting books.

The Elders were a family unit and brought their joint skills to running the Movement's operations. Ruth who was married to Max, boasted a bookkeeping diploma and years of experience working for an accounting firm in outer Brisbane. Max and Reuban both worked in warehousing logistics. They attended one of Sir Raj's seminars where he proselytised about his manifest destiny, channelling love and forgiveness. They found an interest in common and agreed to support Sir Raj establishing 'gospel' type meetings at a local Kingdom Hall on weekends. The Movement grew from these humble beginnings.

Because the real power of the organisation reposed with these three people, they were threatening in a domestic way, as the disciplinarians and the enforcers when youthful behaviour got out of hand. It was a tricky route to transition from cash donations by fickle young seekers to a bonded work relationship with products to import, put together and market. However, Sir Raj's history in sales assisted them to promote themselves as an answer to the eternal search for meaning. For a sum of money.

The Movement's succession plan required a seamless transition from the control and care from one guru – the dying Sir Raj, to his anointed successor, Seth, including conveying his secrets. All the while remaining financially solvent. Once his inevitable death occurred, Sir Raj's body was accepted by the Cryonic Foundation of Eternal Life, who would remove his head and freeze it in the vault of other dead people's heads. These frozen heads were awaiting resurrection, ready for grafting onto youthful vibrant bodies, at some non-specific time in a technological futurist reality, to live again. The science of this project was vague and optimistic and the profound faith in science somewhat undermined the mystical underpinning of the life on earth theology espoused by the Movement. All religions in some way gave succour to their flocks by embracing the ideas of eternal life. For example, the Christians embraced a 'life after death' insurance policy. One could argue this represented the foundational purpose of religion. The Hindus and Buddhists posited corporeal life as a learning process evolving as a series of incarnations. Theological pathfinding. You could go up the ladder to higher levels of being whilst still in the human body and reach the pinnacle, then be freed of the wheel of incarnation.

The Elders weren't counting on the science of cryonic revivification any time soon and once they had sent the body of Sir Raj to the Cryonic Foundation to be disposed of, except for the head, they quietly cancelled the cheque and got their twenty thousand dollars down payment back. The unpaid for head was unceremoniously despatched for disposal to the crematorium with whom the Foundation had a kickback arrangement. More pertinent for the Movement itself was to keep moving on and Seth arranged an appropriate sending off to the spirit world for Sir Raj.

CHAPTER 13

I f asked, Olaf put his career success down to patience, persistence and an insight into the criminal mind. He struck his co-workers and his superiors as distant and unemotional which set him aside from the other law enforcement operatives. He had a strong handshake and was respectful towards his superiors. As it happened, Olaf spoke five languages and had worked at the nexus of policing and organised crime over many years however, he often found the over-weaning bureaucratic control frustrating. He decided to do a Master of Criminal Psychology and chose to join Interpol shortly after his graduation. His immediate boss hoped Olaf's move up the ladder meant he would return rather than leave the force altogether.

'You are a dark horse, Petersen,' Mags Grierson observed when Olaf gave his notice. 'You've always got a place here when you have explored the wide world of international crime.

Olaf shook his proffered hand.

'Thank you, I have enjoyed working here. I do need some adventure, though.'

Mags tilted his head slightly, a gesture indicating he knew there was more, and he was curious to hear it.

'My wife has fallen for a woman.'

'Ouch! You, okay?'

'Yes. I'm okay. Philosophical.'

'Women love you!' His boss replied enviously.

Admittedly Olaf felt surprised when Ida, his wife of ten years, told him she was thinking of leaving the marriage because she had fallen in love with a woman. He wondered about their sex life. Sure, there were ups and downs even for the Danes, who were sexually permissive. They were pragmatic and at times transactional about negotiating sex with each other. His first marriage ended in his twenties, in hindsight, he realised just how young and inexperienced he was.

'It's not about you as a man or a lover,' his current wife commented.

Certainly, his job had kept him working back late at times and, in his defence, he always tried to balance out those times by taking his wife on holidays skiing. Perhaps, if they had children, it would have added another dimension to the relationship. Ida didn't want kids. She was a sporty fit woman who rode bikes and skied. Her assertiveness was attractive to him, as was her independence and self-confidence. They dated for a year before Ida proposed to him. Olaf accepted. It seemed like a good idea at the time. There had been other women during the marriage although they didn't have a specifically 'open marriage', it was more like 'don't ask, don't tell'. When he came home it was always Ida who mattered, he sought her approval and affection. Now she had found someone else. A woman.

Ida was talking as they sat in their living room on low white leather couches overlooking the city through tall glass windows. She held a drink in one hand. Olaf felt as though she was on the other side of a door, and he could only make out some of the words.

'I care about you...' then fading out. 'It just happened...,' Olaf tried to listen harder. Maybe it was a defensive place he went to block out what he didn't want to hear. His parents fought when he and his sister went to bed and Olaf learned to shut them out. They would be there in the morning with lovey dovey touches and knowing looks.

'Olaf!' He was startled out of reverie. 'Answer me!' Ida raised her voice and commanded him to answer her question.

He snapped out of the buffer zone around his emotions. 'I'm sorry. What do you want to know exactly?'

Exasperated, she was searching for a solution to the marriage. She loved the other woman but was uncertain the relationship would last. So many times, Ida felt that Olaf was unreachable, he retreated emotionally and, although he was tender and expressive and yes, he was a damn good lover, it was nothing like the intensity of her new lover, Inge. Ida longed to be in her arms now, where the depths of their kisses and the total emotional connection she never felt with a man.

'Could you live with me taking a lover and staying married?'

Strangely, Olaf felt released by this question as face to face, they talked about who they really were and what they really wanted. Where they imagine living out their authentic selves and having the freedom to unfold and self-actualise.

'I don't think that will work for either of us, Ida.' He sounded pleasant and unruffled.

'Why not? I have tolerated your dalliances, haven't I? Not asking you jealous questions; not spying on you or divorcing you.' She became angrier, randomly shooting verbal bullets.

'Yes, true. We both know that you benefitted too because I looked the other way when you had affairs, so long as you came home.'

From her chair, she threw her drink over him. 'Fuck you, Olaf!' He leaned back and it landed on his legs and the glass bounced away.

'Sure. But that won't solve the problem, Ida.'

'Why won't you get jealous then. Why won't you fight to get me back?'

'That may absolve your guilty conscience and it's exciting. Why, because I think you're in love with this woman. I think you want to be with her and not me. I think you are scared she doesn't have the same feelings for you. You are having a bet each way.' Ida was stung into silence by the inarguable truth of his retort.

In the past they used to argue about him being distant and not talking about his job because he had to separate emotionally from the things he witnessed. During their first years of marriage, he rationalised that his job with criminals meant that he was quiet and thoughtful at home. He tried hard to be there for her, to listen and discuss her life. If he was brutally honest, he was bored with Ida. She was a dominant personality and held a high-powered position in an energy company where she wanted the floor and got it. Ida always wanted more. She wanted emotion and adoration and power. The marriage was over. As a man, he didn't feel undermined by his competition being female. In a way, it didn't surprise him. He wondered what the other woman was like perhaps, sporty and competitive like Ida?

Back and forth the couple argued. Ida wanted the details of the women he had sex within the past years. Olaf deflected her and claimed she was being dishonest. How many other women have you had sex with during our marriage? As it happened, quite a lot. The whiskey and talk of sex aroused her and, incensed, she jumped on him and began pummelling his chest. She cried out with longing as he held both her arms and flipped her over onto her back, and ripping her pants down, he buried his face in her crotch. She moaned deeply. Sex was so thrilling and raw because he'd lost her to another.

CHAPTER 14

Lucy caught the bus out to Nimbin from Byron Bay, having told her boss that her mum needed her. She stayed at a friend's house in Byron that night, after seeing the gangster at the cafe she disappeared into the hinterland without saying a word to anyone else in the Movement, not even Hilly.

The Nimbin bus departed from the terminus opposite the Byron Bay Post Office, and was easily recognisable by its decorations of plants and flowers along the sides and a hippy couple holding hands looking up at a rainbow. It was the first time in almost a year that Lucy returned to Nimbin, and she experienced a mixture of emotions when she climbed out of the van and swung her bag over her shoulder. She decided to go straight home to her parent's place at Paradise Falls, rather than hang around the town.

She put out her thumb and hitched a ride from the corner of the main street in Nimbin to the commune where she grew up several kilometres away. During the past twelve months she spent with the Movement, she had missed her parents from time to time, but she felt that being independent and earning money was important and grown-up. The region was renowned for its extraordinary beauty, rolling green hills, dense rainforests, and spectacular rainbows hence, the Rainbow Region. When she reached the Paradise Falls carpark, a rutted red dirt allotment, she spied the familiar figure of Daniel Pendragon. He was someone she and the kids on the commune thought was a bit weird. Right that moment he was striding purposively towards the meeting hall wearing his Gandalph cape, his stave in hand.

Daniel Pendragon, (not his real name) claimed he found God in the nineteen eighties and, as it turned out, God informed him via 'voices in his head', of his elevated status in the society. Daniel carried his mantel with petulant arrogance which did not endear him to others who thought he was a phoney. Many of the residents harboured delusions they too possessed spiritual or magical powers, just like Daniel. For example, they believed they could change the course of the region's weather patterns or secure easy parking for themselves in the local township. In short, a rabble of believers in anything and everything and Daniel was not unusual in this respect but regarded those who belonged to religious sects and cults and glowing with inner peace as smug! True, he'd been through a period of soul-searching before Yahweh beckoned him. Previously, he flirted with the Wiccans and Warlocks of the Southern Cross, a loose affiliation of men and women enchanted by a real-life commune called Findhorn.

As the self-proclaimed Lord of the Mystical Valley of the Reborn, he wanted to debate with the warlocks, but now was not a good time. Daniel had a Tribal Meeting to attend and important matters to rectify. Daniel was an ordinary human being, with pale skin, wide hips, fair hair and blue eyes thus making his genetic links to Abrahamic Jews, tenuous at best. He got around this sticky problem by claiming he was the reincarnation of King David.

When Daniel arrived at the Tribal Meeting, the vibe seemed surly and tribal members openly mocked him when he rose to his full height, stamped his stave on the ground and demanded their attention. They claimed his incantations and prognostications were rubbish and the rantings of a sexually frustrated, madman. Certainly, he was sexually frustrated. What man wouldn't be when their wife claimed that pregnancy and breastfeeding squashed all sexual desire? And she was either pregnant or breastfeeding for the past five years. Great men of history were marked by rejection by their peers, he rationalised.

His motion was at the top of the agenda for the Tribal Meeting and entitled, 'The Tribe Must Reject All Craven Images of False Gods Randomly Displayed on Tracks and in Gardens as Blasphemy'. Someone suggested to the Chair that his item be bumped to the bottom of the list, as there were far more pressing issues such as approving home sites and resident housing plans, as well as dealing with weed infestations.

'Don't you mean a graven image?' The Chair asked Daniel making a point of correcting the record.

Daniel didn't deign to answer her instead he willed them to vote against the displacement of his agenda item.

'All those in favour of putting Daniel Pendragon's motion at the bottom of the agenda in the Miscellaneous section, raise your hands.'

Everyone at the meeting raised their hands.

'Right, that motion has passed,' the Chair stated perfunctorily, 'let's move onto the flag raising on prospective building sites.'

Stymied again, Daniel was furious. Oh, woe to the unbelievers and pragmatists! He sullenly lamented his burden. Daniel had to compete with an alphabet soup of religions and cosmic know-alls who would not defend the establishment of a Judeo-Christian God, Yahweh.

Some years prior, when he had received the Divine Summons from Yahweh, he wrote a treatise for general circulation about the path to fulfilment and the Divine Destiny of the People of Aquarius, of which he was now the anointed leader.

True, many people were searching for 'truth', oneness with the Universe, the Universal Goddess, Gaia. They were ripe for conversion to Daniel's faith.

Pantheists! He harrumphed with contempt. They'll follow any god with the least amount of self-sacrifice and self-discipline and the most amount of sexual licence. No wonder they were always smiling inanely.

While he was waiting for his turn, he reread the cosmic treatise he'd written and thoughtfully photocopied for members of the Tribal Meeting. It included the articulation of problems caused by suspect graven images and the need to repulse them: Deuteronomy had been crystal clear about this, not to mention, the Commandments in Exodus. He decided to sit on a bank with his cowl and stave, an imposing figure, not unlike Rodin's, The Thinker, and wait for his turn. He flattened out a copy of his treatise on his knees and reread it whilst the peons fought over land rights and airborne weed seeds. Domination could wait, after all, the Israelites needed proof of Yahweh's might too. He would have to wait longer because the agenda for the meeting lasted another hour, and his frustration grew exponentially as the residents debated site inspections, road maintenance and fire equipment in the common areas.

His motion was roundly defeated by the six people who remained at the Tribal Meeting. Despondent, Daniel decided to go home. Gloomily he walked along the track until his attention was captured when confronted by the appearance of demonic looking garden gnomes displayed in grottoes on his way. The small ceramic statues were painted to look like fiendish elves with ghoulish eyes and devilish horns depicted on their heads. Enraged and choking back the visceral revulsion he felt, Daniel's face burned red; he grabbed two of the gnomes and bellowed as he bashed them together smashing them to pieces. It was diabolical! Shaking from the shock of blasphemy, Daniel shouted at the heavens. 'Heretics!' The pieces of garden gnomes lay in fragments around him. His chest felt tight and his arms spasmed as he staggered sideways rent asunder by the depth of emotion he was experiencing.

Gradually, he recovered by taking some deep breaths realising that Jesus, too felt belittled and betrayed; his faith had been sorely tested when he cursed the moneylenders and the unbelievers. Daniel drew strength from this comparison and knew that being 'A Chosen One' meant *his* faith would be challenged. Right now, his belief was being challenged sorely.

'Compose yourself,' he chastised himself standing on the track between the hamlets that were nestled in the folds of the valley that was Paradise Falls. Thus, fortified he picked up his stave swung his cape over his shoulder and set off towards home again. He could suffer the slings and arrows of unbelievers, he assured himself, his chest tight.

It wasn't until he had rounded the corner, just before his driveway, that he saw them lying prone in the centre of an enclosed floral grotto like a verdant cul-de-sac, set back from the main track. The two garden gnomes were face to face lying on a bed of flowers and ferns, in the act of coitus. Little horns were visible, and their cheeks flushed with rouge. Daniel let out a scream of anguish from the depths of his being as he lurched backwards clutching his heart. His head roared and the blood pumped through his body. He fell heavily, unable to catch himself and cried out. 'Oh god, oh god, why hast thou forsaken me?'

He became aware he was sobbing when a light shone in his eyes and that he wasn't having a penultimate religious experience. Someone had come across him on the track and was peering into his eyes with a pen light. He heard a distant voice although he couldn't move or speak.

'Yes.' The voice said, 'he's still alive. Go phone triple zero while I give him C.P.R.'

'I'm on my way!' Said another voice.

Fortunately, Lucy's parents Om and Ovum, lived in the house close by and she jogged up the track, burst through her front door and made a beeline to the phone on the wall. No one was home. Lucy waited until a woman answered and asked her some questions like her address and how to find them. Lucy ran back to the scene breathless, to let the man saving Daniel's life know the ambulance wouldn't be long. She looked down at Daniel lying on the ground having his heart pumped and was struck by how vulnerable and mortal he looked. She wondered whether he would die.

* * *

Daniel awoke slowly to find he was in a white bed tucked in tightly with a monitor rigged up to his body and little wires were attached to sticky pads on his chest. He had a drip in his arm with a bottle of fluid hanging above him. The lights were dim, and he became aware a person was sitting next to him. A man in a black cassock and a white dog collar sat serenely on a chair beside his bed, a heavy rosary and cross hanging from his neck.

'Son, you're awake at last.' The priest spoke with a soft Irish brogue.

Daniels's tongue was dry and seemed too big for his mouth. He grunted. The priest held the glass of water up for him and steadied the straw in his mouth so he could sip it.

'Who are you?' Daniel mouthed the words after a few moments. Daniel was trying to remember what had happened, but it was a fog.

'I am Father Gerry,' the priest pronounced it 'cheery'. Daniel just stared at him.

'You don't remember do you, son?' The priest had a benign

and yes, a cheery face, like a man who had no insecurities about who he was or why he was here on earth.

'You've been calling out for a priest,' Father Gerry explained, 'we thought you must be Catholic. So here I am.' He shrugged. Daniel was still confused.

'Did God send you?' He asked urgently.

'Yes, of course, He sent me,' the priest pointed out the obvious, 'I've been sitting here with you for the last hour praying for your eternal soul.' He smiled, revealing an even row of small white teeth.

'Your wife and children were here earlier. She's taken the kids to stay with a friend and will come back once they are in bed.'

'My wife and children?' Daniel repeated lamely. The priest nodded.

'Why did God send you?' Daniel was determined to get to the bottom of this mystery.

Father Gerry was in no doubt about divine intervention although, he was concerned about the young man's current state of mind.

'As it happens,' the priest began pedagogically,' you are labouring under the delusion that you are the chosen one to lead the people of your commune to the promised land. This is not your job but that of our saviour, the Lord Jesus Christ.' Father Gerry waited. Daniel was staring at him transfixed. Father Gerry continued the sermon.

'Your job is to vanquish your spiritual ego that has misguidedly placed yourself above the divine Jesus. You need to humbly accept that he was reincarnated on behalf of all men and that you are not the reincarnated King David of the Jews.' Father Gerry had delivered this sobering news with love and gentleness. Here was a lost lamb of God, he explained, he needed to bring him back into the flock and nurse his soul into the state of devotion it was yearning for. Simple.

Daniel looked at him like a man who finally found his true path in life. Tears of relief filled his eyes. 'Thank you, Father,' he held the priest's hands in his own.

'God bless you, my son.'

'Oh, you are with us?' A nurse appeared in the door frame. The fluorescent light in the hall behind her formed a corona around her body. She wore a starched uniform and carried a clipboard and a thermometer in her top pocket. To Daniel, she was a vision of loveliness. A resplendent goddess of healing.

'Father Cheery is here with me too,' Daniel reassured the nurse, indicating to the chair next to the bed.

'There is no one there, Daniel,' the nurse spoke in a firm, compassionate voice, 'you had a heart attack and hit your head. I'll get you some more water.'

'Hi, Dad.' Lucy was curled up on the couch with a blanket reading her favourite book from childhood, Black Velvet by Sarah King, having made herself a cup of tea.

'Cassie, what a lovely surprise!' Her father was delighted to see his daughter and his eyes shone with love, 'We weren't expecting you. Will you stay for dinner?'

'Love to. Where's Mum?'

'She just coming with the boys. We had Satsang with Siddhartha and Tamsin.'

'Did you see the ambulance on your way home?'

'Yes, we had to pull the car over as it passed us. What happened do you know?'

'Daniel Pendragon was taken to hospital. A heart attack. I called triple zero.'

'Oh dear, is he going to be alright?'

'Yes, I think so. There was a guy doing resuscitation on him when I arrived. What's for dinner? I'm starving.' Lucy could hear the chatter on the veranda from her mother and brothers returning and ditching their shoes.

Later that evening, in the heart of her family, Lucy reflected on Daniel's heart attack. It showed he was not the messiah he claimed to be, just an ordinary man who could have died. All this spiritual stuff they spout, she mused, is nonsense. Her thoughts turned to Seth. He was just as phoney as Daniel, she concluded. It wasn't a big leap. They were both frauds. It proved to be a turning point for Lucy in her transformation back to being Cassie. She liked the independence of having a job and living in a share house and, whilst she enjoyed the company at the ashram and wanted to belong, she never bought into all that cosmic waffle about being weightless.

CHAPTER 15

Each Thursday afternoon, the team at Legal Aid held a staff meeting scheduled into their diaries. This Thursday, the team was feeling overworked and needed to meet as team colleagues again rather than a group of frantic firefighters desperately trying to put out spot fires on all their boundaries.

It was common in their industry, Brenda reminded them, to think they could fix things. She called it professional bracket creep and instructed them they were lawyers and not social workers, housing experts, Drug and Alcohol counsellors or God forbid, hostage negotiators.

Brenda was clear about her role in the bigger scheme of things advising her team in their one-on-one case meetings.

'When you find yourself counselling the clients about their bad choices, stick to the legal consequences of those choices.' She would pop a Nicobate gum into her mouth adding, 'If you still want to change the world, then go into politics.' True, Frank thought. He made a good fist of changing the world while in politics, though it did consume his life, until now.

'Right, you lot!' Brenda would march through the corridors like a hall monitor. 'Five minutes in the meeting room. Be on time.'

A chorus of affirmatives rose after her.

The meeting room doubled as a staff kitchen and fax machine room because the layout of the office meant space taken up with a surfeit of files and storage boxes spilled over into the hall and the kitchen. It was the ongoing bug bear of the legal system that they were required under law to keep the files and documents accrued from the multitude of cases for many years, before archiving and keeping them even longer. The lawyers filed into the kitchen and sat down with cups of coffee keeping the banter alive until they settled.

'Alright, calling the meeting to order.' Brenda barked, as everyone came to order. Madeleine, the legal secretary, office manager and unflappable right-hand woman sat next to Brenda with a notepad open and a hot cup of black tea in front of her.

As a rule, Brenda went around the table asking for an account of how many cases the team were conducting, where they were up to and what sort of resources they required.

'Diana, update the others on your missing woman Natalie Mulligan, will you?'

'Natalie Mulligan's disappearance came to our attention because her family approached Legal Aid to take their case against the police officers for neglect and racism. Julie and Noel Mulligan, are the aunt and uncle while Elizabeth is Natalie's mother.' Diana outlined. 'Elizabeth lodged a missing person's report when her daughter didn't return home after twenty-four hours. She believes that the police were disinterested and dismissive based on Natalie's Aboriginality.'

'Once we were informed our office was under surveillance by the NSW Crime Commission and the mafia,' Brenda interjected, 'we agreed on a strategy.'

'Vic, you're the closest to the door will you check the front door is locked please?'

'Sure thing,' Vic jumped up and went down the hall to check.

When he returned, he gave a thumbs-up sign.

Diana picked up the thread, 'I met with the Police Integrity Unit. Natalie and Elizabeth come from a regional town. The PIU want to bat the case back to the Local Area Command to deal with what they describe as an 'attitudinal' issue. However, I persuaded them there were broader implications, given the Royal Commission's Report. We haven't mentioned possible mafia involvement.'

She looked at Frank when she'd finished.

'I have been investigating a possible connection to the mafia in the region as Natalie's profession is a crop duster,' Frank picked up the story, 'As yet nothing definitive, just that Natalie works for two companies and is a reliable employee and good pilot, by their accounts.

'Anything else from contacts in the area, Frank?' Michelle queried.

'Nope. Her mother gave me the name of Natalie's housemate, Camelia Flintoff. Apparently, Natalie shares a house but stays with her mother when she is working near Lismore.'

'It begs the question,' Vic pointed out, 'where does the mafia fit into Natalie's disappearance?'

Normally, a loquacious fast talker, Brenda quietly weighed up the ramifications for the safety of her team. 'When I received a call from the Crime Commission asking me if our service was representing anyone with links to the mafia, I didn't know the mafia had staked out the office from the other side of the street.' She sipped her coffee as the others waited.

'Of course, we brush up against members of crime gangs and families in our work from time to time and your security is paramount to me.' She recapped sombrely, 'However, this one is curly. I think the mob is watching people who may know the whereabouts of Natalie Mulligan.' Brenda waited for a moment, 'it's the only plausible explanation. Why else would they be interested?'

'Nothing, other than being a pilot, suggests Natalie worked for the mafia or was involved in moving illegal stuff,' Frank although mystified , conceded it was a possibility.

'It would seem an obvious method of moving gear around.' Diana mused, 'I mean there aren't a lot of checks on the coming and going from regional farms and airstrips. Apart from air traffic control reporting.'

'What about registration and licence checks though?' Michelle suggested. 'Frank, did you talk to anyone at the central air safety organisation?'

'You mean the Civil Aviation Safety and Security organisation? Yes, I spoke to a guy there called...umm hang on,' he ran his finger down his notes, 'here we are, Trevor Cane. He wasn't at all forthcoming. I don't think he really believed me either. When I explained we were representing Natalie Mulligan's family because she had disappeared, he clammed up even more and officiously directed me to her employer, AgBlaster.'

'A bit more interagency cooperation would be nice,' Brenda commented acidly.

'Anything else you picked up while you were working the phones?' Brenda quizzed. Frank looked over his notes again.

'Initially, Trevor Cane claimed that the role of the Civil Aviation and Security was to ensure that the planes were airworthy, registered and the pilots with valid licenses. Not to monitor the workplace relations of pilots and their employers.'

'Dead end with the employer too then, I guess?' Vic asked.

'Natalie is a contractor pilot who can work for other employers or individuals if she wants to. I spoke to Craig Bellamy at AgBlaster, who said Natalie was reliable and stayed in touch. They would offer her work and she would tell them her availability. She would take jobs and then clock her hours at the Lismore airport where Agblaster has an office. There's also another company she works for called, Bolt from the Blue. They are a subsidiary company and, like Craig Bellamy, happy to help but no further information of her whereabouts. Natalie calls in and gets jobs from both employers they explained.'

'She flies Agblaster, planes?' Brenda drilled down. 'What else?'

'Yes. Agblaster has a fleet of crop dusters and a workforce of pilots. So does Bolt from the Blue. They act as brokers taking jobs and then matching pilots to planes and jobs.'

Madeleine, looked up from taking notes, everyone stopped talking at once, one of those times when a natural pause in an animated conversation occurs.

'Does Natalie have her own plane?' She wondered aloud into the space.

'Of course!' Frank thunked his forehead with the heel of his hand. 'I am a drongo!' He exclaimed as though there could be no argument. Vic leaned over and patted his back.

'Admitting it is the first step mate.'

'One at a time,' Brenda cut across the conversation that erupted.

'Did you ask this guy, Trevor, whether Natalie had a plane registered in her name, Frank?'

'Afraid not.'

'Ring her mother?' Diana suggested.

'Yes, l did. I didn't ask her about a private plane,' Frank conceded. 'I did get through to Camelia, the housemate. She said Natalie was often not around but always paid the rent. She confirmed that Natalia stayed at her mum's place in Lismore when she was working.' He read from his notes.

"What about a boyfriend?" Vic speculated.

'No one regular according to the housemate.'

'Maybe she got into hot water,' Brenda continued the line of thinking, 'you know decided to get out of Dodge in her own plane without even telling her mother.'

'I'll call Elizabeth back and ask if Natalie has her own plane.'

Michelle, who loved 'whodunnit' novels, extrapolated, 'I wonder where she would go? Being a professional pilot gives you access to all of Australia.'

'If she had done some business with criminals and they wanted to find her she would have to go somewhere far away.' Brenda mulled.

'Natalie would have friends and connections in the bush and with property owners she has worked with over the years she might go and stay there for a while especially if she had a plane. Family would be too dangerous to them which is why she didn't tell her mother and just disappeared,' Diana concluded.

'I think we're working on a supposition Natalie is still alive,' Brenda looked at each of her team soberly. 'Any thoughts on that?'

'We need to,' Frank replied, 'because it takes us in a broader direction of asking what she would do if she were alive and in trouble.'

'Anyway, why would the Crime Commission be watching our office and asking questions about mafia surveillance, if she was dead? It doesn't make sense,' Michelle stated.

The team at Legal Aid now had a connection, based on a hypothesis, that explained the presence of mafia watching their office. They were imaginatively fired up as Brenda pursued the other avenues of the case.

'Diana, what have you got? How did the meeting with the Police Integrity Unit go? Bet they were thrilled to see you?' Brenda grinned.

'Thrilled is the right word.' Diana tossed her an ironic look. 'They asked what evidence I could produce to show this wasn't just a vexatious claim by Indigenous people perceiving bias. Elizabeth has kept scrupulous records of conversations with the various members of the Police Force. Julie and Noel

Mulligan, are the family connection in Sydney.'

'Surely, unless Natalie turns up dead, senior police can claim this is a disciplinary matter, slap the cops involved on the wrists and move along as normal,' Vic pushed his chair back.

'Discriminating against Aboriginal people,' Michelle finished his sentence.

'I believe that Diana's meeting with the Police Integrity has stirred some action, as a local detective phoned Elizabeth,' Frank looked up. 'Ah yes, here we go, Detective Sergeant Paul Condon, of the Byron Bay Station asked Mrs Mulligan if she had any news of Natalie's whereabouts.'

'Interesting that a person in the system chose to reveal their hand,' Brenda mused thoughtfully.

'More interesting that it was Byron Bay and not the Lismore police,' Diana added, 'given that Natalie flew from Lismore and that her mum lives in Lismore.'

'Under the guise of care and concern creating an excuse to drop in see Elizabeth, the most obvious link to Natalie,' Michelle assessed.

'We all need to be vigilant from now on,' Brenda cautioned her team. 'Be careful about what you say and keep a watchful eye when you leave and arrive for work.' Looking around the room, the mood changed. 'We don't know who this young woman was involved with, but sharks are circling in the water.'

'Next. More housekeeping. You will be delighted to learn that I have secured the funds for one full-time paralegal and one part-time just until we can make a dint in this caseload. And before you ask whose arm I twisted to get this momentous deal, his name starts with the letter 'M'.' Brenda cackled at her own joke.

Having one extra staff member was fantastic, let alone one and a half. The whole team felt relieved and somewhat giddy.

Madeleine took over and ran through the work necessary to relocate piles of files, archive them, and put them in storage.

'Then we'll have to relocate the admin bench to the underused corner of the kitchen,' she gestured to the area which ran the length of the house at the back.

The meeting went on for a couple of hours when Brenda called a close and the lawyers began thinking about going home. Frank felt concerned, they were exposed by representing the Mulligan family and he popped his head into Diana's office.

'I'll walk you to your car?' Frank raised his eyebrows. Diana covered the mouthpiece of the phone with her hand.

'I'm alright, thanks. My sister is picking me up out the front.'

Sydney's Autumn weather was blustery as the season prepared to change, it felt close and unsettled. I must see Dad this weekend, Frank remembered guiltily. Regardless of living close to work, it was six o'clock when he walked through his door that evening, dropping his briefcase and shrugging out of his jacket which he threw on the couch before flicking the television on, half-listening. Moving over to the kitchen bench he reflected on his work while taking stuff out of the dishwasher, glad his sister Genie had given him an array of cooked meals in Tupperware containers, which he had the foresight to take out of the freezer and defrost. He put a saucepan of water on the stove to boil to cook pasta placing the precooked meal in the microwave before moving closer to the television to hear the news reader adopt a grave and compassionate tone.

'A young woman's body has been washed ashore at La Perouse beach in Southeast Sydney. Police are appealing to the public for any information about the woman's identity and said she may be Aboriginal. If you know something that will help the police, please come forward or ring Crime Stoppers.' Frank absorbed the news then reached for the phone and dialled Diana's number; it went to voice mail.

His voice sounded hollow.

Diana called him less than a minute later, 'Frank, the body of a woman has turned up dead! Quick turn on the news now!' She hadn't listened to her voicemail.

'I'm watching it too.' They were both quiet for a few moments sharing their fears.

'It could be Natalie,' Diana felt emotional.

CHAPTER 16

Elizabeth felt sure Natalie would not disappear without saying something about her plans or missing her mum's birthday dinner. That certainty was the reason she had gone to the local police and reported Natalie missing after a day and a night. She found the police reaction to her concern was dismissive and thought they were being racist when she showed them a picture of her daughter with brown skin and hair. They even questioned her version of events.

When she phoned Julie and Noel Mulligan a few days after the initial missing person report, they listened to her story and encouraged her search suggesting she put up notices and make a community announcement on the radio.

'Why don't you call her work again and ask about her,' they urged. Still, there was no news of Natalie. Now weeks had passed, and Elizabeth called Julie to ask what else she could do to find Natalie.

'A mother knows when something is not right,' Julie was talking quietly on the phone. 'We called the Legal Aid people.'

'What can Legal Aid do, Julie?' Elizabeth's voice broke with emotion. 'To bring Natalie back?'

'It will put a bomb under the cops, Liz. Make them justify themselves, you know, work harder to find her.'

'But why not Aboriginal Legal Aid? Did you talk to them?'

'Noel went to see them but they reckoned suing the police wasn't going to help further land rights.'

'They are probably right about that,' Elizabeth felt a weight in her chest.

'Maybe. We got a meeting with a lawyer from Legal Aid. Hang on let me find her card,' Julie scrabbled around in her handbag, tucking the phone under her ear.

'Here it is! Diana Gianiovellis,' she read from the card, 'lovely lady. She said she wasn't sure whether they could help us, but she would look into it.'

'Alright, if you think it will help.' The two women talked on for some time and said their goodbyes. She had only just hung up when the phone rang again.

'Mrs Elizabeth Mulligan?' A young woman's voice asked.

'Yes.' Elizabeth was still standing in her hall beside the front door. She glanced down at a photo of the family in younger happier times, smiling up from the hall table. The young woman went on quickly however, her tone had changed.

'This is Constable Audrey Timms, Mrs Mulligan, from the Eastern Sydney police station,' Elizabeth didn't respond waiting for the news, not breathing.

'I am very sorry to give you this news over the phone, but a woman's body has been found matching the description and photo of your missing daughter.'

Diana picked Elizabeth up from Mascot airport and shepherded her into the car, holding the door open until she was seated and had fastened her seat belt.

'We're going straight to the morgue, Mrs Mulligan. Frank is waiting there with Julie and Noel.' Elizabeth felt numb.

'Please call me Elizabeth.' Diana pulled out of the short-term parking area and turned left toward Riordan Street, an arterial road that wound through Redfern. The traffic was brisk and Diana talked while navigating the lights and delivery trucks.

'We don't know whether the person is your daughter, Elizabeth. That's why the police need to make a formal identification.' Diana indicated and pulled out into the right-hand lane to avoid a parked car. She looked in her side mirror before resuming her explanation.

'There were no papers or other identification with the umm...on the person's body.'

Elizabeth was holding a gold cross on a chain around her neck. Her church congregation was such a source of strength and support when she lost Rover.

Diana entered City Road. Elizabeth, just listened in silence until as Diana drove them onto Glebe Point Road, where the morgue was located next to the public school and opposite a corner coffee shop aptly called, 'Bad Manors'.

'Thank you, Diana.' Elizabeth lightly touched her arm conveying her gratitude.

Diana drove past the morgue on their left and made a left turn into a carpark beside the Glebe Primary School.

'Here we are. Are you alright?' She asked gently.

Elizabeth sighed. 'Yes, I think so. My faith helps.'

'Come on then. I saw Frank with the others waiting as we drove past.'

The police remained circumspect about the cause of death. Probably an overdose or a suicide, they suggested. Frank wasn't convinced she had died from an overdose. Why was she in the ocean floating off La Perouse beach? He felt the body was dumped. She didn't just hit up and wander out into the ocean, he reasoned. Surely, she would have been chewed on? Not so, she died of an overdose according to police. Standing beside Noel and Julie Mulligan on the footpath outside the building that served the morgue in a busy suburb of Sydney, Frank's heart went out to the parents and relations. The Mulligans stood in quiet dignity and Frank felt humbled by the sacrifices that people like the Mulligans make to achieve recognition in his country.

'You a Labor man, Frank?' Noel asked looking him in the eye.

Yes. A card-carrying member.'

'Good. Only mob in Canberra ever cared about equality in this country.'

'Here they are!' Julie walked quickly toward Diana and Elizabeth her arms open.

She hugged her sister-in-law and together they turned back to the men. Noel stepped forward took Elizabeth's hands in his and squeezed them.

'So sorry, Lizzie,' he mumbled.

Frank and Diana exchanged a look of sympathy for the people they were representing wondering if their search for

Natalie was over.

'Shall we go in?' Diana gestured towards the steps of the double fronted, Federation sandstone building. The group ascended the steps onto the broad front porch beneath a bullnose iron roof and pushed open the wooden doors inset with beautiful stained glass. The interior revealed polished wooden floors and cream and green walls with elegant period light fittings and an office with a window halfway along the hall. It reminded Frank of those quiet old university libraries where you weren't allowed to talk, where the air was heavy with thoughts and memories. Diana made their presence known to the woman behind the office window and once she signed in all five of them were directed to take a seat on one of the wooden benches along the wall.

Just then the door opened, and two police detectives entered the building bringing the frisson of the outer world with them. This was a job for them, one they were running a little late for, nevertheless they moved forward and identified Elizabeth, before introducing themselves.

'Mrs Elizabeth Mulligan? I'm Detective Charles Savva from the South Sydney Region office. This is my colleague Detective Constable Beth Warne. I'm sorry we must meet under these circumstances.' Both police officers gave Elizabeth a brief handshake.

Diana took over the introductions. 'I am Diana Gianiovellis, and this is Frank Phelan, we are lawyers assisting the family at the request of Julie and Noel Mulligan, close family relations.' There were more handshakes and courtesies and Diana stepped back. 'There is a waiting room for friends and family,' Detective Savva indicated as he led the way back to the first door off the main hall. 'Constable, can you go and sign in for us?'

The waiting room had the same décor in cream and green with ample light streaming through the frosted glass windows. There were half a dozen nondescript waiting room chairs accompanied by a wooden coffee table with a few magazines and two lonely coasters.

'I would like to clarify briefly to you, before we go in, what the process is so that it is easier for you to deal with.' Detective Savva was professional, having done this many times before. 'Only direct family are to be present.' Before he could continue Elizabeth spoke up, 'I wish to have Julie and Noel with me in there for support, they are direct family.'

'Of course, Mrs Mulligan,' Constable Warne assured her.

Frank and Diana stood together as the detective outlined the process, 'We will enter the morgue retention room and meet the medical examiner. He'll have the body under a sheet. He will draw the sheet back from the face of the deceased and we will ask you a specific question - is this your daughter, Natalie Mulligan?' Julie grasped Elizabeth's hand.

'To which you need to answer clearly either 'yes' or 'no'. Do you understand?'

'Yes, I understand, Detective.' Until now Elizabeth had remained dry-eyed and stoical.

'We'll be waiting here for you when it's over,' Frank confirmed. Noel gave both the lawyers a look of appreciation.

The medical examiner made an appearance at this point dressed in green scrubs and green gumboots, he looked 'vocational' reminding one that he examined and dissected dead bodies. Dr Carthew, had a kind and grandfatherly face with grey hair and tufty eyebrows which seemed to have a life of their own. He was carrying a clipboard with paperwork attached.

'Thank you for coming, Mrs Mulligan.' He looked at Julie and Noel.

Diana introduced him, 'This is Julie and Noel Mulligan. They will accompany Elizabeth.' The Medical Examiner nodded.

The two detectives waited until the formalities were finished and followed Dr Carthew. The morgue was everything one imagined it to be. Clinical, white paint and a strong smell of bleach. There were metal benches on wheels and stainless-steel drawers in a bank on walls to house the dead bodies. An adjacent wall had deep stainless-steel sink fittings and hoses with stainless steel benches. Elizabeth became aware of how cold it was. The two police officers stood at the end of a steel trolley on which the body lay with a white sheet covering it. She approached the bench with Noel and Julie on either side. Dr Carthew walked to the opposite side of the trolley his eyes meeting those of the family waiting in trepidation. He had seen so many families over his career and witnessed their grief and loss. 'Are you ready?'

'Yes, we're ready.' Elizabeth bit her lip bracing herself.

The doctor pulled the sheet pack just enough to uncover the woman's face which looked serene in death.

Detective Savva's voice cut through the shock like a knife. 'Is this your daughter, Natalie Mulligan?'

Stunned, Elizabeth shook her head. Even in death she couldn't believe how much Andy and Natalie looked like each other.

'Andy!' Julie howled a primal screen of a mother who has lost a child, as though she'd been wrenched from her arms by a torrent of flooding water.

Julie fell on the body tears flowing down her face in anguish.

'This is our daughter, Andrea,' Julie sobbed inconsolably.

'How did she die, doctor?' Noel stood behind her with both hands on her back, quiet heartfelt tears in his eyes.

'There was pure heroin in her blood. She didn't drown.'

'Can we have a few moments with my daughter?' Julie's eyes pleaded.

'It's our way. Our culture,' Noel qualified.

'We will wait outside,' Dr Carthew, motioned to the detectives who reluctantly preceded him through the heavy door leaving the grieving parents and Elizabeth pressed together beside the body of Andy. The temperature of the refrigerated room seemed to drop when Julie broke the silence tentatively, 'Maybe there was someone else with Andrea? If they found pure heroin in her system?' She stammered a little. 'She couldn't afford that; she was on the dole and begging for money at Redfern Station. Why has she got this pure grade A heroin in her system and why would she be at La Perouse Beach, on her own?' Julie and Noel felt strengthened by her inquiries, but it led to a perilous path that Noel stepped onto when he asked the obvious question, as yet unanswered.

'Maybe someone else injected her, maybe she was killed?' Julie wiped her eyes with her sleeve while Elizabeth's eyes searched his face.

'It just doesn't add up, because she didn't pose a threat to anyone. Perhaps there's another injection hole?' Julie pulled the sheet down revealing Andrea's pale upper body. She picked up one arm examining it closely, 'There's scar tissue though no fresh tracks.'

Quickly, the two women searched Andrea's body for further evidence. They looked at her feet and thighs variously decorated with tattoos accumulated over the years. They rolled her limp body slightly onto her side so they could see the dragon tattoo that curled around one shoulder and finished under her left ear. Julie smoothed the hair away from Andrea's neck where it clung and touched the dragon's tail. Her fingers feeling swollen. The wound wasn't obvious. It was barely noticeable.

'Look at this,' Elizabeth whispered, the two others leaned in, 'Am I imagining a needle mark?' Her voice was tremulous, uncertain as they hung over the neck of the dead woman looking at a dark mark on the scales of the dragon's tail. They'd discovered a puncture wound behind Andrea's left ear into the carotid artery that remained hidden by the tattoo, apparently unseen by the Medical Examiner. Perhaps because he was looking at the old scars on her arms. Jolted out of their reverie by the sound of Dr. Carthew, coming back into the room, Julie spoke first.

'Dr Carthew, you can't release the body yet. There is something not right.'

'Does your report mention the injection site behind her left ear or what grade heroin it was?' Elizabeth sounded like a teacher. Dr. Carthew, not keen on having his judgement questioned, was taken aback however, before he could contradict them and re-establish his professional control over the situation, Elizabeth stepped forward and pulling back Andrea's left ear pointed to a deep puncture disguised by the tattoo ink which covered half the dead girl's neck and shoulder.

'We believe Andrea was on methadone. Was it high-grade heroin doctor?' Julie interrogated the doctor. Noel who stayed quiet until now, spoke up.

'Look, we're not saying you didn't do your job. Just that there are grounds for doubt. If Andrea committed suicide or died accidentally, shouldn't it go to the Coroner?'

'Yes Noel, that's right,' Dr Carthew's facial muscles unclenched a little. In his job, he had come to expect strange reactions to the death of loved ones. Some were angry, some seemed indifferent, almost as though they expected nothing less. This time, the relatives found another explanation for the callous outcome of an overdose, however, he agreed with the premise, that people tended not to deliberatively overdose and die by the ocean.

'If she did inject herself with pure heroin behind the ear then someone else was involved!' Julie spread her hand's palms up. 'It's too difficult a place. Also, she didn't have money to buy that kind of heroin.'

'Rest assured, Mr and Mrs Mulligan, I want to get to the truth of how your daughter died. Finding the heroin overdose was part of my preliminary findings. I will give a full report to the Coroner. She may have died accidentally, or it may have been foul play. In that case, that will be for the police to pursue. Once this is completed you will be notified and asked to attend the Coroner's court hearing.'

CHAPTER 17

Once the Medical Examiner's findings were sent to the Coroner, an inquest into Andy death was urgently convened. The day before the hearing, the Mulligans gathered to talk with Diana and Frank, in Julie and Noel's living room. They lived in an Victorian two-story terrace in Redfern which loomed over the street front on the South side and had a symbiotic relationship with a giant Morton Bay Figtree. Oftentimes, Noel would sit on his porch after work drinking a beer contemplating the tree, whose roots buckled and spread as though a giant subterranean skeleton was pushing through the concrete struggling over decades for space to grow.

When everyone was seated around the coffee table, the two lawyers went through the whole process of an inquest to make it comprehensible to the family.

'Not every death is ruled suspicious,' Diana pointed out, 'if it was accidental or there are unexplained circumstances surrounding the death, then an inquest is required.' She looked over at Frank, 'Andrea's death may look like an accidental overdose but there are questions regarding the circumstances,' she explained sombrely.

'When there is a finding such as heroin being the cause of death, the report by the Medical Examiner triggers the matter being called before the Coroner's court. In this instance the Medical Examiner requested the case be brought forward and dealt with without delay.'

'Does that mean it is the Coroner who will say it was a suspicious death?' Elizabeth queried while Noel and Julie watched intently.

'Yes, that's their job. They review the Medical Examiner's report, and they call witnesses, usually the police and any other witnesses, perhaps someone who saw something happen or found the body.' Diana paused her explanation. 'The Coroner has the power to compel witnesses to give evidence and they can also provide a certificate to the witness stating the information they provide won't be used in a court against them.'

'How does that work, Diana?' Noel resting his elbows on his knees.

Noel was close to sixty, a round and gentle man who spoke softly, with a warm expression, he wore a heavy sense of responsibility and sadness on his sloped shoulders. This wasn't the first overdose he had to deal with as the scourge of heroin had ripped the community in Redfern apart, but it was the first of his own children.

'If anyone was with Andy when she died, they should've

called Triple 000 or an ambulance, but instead they left her because they were afraid or guilty. Or both.'

'Is that what happened to Andy? How will we find out?' Julie's eyes were red rimmed from crying. A mother searching for answers.

'Honestly, Julie we don't know what happened,' Frank clarified. 'We do know Andrea most likely died of an overdose from the puncture wound behind her ear and it looks like she didn't do it herself. It will be up to the Coroner to review the evidence and decide.' Diana put her hand on Julie's arm and gave it a squeeze.

'What will happen?' Elizabeth asked querulously.

'The Coroner can issue a certificate to a witness who tells the court what happened at the time, which means it can't be used as evidence against them,' Frank picked up. 'If it is ruled a suspicious death, that will trigger a full-blown police investigation possibly for manslaughter or murder.' Noel looked at the carpet between his feet as Frank concluded.

'Poor Andy,' Elizabeth shook her head. One child dead and another missing.

'As a rule, Coroners determine the cause of death in accidents, suicides and fire and also when a person disappears, once a certain time has passed, say five years,' Diana answered the question in everyone's mind, 'that won't help us find Natalie, I'm afraid.'

The body had been reported by a passer-by who left an anonymous phone message and the police team that recovered the body would give evidence to the Coroner.

* * *

'All rise for the Coroner.' The Court Clerk announced the arrival of the presiding judge. As the courtroom stood, Frank and Diana exchanged a glance. Not all judges wore silly, ancient wigs that distinguished them from their colleagues. Judge Anna Sierra had thick auburn hair, a stern expression, and a pedantic character. She was a prodigious contributor to the Law Journal of Australia. Diana felt inspired by her serious intellect.

The courtroom, built in the nineteen eighties, was windowless save for a high bank on the wall above the Coroner's bench which looked unwashed since being installed. The light was dappled in the courtroom. As a setting, where the legal world met people living through a death in their family, it wasn't too bad. The long wooden panels were in blonde wood like teak and the benches were crafted of the same material which lent a Swedish air to the room.

'Judge Sierra will probably ask the police to speak first and then the parents,' Diana whispered. The courtroom was full of Andrea's family and extended family while Elizabeth sat quietly between them all with her hands folded in her lap. Elizabeth had been in Sydney for a full week staying with her in-laws. Today she was dressed in her town clothes wearing a smart blue coat and a pleated cream skirt with a pale blue twin set and pearls at the neck with pearl earrings. Bearing herself with dignity, she supported Noel and Julie with her understated sadness as Natalie was still missing. She dabbed her eyes with an embroidered hankie and put it in her purse.

Normally, Frank was considered a tough operator when he was in politics, and he was trained as a lawyer who chose to become involved in the formulation of laws in parliament.

Sitting now in court surrounded by the deep history of loss, death and sacrifice by Aboriginal people, he felt their pain.

Once the police established the body was Andrea Mulligan, they took a seasoned approach to the matter. The Coroner grilled them about their findings about place and manner of the death.

'When you found the body Detective Savva, what was your first reaction?' The Coroner fixed him with a penetrating gaze.

'After the shock of seeing the victim lying face down in the water, I wondered how she ended up there. We dragged her from the water, called the M.E. and locked the scene down to prevent the press and busybodies from getting involved.'

'What did you do next?'

'I notified my superior, Detective Inspector Rye, that we discovered a dead woman, and by her needle marks, possibly a drug addict, at the edge of the sand in La Perouse Bay. We searched the area for any belongings or signs the victim was on the beach before entering the water. We didn't find anything. There was no car or any tracks in the sand.'

'What state was the body in when you recovered it?' The detective looked uncomfortable with the question and deflecting the inference said, 'I'm not a medical person. I can't comment on that.'

'What was your summation of finding the victim in the water, on a beach?'

'The whole thing didn't add up in my experience. If the victim was a practising addict and died of an overdose, how did she get in the water?'

'Can you elaborate?' The Coroner pressed.

'The body appeared dumped. Ms Mulligan didn't just shoot up and wander out into the ocean. We weren't convinced. There were no belongings on the shore, no injecting equipment. Plus, she was wearing her shoes.' He looked across at the Coroner taking her lead to continue.

'If the victim entered the water somewhere else, she would have been chewed by fish. But instead, she died of an overdose of heroin and not by drowning.'

'What you are saying is, the police have questions about the death of the victim, that aren't satisfied by the evidence available at present?'

'That is correct.'

Coroner Sienna, continued her questioning of the other witnesses. Noel and Julie Mulligan both spoke of Andrea's struggle with drugs. They believed she was on the methadone program, but their daughter's addiction had strip mined their hopes and all their cash over years and years. In the end they told her not to come around until she was clean and going to Narcotics Anonymous.

'Andrea hated sand!' Julie stated as though finding her on a beach was impossible.

The Medical Examiner summarised his report and conclusions that the victim died of an overdose of high-grade heroin and not drowned in the ocean and, that the circumstances of her death were suspicious.

'The victim took the heroin before she went into the water?' The Coroner persisted.

'Yes. The victim was a drug user, but she could not have injected heroin into the artery in her neck and walked into the sea. She would have died instantly.'

The verdict handed down by the Coroner was that Andrea Mulligan died a suspicious death in unexplained circumstances. These needed to be answered by a police inquiry into her death. The Mulligans, their legal team and the extended family filed out of the court, vindicated and downhearted. Once on the street, they hugged and comforted each other. Perhaps there would be some justice for Andrea.

Andy's funeral was held at the Memorial Gardens at Rookwood Cemetery. It was packed with family and friends including Frank and Diana. The beautiful service moved everyone there and the whole room filled with voices in song and sadness, as though each life there was cloaked in the collective knowledge of loss and dying.

Noel gave a eulogy for his daughter which moved everyone to tears. Andy, he said, was the wrong woman in the wrong place at the wrong time and now her life had been thrown away.

Rest in peace Andy.

CHAPTER 18

Andy hadn't been back in Nimbin for over a year, largely because some nasty dealers, to whom she owed money, would come after her and menace her. In her befuddled fantasy world, she pretended they'd forgotten. Having died her hair henna red before escaping Sydney, where she also owed bad people money, she added a pair of dark glasses, believing she was less visible in the motley crowd of Nimbin. She was rake thin with tattoos across her back and arms, neck and wrists, she wore chains, ear studs and bling giving the overall impression of an inner-city punk, rather than a dreamy hippy chick.

Out in the countryside, on the commune Paradise Falls, there were empty shacks she could squat in without being hassled. Her priority was to get some money and drugs. She knew the dealers don't hit town till after twelve o'clock and the place is too small to rob anyone, she'd never make a getaway. Sauntering into the front bar of the hotel, her eyes roamed over the men propping up the bar trying to make eye contact with one of them who might need a root. Down the back there was a small shed where the publican kept some large outdoor umbrellas and Andy knew it was open. Sidling over to the bar she wedged her shoulder into a space between some men leaning against it.

'Buy you a drink?' A man in his forties with dirty work gear on and dusty umbrella caps over his boots offered without looking at Andy. He was wearing shorts and a white singlet with an unbuttoned checked shirt over it that smelt of sweat, woodchips and petrol.

'Yeah sure, handsome.' Andy batted her eyes 'I'll have a middy of beer thanks.'

'Anything else I can help you with?' She murmured. The bar man had delivered them both a glistening cold beer and taken money from a pile on the bar in front of the man.

The man took a sip of his beer cutting his eyes to the woman standing beside him looking down at her cleavage.

'How much?' The tree feller's ears pricked up and his loins stirred. He took in the woman's breasts visible beneath her tangerine silky top. She had a floaty, floral hippy skirt on but didn't look like a local.

'Fifty bucks,' she bargained knowing that soliciting for prostitution services in the hotel front bar was frowned upon.

'Lucky I've been paid,' the bloke chortled. He put a hand into his pocket and peeled off two bills and put them on the bar.

'Give you the rest when we get it on.' Andy quietly pocketed the bills.

'Follow me out and round the back there's a shed down there.'

Having downed her drink, she picked up her bag.

'I just got to go to the ladies.' She exited as quickly as she'd turned up, closely followed by the tree feller.

They intersected at the door of the shed at the back of the overgrown beer garden where it was shady and cool. She had the door ajar and her hand out. 'Another twenty bucks.'

'Yeah well, you'd better make it worth my while,' she could see that the guy was weighing up whether to rip her off.

'Don't worry it will be worth it.'

Begrudgingly, he gave her another twenty bucks. Andy pushed the shed door open revealing a clutter of outdoor materials and a circular wooden table they could do the deed on. Leaning against the edge of the table she slid one knee between his legs and massaged his inner thigh then pressed her breasts against him. She groaned with confected lustfulness.

'How do you like that?' She asked throatily. The man was aroused, his cheeks flushed. She noticed his bad breath. Dropping to her knees and undoing his fly she fellated him briefly before she disengaged and stood up and lifting her skirt up to reveal her bush, she undid her blouse and let her breasts hang out. The man grabbed her breasts roughly and began kneading and rubbing them before pushing her roughly onto her stomach across the table. She gave him a condom from her skirt pocket and heard the rustle as he slipped it on and, commenced with a thrust and a groan. They concluded the business and went their separate ways. Andy ducked into the toilets at Birth and Beyond, the prenatal clinic on the main street, washed her hands, face and vagina with warm soapy water then snorted her last dose in a toilet cubicle before crossing the road again to the Nimbin Post Office. The Post Office, was a quaint stand-alone weatherboard house in cream and red trim which had stood the test of time for almost a century.

'Any mail for Mulligan?' Natalie might have a cheque in the mail from her employer. The man behind the counter wore a clean white shirt with short sleeves and a nondescript tie. He combed his hair over neatly to hide the thinning and his complexion was a waxy yellowish colour like a cigarette. His fingers were shaky and stained yellow from nicotine on both sides. As it happened, he tried to smoke at least a packet a day and, while his work hours restricted his habit, he made up for it at the end of the day, at the front bar of the pub.

He turned around to the pigeonholes and took out a letter then he read aloud, 'Natalie Mulligan?'

'Yeah, that's me,' Andy put out her hand.

He raised his rheumy eyes and regarded the woman, confirming that she resembled Natalie Mulligan, who came in for her mail. He handed her the letter which she stuffed it in her bag. The moment the woman left, the post office man picked up the telephone and dialled a number. There was only one other person in the Post Office at the time and she was addressing a parcel on the bench below the window. The phone rang several times before someone answered the call.

'Natalie Mulligan just picked up her mail,' he said. 'No, I don't know where she went.' The man hung up the phone and stepped into the mailroom his hands shaking.

A grey Landcruiser 4-wheel drive pulled up alongside

Andy, a little way past the fork road at Diggers Park, in the middle of Nimbin. She was contemplating hitching a ride out to Paradise Falls to score some weed. 'Want a lift?' A tanned man in the front passenger seat had his arm resting on the open window. Manifestation! She foolishly thought, I need a lift and some gear. She climbed in the back of the vehicle. A bit further down the road it pulled over and the guy got out of the front passenger seat and climbed in the back with Andy. He grabbed her bag and found the letter proving she was Natalie Mulligan. She struggled to get free and tore a nail then, ferociously bit the man's arm tasting blood in her mouth. 'You bitch!' He was angry. He slapped her hard across the head.

'I don't want to die,' she whimpered, one hand grabbing the seat belt anchor trying to escape.

'Nobody does. Don't take it personally.' Her killer replied.

On their way out of town he injected her in the carotid artery with heroin. Andy slumped sideways. Instantly dead, her eyes rolled back. The man threw a picnic rug over her body before climbing back in the front seat.

The young Aboriginal woman's life was over. Just thrown aside with casual cynicism. Drugs and money were powerful socio-economic drivers pushing people into despair and crime compounded by a recession that created dislocation and job losses. It was an Australian story in 1994.

CHAPTER 19

Natalie knew it would be at least four hours flying to the outskirts of Alice. Rover flew her there once during the school holidays when she was about fifteen years old. The boys were on holiday camp and Andrea was staying at a friend's place. Rover's kinship uncle ran into a road train and was banged up in the Alice Springs hospital for weeks. He claimed never to have eaten so well in his life and all the families from hundreds of miles stopped by, talked in their language and joined him for a cup of tea. Despite the Mulligans coming from the Eastern seaboard, Uncle Fred made his home in the Alice, a place he described as 'the centre of the ancient world'.

Natalie was completely at home flying high above the land that stretched out into infinite sky. The Beechcraft was like a tiny gnat buzzing along a what seemed like a preordained path. A few fluffy clouds danced around the sky while

Natalie went through Rover's instructions on finding Uncle Fred's place and how to land there safely. Rover was always explaining stuff to the kids who most of the time switched off unlike Natalie, who listened and tried to commit stuff to memory. She was watching carefully for the markers on the landscape leading her to Alice Springs. She set her coordinates and checked her times against them still felt nervous she might miss something.

The dog was still coming to terms with airsickness and had thrown up the last salami sandwich and keeled sideways. He slept with a paw over his face and when he woke up, ate the chucked-up breakfast and lay down again.

'Not long to go now Buddy,' Natalie turned slightly in the cockpit and spoke to the dog. He wiggled over and stuck his snout under her armpit and whimpered. She patted his head and scratched under the nearest ear. 'You must be dying for a drink. Here we go! Look up ahead there's a creek bed and an old road running beside it.'

'Just act like a normal croppy Natalie,' Rover counselled, 'fly in low to the ground between the two rocky outcrops like you're checking out the field.' He showed her how to keep an eye out on her right side for a deep, green crevice in the land. 'That's a watering hole that runs all the way through to the aquifer,' he went, on sounding like her geology teacher. 'Fred would hook up the pump and generator each night and fill the tanks and then pump water into a little terraced dam he'd filled in the dry creek bed, so all the critters shared water.'

On the Southern side of the dusty red road a long wire fence separated the fields from the road itself which served as a stock track bulldozed and rolled periodically. The world here in the centre was so red. The dust that blew off the surface soil and hillocks coating everything from the flora to the fence posts. The sky, by contrast was a dazzling lapis lazuli, iridescent blue. 'Wow!' Natalie was enthralled.

'See this little range coming up Nat?' Rover had pointed to a crumpled, ancient line of hills covered with scrub and native grasses, 'they're just high enough to block out the radar tower at the airport and any equipment at Pine Gap, where the Yanks are over on the other side of Alice.' Rover looked at his daughter seriously. 'Sometimes our mob need to move about our land without drawing too much attention.' Rover observed with finality.

'Now watch this Nat, cause you need to bank the plane before you get to the hills then, make the turn and slow down bringing it down to taxi along that strip of road. You'll see the fence goes left and you've got a big paddock to turn the Beechcraft around and head back up the road.'

Natalie followed his instructions gauging the distance to the hills before banking the Beechcraft before the thermal's up-draught where a majestic eagle with a wingspan of two metres hovered. Managing the turbulence across the rocky cliff faces, she straightened the plane and lined up the road surface. Carefully, winding back her speed she descended at a steady rate as the road came up faster than she had anticipated, the plane bumped down hard and swerved sideways before she could correct her path. Having slowed down, in control of the plane again she sped up a little to taxi up the road. Sure enough, they came to the end of the fence and a broad, open grassy paddock. She took a broad sweep and turned praying there weren't any large rock or unseen ditches and motored back towards Fred's place. It looked like a shambles of corrugated iron, weathered timbers, and railway sleepers and indiscriminate foliage over everything. Seeing the spread up close surprised her, as it was barely noticeable from the air where the overall impression was of an abandoned camp.

A weathered, old Aboriginal man walked out past the miscellany to greet her. He was short with snowy white hair and shiny white teeth while his coal black eyes sparkled with humour and hospitality. Natalie pulled up at the end of the road only fifty metres from a shed with two open sides and screeds of camouflage netting and tarps across various parts of it. A wave of relief washed over her as she opened the cockpit door. Seeing the opportunity, the dog barged past her only to slip and slide along the wing before falling and jumping down to the ground. A yellow kelpie cross shot out of the barn barking furiously at this canine intrusion. Uncle Fred clucked to settle her down while Buddy trotted over to sniff the yellow dog's bum, his tail wagging. Natalie felt a surge of release being on land again, in the middle of nowhere greeted by this beautiful old man. She slid off the wing and landed with her knees bent.

'Hey, Nat how ya goin'?' He held out his warm, brown hands and took both of hers in his.

'Welcome to my camp, let's have a cuppa tea? I knew you were comin' didn't know you bring your dog with you.' He chuckled at his joke. Natalie wondered how he knew she was coming but didn't want to seem naïve by asking him. He was delighted to see her rather than surprised.

'Your mum alright, Nat?'

'Mum's okay she just misses Dad all the time. We all do.' They had reached the camp site where Fred had an open fireplace with railway sleepers and stumps as seats and over to one side where the site became the shed there was a big freezer next to a barbeque outfit.

Fred reminded her of the photos she had seen in books about WW11 where smiling men are standing next to a jeep. Like them, he wore khaki shorts held up around his skinny hips with an old-style leather belt and a navy-blue singlet tucked into his pants. His brown arms were strong and sinewy with muscles and ropey veins that stood out from his neck. He radiated deep harmony and happiness.

'Nice set up, Uncle Fred.' Natalie shyly approved.

'Got everything here, bub. Harold did a TAFE course as an electrician and we jerry-rigged a direct line to the overhead wires to run the utilities and the television.'

As she studied Fred's extensive home, she realised very little of it could be seen from the sky, or the road for that matter. She was aware Fred was watching her his black eyes shining with merriment.

'Got a lot of stuff for the place at the local recycle centre,' he jerked his head pointing out the freezer and a generator. 'Them walls have pulleys and hinges, and I can fit two vehicles and a home under the same roof. We can have a cuppa and then put the plane out of sight, eh?' Fred winked and nodded his head.

A heavy metal kettle with a spout sat over the coals of the outdoor fireplace. While Fred looked about for clean cups, he indicated to her to sit down. She felt the air on her skin, it was surprisingly cool in the shade. The two dogs had taken off exploring and playing like long lost friends.

'Take the weight off Nat and I'll fix up the animals and get a cuppa organised,' he whistled to the dogs who came in wagging their tails and talking to them filled up two enamel plates with roughly cut pieces of animal. 'Kangaroo tail,' Fred said over his shoulder. Then he turned on a tap and filled up a big saucepan with fresh water. Natalie watched the dogs eat and drink.

Fred plonked a cup of tea in front of her and took a seat in a fold open director's chair.

'How much trouble are you in, Nat?' The old man stirred his sugar in and then casually chucked the tea bag in the fireplace.

'Honestly, a lot of trouble, Uncle Fred.' By nature, she was a resourceful, down to earth woman, but facing up to the events of the past she felt remorseful and insecure. Fred sipped his tea and waited.

'I got my pilot licence and now I do crop dusting for a living. The authorities at the airfield asked me to report on any contraband trafficking I found out about. They are going to pay me for proof. I did a run of dope into Sydney with a guy.' She spoke quickly trying to get it all out.

'Then what happened?'

'Then I set up a camera and sound system and filmed this guy, the mafia and two bent coppers doing a deal over buying and selling dope and probably planning to kill me.'

'No one else knows about this film. I haven't even watched it myself yet. I just switched the camera off in the plane and flew here while it was dark. I didn't know where else to hide.'

All this came out in a rush and Natalie's coffee-coloured

cheeks blushed with the truth and the danger of what she'd done.

'They are pretty deadly enemies, Natalie. Why d'ya reckon they want to bump you off if you done some flyin' for them?'

'Because I am an unknown. I was having a thing with this Māori guy Brendon, the other pilot. He asked me did I want to run some drugs as co-pilot. I figured once is proof. Then he meets these mafia type guys, and we load the bales on a Cessna and fly it into Campbelltown. Brendon paid me a couple of grand and said there will be another shipment soon. I stashed the money. Haven't spent it.'

Uncle Fred chewed a twig without taking his eyes off the young woman in front of him.

'Then a few days later, I'm there at Brendon's place in the morning. I heard him on the phone talking about a meeting with this mob and some other guys he calls our 'friends' and how they are meeting at the Tyagarah airport. That's when I decide to rig up the film in the Beechcraft and go into hiding until I can give the film to the right cops.'

'You wanna give the money back, bub.'

'I wanna stay alive first, Uncle Fred!' Natalie took a drink of her tea then looked up again. 'It was just pure luck that it rained the night those bad guys had a meeting otherwise they wouldn't have gone into the hangar, and I wouldn't have got the recording of what they said.'

'Luck is a strange spirit, bub. It hovers around some people. Can change the course of history, I reckon.'

* * *

Natalie was beginning to feel at home in this ancient sandy ecosystem with Uncle Fred, who didn't follow the course of life by the weeks and days of a calendar, he watched the ebb and flow in the rhythm of seasons around him. The sun came up and went down, the moon waxed and then waned, the desert flowered, and the rains came. Poetry!

Fred was listening to the news on the radio early one morning when he heard the piece about an Aboriginal woman's death. The police had identified her as Andrea Mulligan, and they were asking for people to come forward with information. He kept the news of her cousin being killed from Nat, knowing the cycle of headline dramas would pass and he could break it to her later. But he felt the need to act and send the tape Nat had made, to some people high up in authority, because he didn't trust the local cops. Nor did he believe it was a coincidence and pondered for a while on how much the two cousins look like each other.

One night a few days later, they were both reclining in canvas deck chairs near the campfire staring up at the sky. Nat was transfixed by the multitude of stars brightly shining in a constellation that seemed to swirl and move as she watched. The stars and galaxies appeared to flicker and sparkle at her when she focussed on a special cluster. She felt sure they coalesced and shone brighter just for her and searched for words to describe the sense of boundless space above her. It truly was like the centre of the universe as space seemed to stretch and absorb her and, any sense of separation from nature dissolved. Every nerve vibrated, attuned and sensitive to the noises of the night, to the soft cool breezes. The earth pulsed slowly and rhythmically beneath them, and she felt more alive and deeply connected to the land than at any other time in her life. The dogs lay asleep at their feet.

Uncle Fred sat staring into the distance with a peaceful smile creasing his face.

'See that cluster of stars up there, bub?' He waved a hand in a circular motion.

'You mean that dense cloud mass which seems alive?' She followed his hand.

'Yeah, that one. Can you see the dingo shape?' She looked for a shape in the starry field.

'See up there,' Fred drew a picture for her, 'there is his nose. Then look along the line and see them two strong stars shining close? Those are his eyes.'

'Yes, yes. I see him. There's his back and his tail.' She scooped a line across the sky painting the shape of the dingo.

'He's one of the guardians for us desert people. We can follow his tracks across the sky and see them mirrored here on the ground. That way we never get lost. He is our guide.'

They both went back to their thoughts and after a while, Nat asked Fred.

'Does Mum know I am alright?' Her voice was small. She prayed her mum would know intuitively, that she was safe. Fred just made a sympathetic sound like a soft hum.

'I just don't know if being here keeps my family safer, or if I ought to hand myself in to the police...' she trailed off. It was a dilemma, and she didn't have all the facts.

* * *

A week passed before another news item covered the inquest into the death of Andrea Mulligan, the woman found washed up at La Perouse Bay. Natalie let out a wail when she heard the announcement while Fred leaned in closer to catch the names of the lawyers representing the family. The words 'Legal Aid' were clear as the reporter asked if there had been foul play. Natalie walked out into the surrounding desert distraught that her cousin was dead. Both dogs followed her, she returned with teary red eyes. The sun set with long red slanted eyelids closing as the horizon rose to embrace its return to the other side of the earth.

'That could have been me. It's so sad, Uncle Fred.'

'I sent the tape along with a coded message to your mum, so she knows you're safe.' He wondered whether Elizabeth received the Freddie Mercury tape yet and had passed it on to those lawyer people.

'We need to wait see if them lawyer folk got the evidence, and they take it to the right part of the law to get them bad fellas busted,' Fred cautioned patience, 'You don't want to come rushing out trying to fix up the mess, bub. Dangerous people – might be counting on getting information about you.'

'I'll wait,' she took a deep breath and sat back down nearer the camp oven. 'Tell me a story, Uncle.'

'You got a thousand years?' Amused by his own joke, Fred poked the fire.

'Why did dad and his friend set up at the Tyagarah air strip? Didn't it used to be owned by an American developer or something?'

'You got the American part right. It was owned and run

by big knobs like generals and CIA out from the Vietnam war, an' the only thing they were developing was their bank accounts.'

Natalie felt a shiver run down her spine she looked wide eyed at the old man and goosebumps rose on her arms.

'What were they doing?' Her voice betrayed a quiver of terror. The shard of glass she looked through helped her comprehend being on the airstrip loading drugs. Maybe the mob always knew about it? It would make sense.

'Rover reckoned the army brass and the secret squad, over in Nam, were making a mottsa out of the war, running drugs, selling ordinance, stuff like that, so they set up operations here in Australia.'

'You mean running drugs?'

'Yeah, that and laundering money through some bank they financed.'

'Which bank?'

'Not the Commonwealth, that's for sure,' Fred quipped. 'Your dad was like a dog with a bone. He followed all the stories about this bank, Nugent or something, it was called. He talked to the locals around Tyagarah. Just a yarn at the pub ya know? Didn't want the mafia mob takin' notice of him.'

'The mob? What happened?"

'It was a catastrophe waiting to happen. The mob and the CIA been trading drugs and money for ten years. Then the owner of the bank got executed and it all goes belly up,' Fred chortled with delight and shook his head knowingly. 'Hand, that's it! The Nugan Hand Bank. Hand in the till I reckon!' He rocked back laughing until his eyes watered.

She waited for him to continue.

'One gang ran to the bank and shredded all the files then disappeared. The big brass ran in the opposite direction – denied all knowledge. Millions of dollars owed to people. A royal commission. A big cover-up, Rove reckoned. Only the bank secretary and lawyer got blamed.' Fred rubbed his chin in the way men who shave assess their growth. 'Rover worked out there were twenty six high level brass and CIA people named as parties in the bank scandal. All got off Scott free.'

'Your dad and his mate Norm, saw an opportunity to lease the airstrip from Council. They had dirt on their hands from corrupt deals over the airstrip and land sales.'

'That's how the Beechcraft got a home!'

'That's right bub, Rover and Norm did a deal, a 99-year lease for the glider club plus the Beechcraft rent free for life.'

* * *

Natalie relished the time she spent with Uncle Fred, and their daily rhythm was collecting old engines from the local tip, stripping them down, fixing them and reselling them again.

'You pull your hat down low, bub,' Fred would caution when Natalie came to the tip with him to salvage things, 'look like a young lad, keep that bandana round your face too. Can't be too careful.' As they drove along the dusty corrugated road Fred had a CD player duct taped into the gap where a radio once sat. A woman's voice rose higher and higher each time they went over a bump.

'Who's that singer, Uncle?'

'That's a Māori woman, Dame Kiri Te Kanawa. Opera singer. I love her voice.' Fred turned the steering wheel to avoid a pothole.

'It's beautiful,' she agreed, 'like soaring in the sky.'

Fred enjoyed the companionship of the young woman who was an expert with motors.

'Your dad taught you to fix them engines, I reckon?'

'Yep,' Natalie glowed, 'I learnt everything from my Dad. Even how to fly into your camp without crashing the plane.'

'Good thing you learnt that. Here get on the other side of this will you?' Together with a couple of planks and a pulley, they hefted a compressor onto the back of the Ute which sagged under the weight while the dogs wobbled around trying to find the highest point on the load without falling off.

The two set out from the tip driving slowly as the back was weighed down, pulling over at a lean-to beside the gate where Fred always gave Roy, the tip custodian, some money from his salvage works, though since Natalie had arrived, they'd had been making twice as much money on his motors and repair jobs. He handed over a wad of money and muttered some words through the open window. Roy took the money pocketing the cash.

'Married to one of me sisters. Never seen anyone helping me.'

'You mean me?'

'Everyone passes through the Alice. Don't want word getting out.'

The odd couple trundled on home in companionable

silence with the dogs hanging their heads out of the truck, their ears streamed back and eyes closed smiling.

'Look at them cheek flaps,' Fred chuckled seeing Buddy in the side mirror, 'they're waving in the wind. We should call him Flaps.'

'Here we are,' Fred pulled the Ute off the road onto the track that led around the side of the work shed. He set up pulleys and levers beside his work benches and wooden pallets to put machinery on. 'Gotta look after me back,' he said. The dogs leapt off to find some water. 'I'll fix us a cuppa.'

CHAPTER 20

'Being on the rebound meant redefining myself,' Diana opened the conversation sounding as though she had practised saying this out loud and not feeling angry. Frank looked at her encouragingly making a 'hmm' sound.

'I can make clearer choices,' he hoped those clearer choices meant choosing him.

'Have you divorced this guy yet?'

'No, he wouldn't marry me in the first place. We owned a flat in joint names. I put it on the market when I changed the locks and threw his belongings into the foyer.'

There was a defiant tilt to her chin.

'What led to that chain of events?' Frank prompted.

'I was triggered by the conversation I had with a certain Tiffany, who answered his phone in the motel, at a Gold Coast convention.

'Ah. That will do it.'

'Do you want to know what he said when he rang me back?'

'In your own time.' A slight inclination of his head. Frank was glad the love of his life didn't have to go through a divorce. Unexpectedly, Diana threw back her head and laughed sardonically.

'I feel I've wasted five years of my life with that rat!' She shook her head philosophically. 'Oh, I wanted to be in love with Troy. I tried to find qualities and character traits that were endearing,' she articulated.

'Truthfully, I succumbed to peer group pressure and got involved with him, thinking we'd grow closer over time. Not so.' Their food arrived and the waitress served the rice while the two friends waited feeling warm and connected and wanting to keep talking.

Diana began spooning Thai Chilli Chicken onto their plates.

'Both of us worked hard, however we didn't get past the mechanics of life.'

They stopped talking to eat for a time.

'We would take holidays together which passed for love, I guess,' Diana continued, 'I think it was the feeling of having a break from work.'

Frank spooned some rice onto Diana's plate and raising his eyebrows proffered the green curry and then topped up his plate. He found that eating together was comfortable as they enjoyed their meal murmuring agreement about the food.

Diana wiped her mouth with the soft white cloth napkin.

'My mother loved the fact I was dating a regular boyfriend. She was always cooking things for him. When we moved in together, she was sure there would be wedding bells and babies. Mum is obsessed with grandkids. She's like a soap opera diva.'

'She loves you,' Diana nodded agreement.

'How did your dad feel about Troy? Did he approve of the match?'

'Dad knew he was a cheat and a bum. Fathers know these things, I'm sure,' Diana's guileless description of her ex-boyfriend was refreshing.

'They do,' Frank concurred. 'I believe fathers know about men and their honey words, which aren't always the same as their deeds. They don't want to see their daughters hurt.'

They concentrated on eating again as they were both hungry. It had been a trying and tiring day at the morgue.

'Is everything to your liking?' The young waitress in traditional Thai dress, stood tactfully to one side of the couple's table.

'It's lovely, thank you.' Diana pushed her plate away.

'Would you like some jasmine tea?'

'Mmmm, I want some. Frank?' Diana questioned.

'Yes please,' Frank gave his plate to the waitress who cleaned the table and disappeared to get the tea.

'What about us, Diana?'

Her cheeks coloured then she flicked her hair over her shoulder to create a space.

'Do you think about me?' He pursued.

'All the time.'

'Good, I'm glad.' Frank eased himself back breaking the tension.

The willowy waitress delivered a white porcelain tea pot and two small bowl like cups. The aroma of jasmine infused the air around them. She poured them both a cup of tea, bowed and left. Diana took a sip while Frank waited until his cooled.

'I'm lost to you Diana. I want to wake up with you every morning.'

Diana put her handle less cup down and put both hands around his. He noticed her dark red nails.

'I just need a little more time, Frank. I rushed into my last relationship and pretended to myself I had certain feelings. I am embarrassed by that. I need a bit of time.'

He waited.

'But I can't imagine my life without you either and, because it feels so natural, I want to take our time and get to know each other.' He was beaming.

'Perhaps we need to go on dates? Not just work lunches but walking, going to movies and doing things we like. What do you think?' They hadn't let go of one another's hands during this intimate conversation.

'I think I'd like that, Frank!'

Frank hadn't fallen for someone like this before. Sure, there were the high school crushes and the head over heels university affairs, and after that he joined the Labor party and became involved with the prime minister's daughter, Stella. He felt like a boyfriend minder to her. It was a complicated relationship, and they broke it off when she had met someone else. Frank, would come when she called, and Stella knew he would pick up the pieces of her life. Keep it out of the papers. They fought over the fact his primary loyalty was to the party and the prime minister and she accused him of 'managing her'.

'What about your romantic life, Mr Phelan?' Diana teased, her eyes mischievous and curious.

'There was April Moreland, you may have read about the murders and mayhem in the papers last year?'

'In passing,' Diana commented archly, 'what happened between her and you?'

'April wanted to be a war correspondent more than a girlfriend and we parted as friends.'

'That's it?' Diana didn't believe it could be that simple.

'Not really there was more, however like you, I wanted love. She just wasn't interested.'

Frank described meeting April when he visited Bill Falco, his former boss, at the cancer clinic and her audacious bid to get involved in the mystery and write a story of Stella's disappearance and the great man's life.

'She won a Walkley.'

'Yes, she did,' he was proud of her. 'April is a comrade in arms,' Frank clarified. 'We went through life and death together.'

'That's a bond.'

'It is sort of brotherly, but not. Like Stella, I never imagined marrying April or having children.' He shrugged, 'or even having her undivided attention for that matter.'

'Then I'm glad it didn't work out, Frank.'

'We were only together for a few months after our adventure at Paradise Falls.'

He stretched his legs under the table.

'You have nothing to worry about, Diana,' his expression devoted, 'I am captivated. When we met, do you remember you asked me for a cigarette outside the office?'

She giggled remembering that first meeting.

'How can I forget. You thought I was Claudia Karvan!'

Frank paid the bill. He put his arm around her shoulders and opened the door for her. 'Drop you home?'

'Hmm,' she smiled 'that would be nice.'

Frank exhaled slowly.

CHAPTER 21

After the separation, Diana moved into an older style apartment in Petersham, an inner suburb of Sydney. The building was a dark brick block built in the 1940s, that comprised eight flats with an English style box hedge on three sides. Her place was on the first floor and had a long and narrow marble top table dividing the main living room from the adjoining front entrance and door.

Her feet hurt as she climbed the carpeted stairs to her front door reaching into her handbag for her door keys, she looked up. It was ajar. Startled, her heart constricted in her chest, as she pushed it open, ready to run if there was someone inside. Nothing happened. They were gone. Everything in sight was searched and gone through, every cushion cover opened and even the covers of her couch were pulled back as the intruders made their way from room to room searching for something. She went into her bedroom and then the kitchen checking for signs. The condiments from her fridge were lined up on the sink and the waste bins searched. Numbly, she walked back into the lounge room bending to retrieve a fluted, red Italian Murano vase that fell off the table onto the floor where it lay. A silent challenge to be picked up and returned to its place next to the glass urn.

Diana felt as though she had been punched in the stomach and winded and it wasn't until she understood that contrary to a sea of chaos, nothing the searchers looked at was strewn recklessly. The search was systematic and thorough as though everything had been inspected and lined up. A sob escaped. Involuntarily, she wrapped her arms around herself with her leather bag still hanging over her shoulder.

It is confronting when your own house is burgled, especially as this was more of a home invasion with a specific purpose. Who does this, she puzzled? What were they looking for? Think Diana! The mafia! Of course! Who else could it be? She went back through to the bedroom where the same scene greeted her. In the bathroom, it was the same search pattern. The bin had a pile of things tossed into it presumably looking for something small and incriminating. Diana returned to the front door. A cold chill settled on her when she saw where the latch and lock separated and a missing a piece. The intruders had unscrewed the mechanism to get inside. She shut the door and put a chair into place thinking any barrier was better than nothing until the police came.

Time to call the cops she decided to regain some control over the situation. And a locksmith. And Frank. She called Frank first and left a message on his phone at work. Then she dialled his home number and left a detailed message giving more information about the break-in. Next call, the Petersham Police Station.

'Sergeant McManus, how can we help you?'

'My name is Diana Gianiovellis and I live at Flat 4, 44 Blenheim Place, Petersham. I want to report a break-in officer, the lock was dismantled. Please could you send someone to take my statement and get photographs and fingerprints?'

'Don't hold your breath, Miss Gianiovellis,' Sergeant McManus cautioned her, 'could take them an hour or so.'

'Sergeant, I am a Legal Aid lawyer, representing a family in the disappearance of an Aboriginal woman, moreover,' she stressed, 'there is probable involvement by the mafia. This isn't a normal robbery. I think you need to send someone right now.' She instructed, waiting a few beats before adding, 'because it would show you're responding to a present danger by organised criminals.'

In a flush of law enforcement solidarity, the Sergeant ordered two officers to attend the scene of the crime immediately.

'You stay right there, madam, we'll have a couple of officers over in a jiffy. What makes you think there is mafia involvement?'

'Confidentially, we were being surveilled by persons known to have mafia connections. My place has been systematically searched and nothing stolen that I can find.'

'Right! Can you prop a chair on the door?'

'Yes, I can. Thank you, sergeant.'

Next, she got the Yellow Pages telephone directory and found a locksmith with an after-hours number the phone rang and rang while she waited and eventually a man answered the phone whom she assumed was the Bernie Sanders from the advertisement.

'Sanders Safety Locks,' a deep voice answered, Diana could hear a television going in the background.

'Mr Sanders, my name is Diana Gianiovellis, I found your advert in the Yellow Pages.'

'What's the problem, love.'

'There's been a break-in, and I need a new lock on my front door,' her voice quavered sounding vulnerable, 'I can pay you a bonus if you come over now.'

'Certainly, what's your address? My fee is a hundred dollars. I'll be there in about half an hour.'

'I'll be here, have you got a pen to write the address down?'

Diana tried not to touch anything else that may reveal fingerprints though, she doubted the intruders had left prints as it was a professional job. She went to her bedroom where she had an Instamatic camera in the wardrobe. Keeping busy suppressed her anxiety and after she had used up all the film she went and checked the door again. Then she phoned Frank again and left another message. Where was he? 'Frank, I've been robbed. If you get this message, call me. Please.' She needed him.

* * *

Meanwhile, Frank was having a beer with Mike Purcell, whom he knew in Canberra when they both worked at Parliament House. They would go running together regularly and Mike had been involved when Frank was on the trail of Stella Falco. Mike moved from the Australian Federal Police to the Major Criminal Gangs Division, with NSW Police. The two friends were leaning on a bar in Pitt Street, in the Sydney centre sipping beers and catching up after work.

'Sorry to hear about Bill Falco dying.' Mike commiserated.

'Thanks, mate. He was a good friend to me,' Frank set down his glass, 'though it was a fitting end and a good funeral.'

'You still seeing April, the journalist?' Mike hitched his eyebrows.

'Nope. That's over.'

'What happened?' Mike was curious but not surprised.

'She got a job as a war correspondent in Lebanon.'

'That right? Tell her if she ever wants a job, I know a search and rescue team who is deeply impressed with her abilities.'

Frank's eyes twinkled, 'she is impressive. I owe my life to her.'

'How's the new job?' Mike looked at his friend. 'Legal Aid seems a bit,' he cast around for the word, 'domestic, compared to your other roles.'

'I needed less drama while I worked out what I wanted longer-term.'

Frank took a sip of his beer, 'As it happens, I've met someone at work.'

'You mean romantically?'

Frank was conscious his feelings were transparent when Mike scrutinised his face.

'Oh, I see. You're completely gone on her.'

'Yep. Her name is Diana Gianiovellis, and she is drop-dead gorgeous!'

'Well good! You're serious about a woman. You should let her know, mate.'

Frank agreed wholeheartedly.

'Apart from your love life, what's the work like?'

Frank debated telling Mike about the mafia and Crime Commission.

'We appear to have attracted the interest of the Crime Commission, who are watching the mafia surveillance of our office.'

'Fair dinkum!' Mike cast his eyes around, ever cautious of being overheard talking shop. 'Not my area. I am on the Middle Eastern and some Asian syndicates. Go on. Captive audience, as they say.'

'We think a client we're representing may have got mixed up with the mob. She's disappeared but her cousin turned up dead.'

'You mean the woman on La Perouse beach? Nasty bunch to get mixed up with.'

'Yep. It's a mystery.'

* * *

Having closed the door, Diana went to the bathroom. She wondered how long it would take the cops to come or if indeed, they would take it seriously. She washed her hands and went back to the kitchen and considered letting her neighbour know what had happened.

Meanwhile, Frank picked up the message on his phone when he got home, turned around and immediately drove straight over to Diana's flat and rushed to the front door of the apartment building arriving at the same time as an older man dressed in a warm tweed jacket and carrying a briefcase.

'I'm here to see Diana Gianiovellis, I am a work colleague,' Frank explained as the gent opened the front door to the block of flats. The man looked Frank up and down, decided he was trustworthy, and held the door for him saying goodnight as he opened his apartment door.

Just as she was about to go to her neighbour, Diana heard a fiddling sound at the door and crept over to a chair, having grabbed a vase on the way. Frank carefully opened the door noticing that the lights were dimmed. You are imagining things mate, he thought to himself, no one is going to come back. Tentatively, he pushed the door and stepped forward when something caught his attention on the floor. It was a small piece of paper. He bent over to pick it up.

Crack! Diana lifted a vase over her head and brought it down on the man's head. Frank yelled out in pain and lurched sideways trying not to collapse instead falling to his knees and cradling his swimming head in both hands and trying hard to stay conscious. A cloud of dust swirled around his head and shoulders covering them with a layer. He slumped forward face down.

'Frank!' She cried throwing the chair to the side. Frank's legs were stretched out where he fell and were holding the door open but there was no mistaking his shape and size. All around him was dust and his head was bleeding where Diana had broken the funeral urn on him making him look like a zombie.

He opened his eyes and stared at her in shock, before his eyes rolled back. She raced to the bathroom got a wet washer and towels and applied them to his head wound then moved him on his side pressing the cloth against his head. She padded the towel around it to staunch the bleeding, placing another towel under his head and neck. Frank groaned.

'Oh God! Frank, I'm so sorry. I thought you were the mafia coming back.' She felt frantic. He must wake up! With a supreme effort, he propped himself on one elbow his mouth tasting dry and burnt while his head throbbed.

'Water, can I have some water?' He croaked and then coughed, his face and mouth covered in dust. She went to the kitchen returning with cold water from the fridge and sitting on her haunches she held the bottle up to his mouth cradling his head in her arm.

'What's all this grey stuff?' He wiped his neck with the towel and felt his hair which was damp and stiff from the powdery stuff.

'It's ash, Frank.' Diana confessed, knowing it would come out anyway. 'I hit you with an urn.'

The police found them moments later, having taken the stairs to the first floor two at a time, on hearing noises coming from above.

'This is not what it looks like officers!' She announced straightening up brushing dust off her skirt trying to sound matter of fact.

'This is Frank Phelan, my colleague, we are lawyers. I have inadvertently hit him with a vase thinking he was the intruder returning.' She sounded as though she was swearing to tell the truth, the whole truth and nothing but the truth. The two officers appraised her and one of them reached a hand down to Frank offering to pull him to his feet before slipping the chair under him.

'Are you going to be alright, sir?' The other cop looked

around the flat before pulling his notebook out.

'Yes, I'm okay, thanks,' Frank looked at the cop's name badge, 'Officer Petty, 'I'll get checked out by a doctor once Diana's place is secure.'

Over the next half hour, the two police officers took photos and notes and asked Frank and Diana, why they believed this was a professional search and not a robbery, suggesting it was unlikely the intruders had left fingerprints. Finally, they pocketed their books and offered to drop Frank off at the Emergency Unit in Camperdown. Frank wiped down his clothes and hair whilst this was going on and took two Panadols pressed into his palm by Diana.

Bernie Sanders, the locksmith walked into this scene of domestic mayhem carrying a new deadlock and a tool bag. He was a solid Englishman, with a neat moustache, grey dustcoat and lace-up leather boots, unfazed as he moved aside to let the police leave.

'Big mess the intruders made here,' Bernie look sideways at Frank. 'I'm guessing you tried to stop them?'

'Something like that.' Frank grunted. Once the new deadlock was fitted and Diana paid the locksmith, the two friends faced each other.

'You might need to get some stitches, Frank.' She was contrite.

* * *

The After-Hours Clinic was busy that night with injuries, drug addiction and accidental poisoning. Diana sat close to Frank and held his hand. Neither of them spoke.

'Mr Phelan. Mr Frank Phelan?' A nurse in uniform called out walking toward them in a hallway.

'I'm so sorry Frank,' Diana repeated. They were sitting in one of the sterile treatment rooms having been looked at by the doctor on duty and stitched up by the nurse.

'I have to wait until the doctor releases me before I can go home and lick my wounds.'

'I'll stay here, and I'll bring the car around once you're released.'

'Maybe stay at your mother's place for a few days?' The Mulligan case had taken a sinister turn and Frank felt scared for her safety and security.

'I'm not going to knock you out and then dump you, Frank. But going to Mum's after is a good idea.'

Dr. Vajarasparam, walked back into the room approaching the two lawyers looked up from his clip board studying the couple.

'Are you the person who inflicted the injury, Ms Gianiovellis?'

'Yes, doctor, it was an accident and completely unintended.'

The doctor shifted his attention to Frank, 'You are concussed. You need to rest,' the doctor inspected the white gauze pad that was lightly taped around the wound.

'There are three stitches into the wound Mr. Phelan, and you will need to change the bandage and not get your head wet until the stitches come out in a few days. You can go to your local GP to get that done.' The young doctor pulled a prescription pad from one of his roomy coat pockets and began scribbling on it before whipping the page off and handing it to Frank.

'Here is a prescription for painkillers, Mr Phelan.'

'Thank you, doctor,' Frank took the prescription obediently.

'Concussion is a serious thing so take it easy.' Throughout this interchange, Diana stood with her arms crossed.

'Is there anyone at home, Mr Phelan?' The doctor tilted his head suggesting with his eyes that an alternative to the stern brunette who brought him in, would be beneficial.

'No, not really.'

"I shall take him back home and ensure he is well cared for,' Diana stated firmly.

The doctor bridled, hesitant to release Frank into the hands of that woman.

'Is that suitable for you, Mr Phelan?'

'That would be wonderful, Doctor,' Frank reassured the solicitous young man, 'I would like that very much.'

The basement garage door rumbled open slowly and Diana drove her car down a steep ramp and into the nearest parking space next to the lift doors.

'I am on the third floor.' The goods lift was hung with ceiling-to-floor canvas padded protectors that smelled of creosote.

'Sit down, I'll make you something to drink like tea and some bread maybe.'

'Everything is in the kitchen.'

'You can have a shower in the morning,' she bossed tenderly. He felt dizzy.

He swung his legs onto the couch and pushed a cushion under his head letting his eyes close. Diana had two mugs of tea on the breadboard she put them down on the coffee table and sat drinking one of them looking at Frank asleep beside her.

When she'd finished, she got up and took his shoes off before going to the bedroom and collecting a doona which she tucked around him then bent over and kissed him on the forehead, 'I'll be back in the morning.'

* * *

Claudia threw her hands up in consternation and alarm. 'Now these criminals are breaking into your home?' Diana downplayed the whole incident, stating that they had a difficult case and there had been a break in, but Frank and the police both came to help.

'Mum! Mum!' Exasperated she had raised her voice to puncture the assumptions spilling over from her mother's overactive imagination.

'Why do you make everything a Latin soap opera? I drove Frank back to his place after the accident.'

Her mother regrouped.

'We will go to his house first thing in the morning.'

'I'm sure he will be alright,' she reassured her mum.

'Darling, this is our culture: food is our culture and caring for each other in time of need, is our culture. We are going over to Franco's house like a good Italian family and make sure he's got enough food while he's recuperating.'

She was outgunned. 'Can I stay here overnight, Mum? I don't want to go home?'

'Diana, I know you. You are feeling guilty. Has he got a concussion if he knocked his head on the door?' Diana had excised some details out of the evening.

'I'm tired, Mum.' She kissed her on the cheek, 'goodnight.'

In the morning, Claudia was busy packing up a box full of sauces and pasta.

'What's going on? 'Her father asked mildly.

'Mum is on a mission.'

She and her mother drove to Frank's place and when he answered the door, he was surprised to see both women.

'Hello Mrs Gianiovellis, Diana, come in,' he searched Diana's face. She shrugged.

'Tell me the truth Franco, how did you get that big bump on your head?'

'Mrs Gianiovellis,' Frank's spoke hesitantly. 'Some bad people broke into Diana's flat looking for evidence about a case. She called me to help and mistook me for the thieves. She hit me with a vase.'

'I knew it! It's a sign!' Vindicated, Claudia crossed herself fervently. Diana rolled her eyes.

CHAPTER 22

Far away on the other side of the world, the woman felt a sense of not being in her body despite knowing her body was there. Somewhere. She was aware of her consciousness for the timeless moments before the drugs and the sleep softly escorted her away. She had no idea of time nor where she'd been taken. A local hospital perhaps or out of the country? She clung to the shoreline of her humanity and as the tide washed out, she perceived her life slipping away too. Just as she wanted to let go but the tide washed in again. A lapping tug of life echoed in her cells calling her name over a canyon.

A shard of memory entered the dispersed arena of herself. Sharp and crystalline, a thin connection back to before. Some invisible thread of cause and effect. It was the moment before the bomb exploded under the taxi, that she shared with Salma on their way to visit Salma's parents in one of the outer suburbs of the city. The two women, both excited about leaving the compound together.

'Headscarf.' Salma prodded to her new friend. April pulled her light scarf over her hair and tried securing a length around her neck.

Salma laughed aloud as she lowered her sunglasses down her proud nose, her skin a burnished brown, was glowing in the sunlight.

'Here, lean over. Let me show you how,' Salma took the two ends of the scarf, deftly rewrapping it around April's head.

'Thank you, Salma you are a whiz.'

'Don't worry you'll get the hang of it. Come on.' Her voice was sisterly, assured.

They called a car to pick them up. Safer than taxis Salma explained. The car looked like a dilapidated New York cab. The bright yellow body was distinctive though somehow not out of place in the colourful, kaleidoscopic melee of people, vehicles, animals and stalls that constituted life on the streets of Beirut.

'Never, ever get in the front seat, April,' Salma cautioned her on a serious note.

'Sexual harassment?'

'That is putting it mildly,' she said before giving directions in Arabic to the driver, who sat waiting behind the heavy perspex divider that segregated him from his passengers. The grizzled old man in white robes and a straggly white beard rested his large, veined hands on the steering wheel. On receiving instructions, he clunked the car into gear moving off from the kerb at a slow pace.

April believed in intuition and as they set off a feeling was nagging her, like when you leave home and a voice whispers, 'Wait, you've forgotten something.'

'Pull over, driver,' she put her hand on the back of the seat, 'I have to get a gift.' That was it! A gift. She needed to take a gift.

Salma interpreted and the driver slowed down. A throng of people and dust pressed against the car urgently yet indifferently. They were passing a pavement bazaar housing a myriad of scarves, rugs, pots, perfumes, dried goods, and tourist trinkets. An endless array. Pulling over directly outside a ceramic pottery shop, on the roughly cobbled road which held the bizarre stalls, spilling out all over it like swathes of bright fabric thrown across a workbench. The street was narrow and filled to the brim with noise and people going about their daily lives.

Espying a beautiful vase, the colour of the Mediterranean, April was halfway out of the back seat when the bomb went off ripping the vehicle in half and killing Salma and the driver in an instant. She screamed Salma's name before the shrapnel scarified her body. The pain was instant and searing. Her second sensation was that she was going to die.

* * *

April Moreland didn't take the job as a foreign correspondent believing it would be easy. Quite the opposite. She knew her first assignment would be tough and gave herself another pep talk on the plane going over to Greece. 'Fake it until you make it,' she braced herself. Not that she lacked confidence as a person or a journalist. It was the unknown. Propelling her through her career, was the serious intention of the fourth estate as a mirror to the world. A fundamental instrument of a healthy civil society, she believed.

She had researched the Gulf states, talked to her brother Hugh, who worked for the Australian Government, as an engineer on developing commercial projects. She learnt of the 1990 invasion of Kuwait, by the United States and thirty-three other countries including Australia. She phoned numerous journalists to ask them about their experiences and what drove them to go back to conflict zones. What scars marked their souls?

Having a Walkley Award, opened a lot of doors she realised when she hung up from speaking to Jake Abraham, at the Boston Globe, late one evening. He sounded like the last one to leave the office, his tone curious and slightly surprised when she explained she was about to go on assignment in Lebanon.

'What do you want to get out of this assignment, April?' He asked, his voice resonant. She found his accent and cadence pleasant.

Not knowing how to respond, beyond the platitudes of wanting to report on world events, she realised mostly she wanted to be taken seriously.

'I am fascinated by the world Jake, including international struggles for power.'

'What about finding the 'truth' behind the story?'

'I doubt that there is just one truth, with a capital 'T'.' She relaxed and spoke while formulating her thoughts. 'However, I am interested in the ideas represented by the various parties about truth.'

'What do you mean by that?' She hadn't explored her motives deeply beyond needing to feel she was a serious reporter, whose work held meaning.

Being a journalist was what she did, it was her profession. It was an expression of herself. However, she had made an intentional decision about what sort of journalism she wanted to do and what she didn't want to do anymore.

Her friendship with Frank, had been sealed by adventure and she vividly remembered every detail of that thrilling, perilous night on the mountain, kidnapped together by a gang of bikies, escaping and defying death before discovering a dead body and capturing a murderer. It had fuelled a hunger in her to be engaged in a larger life. A burning point beyond the mundane.

'I mean, more than the headlines or the stereotypes you know. 'Saddam invaded Kuwait and killed a bunch of people' that sort of thing.'

'Many strong men grow to power in the Middle East.'

'I'm not searching for myself you know. But I am hooked on the adrenalin. There it is.'

Jake made an understanding sound. On the other end of the phone, on the other side of the world, they shared an intimate moment revealing what spurred foreign journalists on in the face of adversity. April shifted her weight wishing they could be in a bar talking to each other over a drink. She found his professional recognition validating. Not something she had experienced on the sports desk at the Daily Tribune in Australia.

'Sad but true.' A little on the defensive. 'I want to be committed to doing something more meaningful.

'That's good, April, don't be embarrassed to own it. You'll need everything to get through the tough times. And remember the truism, you can't save the world.'

April knew Jake's work and had followed his career for some years. Here she was talking to him as a colleague about her deepest thoughts, beliefs and motivations.

She began to understand that the glue of the journalist's tribe was forged between them as they went into the foreign countries and the conflict zones giving them a bond of shared experience and emotion. Shared recognition and pain too.

'You realise the murder story you wrote last year was covered over here too? And you got a Walkley for it.'

'I saw some coverage.' Modestly.

'You still with your partner in crime? What's his name again?' Trailing off.

'Frank Phelan. No, we agreed to part ways. Frank wanted a desk job, and I wanted a war zone. They weren't compatible relationship goals.'

Jake laughed spontaneously, finding her forthrightness refreshing and funny.

'Well, I hope we get to meet someday, maybe covering a story?' There was hollow in the background as he was packing up his desk. Neither of them wanted to say goodbye or cut the connection.

'Take care of yourself. If you are ever in Boston, I'll buy you a drink.'

'Why thank you,' April felt good, her cheeks flushing, 'the invitation is reciprocal. See you Jake...and thanks again.'

'Yep, see you April.' Click.

April got out of bed and switched off the lights before going back and trying to sleep. She tossed fitfully and eventually dropped off.

* * *

She arrived at Beirut airport late in the afternoon on her first overseas assignment, having flown from London's Heathrow Airport. She hadn't slept properly for days from tension and excitement. Feeling gritty, and tired, she attracted unwanted attention from men fascinated by her height and mass of curly red hair. Eventually, she dug out a light muslin scarf to wrap around her head. She had packed clothes appropriate to the climate and the culture. Loose pantaloon pants with long tunics and lightweight floaty scarves to cover her head. The dust was choking but the temperature was bearable. Apparently, the temperature reached 48 Celsius in July and August however, autumn and winter had milder days albeit, very cold nights.

Her employer scheduled her flights, food and travel vouchers plus, there were emergency numbers and arrangements for her arrival. In addition, an escape plan should things become deadly for foreigners. She cleared customs and pushed through the barrier spotting a young awkward-looking man and an local driver standing together holding a cardboard sign with her name.

Beirut was noisy, overcrowded and historic. There exists a perpetual sense that the city and everyone's life exists deep within history itself. There is the clamour and the intense interactions of a heaving human base load, all shouting and bargaining for the next sale, bartering transactions, putting the next meal on their tables.

The newspaper's compound was co-located with the American Embassy behind a wall and a curved set of heavy wooden doors embossed with carved insets from the seventeenth century when the Ottoman Empire was the hegemony. The walls were made from solid brick covered in whitewashed stucco and there was a row of forbidding razor wire on top. It was a fortress. Lebanon was not a safe place for Western journalists harbouring, as it did, ancient resentments and hatreds. It was an utterly alien world, one that April's life experiences had not prepared her for. The gap year mountaineering in Europe and Canada certainly didn't count for anything though her shooting abilities gave her some comfort.

Her boss, Joe Metternich, had a phone cradled against his ear when she entered the office. He put one finger up to indicate he'd be another minute. The whole place looked like a newsroom from a movie set with piles of papers, computers and printers on every desk, people's phones were ringing and the team absorbed and serious.

Joe was a scruffy, dishevelled man with salt and pepper hair, a matching beard and a Scottish accent, who wore clothes that looked as though he slept the night in them. He had slept the night in them! April estimated he was in his early fifties however, he could be a study in bad habits that made him seem older.

Joe hung up the phone standing up from behind a mountain of papers.

'I'm Joe. Your boss. You must be the new girl?'

April had put her bags on the floor, took two long strides and grasped his hand in a strong grip pumping it and, without missing a beat, put him firmly in his place.

'April Moreland. You must be mistaken Joe. I haven't been 'a girl' for twenty years.'

Joe observed that the recruit was not only incredibly good-looking but stood a head higher than him. Trouble, he concluded. Delicious womanly trouble. Joe was not the first man to make ill-advised decisions when it came to women.

April looked around the room at the others smirking and enjoying the 'touché' moment.

'Right.' He recovered and swept his arm across the office to the other team members.

'I'll introduce you. This is April Moreland.' He started on his left.

'This is Salma Rizvi,' a striking woman with fiercely intelligent eyes lined with kohl waved and smiled. 'Great to have you on board, April.'

Her raven hair hung loosely on either side of her head scarf and tied at the back in a loose thick plait past her shoulders. She looked Egyptian, in traditional loose clothes with flawless skin.

Joe moved on to a short, round, bland-looking white guy. 'Over there is Fred Weatherby, he's from our European office. Don't let his looks fool you, he's a lethal weapon.'

'A spy you mean. Hi Fred.' April lifted a hand in salutation.

'Hi April,' Fred had a distinctive drawl, 'you'll be with me for the first month or so.'

'Righto.'

Joe cast around, 'where's Bryan?' He asked no one in particular. 'Never mind you'll meet him later.'

'Remember you run the risk of being kidnapped at any

time and you must never, ever get in a cab without a guard or one of us. You got that?' He ran the flat of his hand over his two-day growth and then through his hair seemingly aware that he looked like something the cat dragged in. 'Assume that we are being bugged, Moreland.'

'Feel free to call me by my first name. No need to be formal.'

April was aware of how tired she felt. Joe ignored her quip.

'OK, what else? Keep your head covered when you're out of the compound.'

'Salma will run you through the cultural protocols.' April had been mentally ticking off the safety list.

There was a hiatus while Joe eyed her salaciously before lobbing an offhand, sexist question.

'So, who did you have to screw to get this gig?'

'What makes you think that?' April retorted. It was always the same with these men. 'I won a Walkley for my last story. Did you miss that memo, mate?' It was a perfect putdown.

'That shut him up,' Salma chimed in delighted.

* * *

Diana and Frank decided to meet for a meal in Chinatown when she had finished her meeting with a client. He was putting on his jacket just about to leave the office when he got the phone call from Neil Moreland, April's father, Frank knew something was wrong.

'Neil, what's up?'

'April has been injured. A car bomb. They've flown her back,' the older man's voice choked with emotion.

'Where is she?' Frank felt his stomach sink.

'They've taken her to the spinal unit at St Vincent's. Could you go and see her?'

'Yes, of course. Are you and Helen on your way?'

'We will be there in a few hours. Our son Hugh is meeting us at the airport. We'll stay with him until they release April.'

'I'm so sorry, Diana. I'm going to the hospital. I'll be late. April's car was bombed.' He told her home answering machine then at home knowing she generally checked her messages at the end of the day. Then he rang her parents and spoke briefly to her mum, asking that she pass on the message should Diana call. As a last resort, he rang the restaurant they planned going to and spoke to a person, who spoke little English. When he reached the hospital, he learnt that April was in an induced coma. He was forty minutes later, when his cab pulled over on Hay Street, and he could see Diana standing on the pavement. He paid the cabby and walked up to her quickly anxious to apologise profusely.

'You stood me up, Frank Phelan.' She challenged him hurt and angry.

'I needed to check on April in hospital,' he stated, 'her father rang and asked me. Didn't you get my messages?'

A mixture of emotions crossed her face.

'Diana, I tried so hard to let you know.' Frank defended himself remorsefully.

'How hard" she cross examined him.

'I rang from work and left messages at your home, your mum and the restaurant to say I was running late.'

'You rang my mother?' she seemed unconvinced. 'No. I didn't get any of those messages.'

Frank stumbled, sensitive to the fact he was at a trust crossroads in his love relationship.

Accustomed to being confident, he combed his vocabulary for the right phrase to convey his sense of duty to a friend and her parents.

'Yes, I did,' then sensing it still wasn't sufficient, he added, 'I was desperate to contact you and explain.' She made a small noise in the back of her throat, one Frank interpreted as her accepting that explanation.

'Don't ever stand me up again, Frank Phelan! Come and get me and we'll go together to see your friend.' This surprised him.

'I'll make it up to you, Diana.' That mollified her slightly as she stood on the street looking at him intently.

'If we are to have a serious relationship, Frank, then I come first, not your ex-girlfriend.' It dawned on him that she felt jealous. He was secretly pleased. She stepped back from him and pulled her coat closer.

'Take me home please.' They hardly spoke in the cab and when they arrived at her place, Frank jumped out and opened the door as she gathered her bag, climbed out and walked toward her flat leaving Frank standing on the pavement. The cab driver leaned around catching Frank's eye.

'Want me to wait?'

'Yep. Hang on,' he followed some of the way toward her apartment building.

'Good night, thanks for seeing me home.' He was ensuring her safety. 'I hope April will be alright,' her tone had softened.

'Good night. I am sorry I let you down. I will see you

tomorrow.' She gave a small nod accepting his apology and walked through the door without looking back.

He climbed back into the cab and gave his address to the driver.

'Woman trouble?' The cabby enquired genially.

'Big trouble!' Frank sank back and sighed. It was late when he got back, feeling drained and emotional. He had left a message for Neil and Helen Moreland at the hospital desk where April lay injured, saying he would visit.

Then he rang his friend, Mike.

'Frank, what's up?'

'Want to catch up for a beer later this week?'

'Have to be Friday afternoon. What's happened?'

'Why do you ask?'

'Just one word. Tone.'

'Ah. Diana and I had a row.'

'What about?'

"I was late for our dinner date.'

'Oh boy. You let her know?'

'Three different places.'

'Why were you late?'

'April was medevacked to hospital in Australia. Car bomb.'

'Is she okay?'

'She was jealous.' Talking about Diana.

'I would say she is seriously falling for you, Frank,' Mike replied.

'Oh. Right. See you Friday.' Frank hung up. He felt inexperienced in the emotional complexities of relationships. He needed to learn more.

CHAPTER 23

t had been almost a week since Frank was late for his dinner date with Diana. He had sent a card to April and called her though she wasn't up to chatting. Both her parents had arrived in Sydney, and thanked Frank profusely for rushing to their daughter's side.

The Legal Aid contingent was excited about the Law Ball, and this year the Law Association of New South Wales, had scored the Sydney Town Hall for the event. The office was abuzz including Brenda, who joined in the banter. At one point she gave Frank a lingering, seductive look which Frank pretended not to see.

Now was the moment of truth, Frank needed to ask Diana to the Law Ball and if she declined, he would be bereft. He was leaning against a three-draw government grey filing cabinet in the larger office she shared with their colleagues. The top drawer held stationery and Frank opened it and pulled out an envelope plus a yellow sticky pad and a biro on which he wrote.

'Please forgive me and be my date for the Law Ball, Diana?'

He folded the note and put it in the envelope then wrote her name on the front. He hadn't felt like this since he passed a note to Jenny Mercer in high school.

Michelle picked up the phone and when Brenda moved off to her office, Frank took the opportunity and gave Diana the note.

'Let me know what you think,' he added enigmatically.

Michelle, the phone to her ear, shot Diana a puzzled look while Diana took the note and slipped it between the pages of her diary.

'Sure.' Sounding non-committal.

Later that day, Diana coolly slipped the note back to Frank, and to his relief she had written on the bottom 'Yes. Pick me up at my place at 7.30pm.'

It was a good start and his heart leapt in the air with hope. He had gone all out to impress Diana with his earnest wooing of her and he brought a huge bunch of roses and stood at her door in a black suit and bowtie feeling unbelievably nervous. When she opened the door, he was smitten! Her dress, which was strapless, black and fitted accentuated her décolletage which swelled under the push-up bra. Oh boy, he thought. Frank wanted to sweep her up, kiss her passionately and bury his face in her cleavage. Steady Frank, he told himself. Breathe. Breathe. He looked down taking in Diana's dress which flared out at the waist in satin and net folds to just above her knees where her legs swished when she moved swathed in shiny black stockings and seams down the back.

'Frank! They are beautiful. Thank you!' She exclaimed delightedly taking the flowers from him and giving him a moment to recover himself. He smiled down as she took the flowers into the kitchen, 'I'll put them in water before we go.'

Diana put the bouquet in the sink and opening a cupboard pulled out a long glass vase with a wide mouth which she positioned under the kitchen tap, filled it with water and put the bouquet into the water wrapping and all. He stood at the kitchen door and admired them. He admired her for longer.

'I'll just get my wrap and purse.' She led the way back through the hall.

When she returned, he knew she was just as delighted to be going on a date.

'Diana,' Frank relaxed, 'you look absolutely gorgeous!' He meant every word.

'You like?' She swirled and the dress skirt shimmered and rustled catching the lights in the hallway.

'I like it very much,' Frank had got that part right too, she lowered her eyelids.

'Thank you, Frank. I am glad .'

'We can walk up to the cross street and get a cab if you like.'

'I have a car downstairs,' he pointed out,' here let me help.' She had a fine, wool silk, black shawl with heavy, soft crushed velvet pieces on each end. Frank held the wrap out with two hands and Diana turned her back as he draped it around her. She gave a little shiver of frisson as he touched her shoulders. With her black diamantine clutch in one hand, she stepped forward and opened her door Frank absorbed the exquisite smell of her perfume and beamed. He hoped she would like the Rolls Royce Silver Ghost waiting downstairs.

'This is fun, Frank.' She hadn't gone on a dress-up date, let alone a black-tie ball for some time.

'Me too. I am a bit nervous about the ballroom dancing part. Hope I don't embarrass myself.' She giggled imagining him dancing, something that required suave grace, for a tall guy.

'You'll be just fine, Frank Phelan,' she slipped her hand in his arm as they moved down the last set of stairs and through the double glass door with etched zig zags.

Frank held the door open. 'Glad you are confident. Here's our car!'

'Oh my God! Where did you find this car? How fantastic!' She gasped, delighted by the Rolls Royce parked at the kerb.

He beamed. Inside was a chauffeur in the livery of seriously luxury cars, he opened the door, and she climbed in without needing to bend over and sank back into the deep, luxurious leather seats wiggling a little as he followed her in.

'Hi Fernando,' he greeted their driver. 'Let's go. The Town Hall on George Street, in the City please.' Diana stroked the leather seats and strained forward to see the motor with the Silver Ghost badge riding proudly up front.

'Wow! It's so classy.'

Having set off, he set about further impressing Ms. Gianiovellis, by pulling down the exquisite, tortoiseshell bar console in the back seat and popping a bottle of Verve Clicquot without spilling a drop.

A wonderful evening had begun. The ballroom at Town Hall was magnificently decorated and bedecked with flowers and white damask covered tables and chairs with similar bars and tables set up on two sides. There was a five-piece band playing on the stage while streams of dazzling men and women moved into the space greeting each other, grabbing drinks, talking loudly and happily, pleased to be celebrating together as a coterie of professionals having fun and not enacting the grim business of the law.

On arrival, the couple spied their table where Brenda was holding court and held up a glass of red wine beckoning them over. Vic Barraclough and his wife, Sulari waved warm hellos while Brenda conducted introductions.

'Look at you two!' she announced. 'Welcome! You scrubbed up divinely. You know Marcus Guthrie, don't you?'

'By reputation only, Your Honour,' Diana reached over and shook his hand.

'We met during the attempted escape of my client, I believe,' Frank reminded him.

'Ah yes, excellent save,' the judge boomed.

Brenda swept her arm around the table where the Legal Aid team were seated with lawyers and partners from several private companies, 'Sit down, sit down and talk amongst yourselves.' People mingled, chatted, and laughed, ties were loosened and somewhere between the main and dessert plates of Fruit and cheese, when the band dialled up the tempo it encouraged scenes of dancing and lashings of wild frivolity. Frank, whose attendance at the traditional Parliamentary Midwinter Ball, was obligatory, turned out to be a good dancer, a fact Brenda took advantage of grabbing him for a set. Following some provocative behaviour and hip swaying during the rumba he threw a glance over Brenda's shoulder at Diana who slid over the dance floor and tapped Brenda on the shoulder.

'I think I need to take this man in hand,' she tapped her boss.

'Of course, you do,' Brenda released him, spun about and tapped the next passing male and continued dirty dancing with zest. Frank pulled Diana into his body breathing in her intoxicating smell wondering whether it was too early to suggest they go home and make love; they danced cheek to chest mooching their way out of the crowd gyrating on the floor. Gallons of bubbly, music and disinhibition created a dazzling, boisterous and raunchy atmosphere. The stars lined up. Everyone was having a ball.

'I need you now, darling,' Diana urged him. He followed her hand in hand as they found their way upstairs past the Council chambers, they slipped into a wood-lined office with a stately desk. Diana pushed Frank back into the director's chair which virtually turned into a bed when you lean back. She dropped her panties and kept the suspenders and stockings on then she kissed him deeply on the mouth as she straddled him. Tongues were involved. It was so erotic Frank didn't know if he could hold back. He kissed her with all his heart and held her body tightly against his.

'I'm not wearing panties,' she teased holding his bottom lip gently between her teeth.

Frank gasped as she let go and unzipped him.

'Diana,' he whispered, 'I haven't got any protection on me.'

'Nor do I. It's okay. I just finished a period.' Famous last words a little voice said somewhere in his head.

'If I get pregnant, you'll have to marry me, or God will punish us.' With that she was astride him, putting him inside her as she kissed him again, deeply luxuriating in the feeling. Oh God, how fantastic! That glorious sensation when the man you desire is inside you.

Frank was desperately thinking of how not to climax.

'Oh God. Oh god.' She moved on top of him as though nothing else mattered anymore. When she came, it was intense and focussed as they rocked together. He thought he would explode and his whole body convulsed holding her buttocks with his face buried into her breasts to stifle his joyful yell.

She leaned in and kissed him as they locked together for what seemed like forever.

He longed to say, 'I love you,' Diana. He had never experienced what he felt for her with any other woman. It was an acute, exquisite sensation. He understood the agony of love.

After a while, warm wetness spilled on him and she slipped off him, leaned down and grabbed a packet of tissues. Together they mopped up the juices on his damp belly hair.

'I thought you weren't religious.' He said.

'I was thanking God for giving me a man that makes me come. We should sneak back downstairs.' She stood up leaned over and kissed him again. A promise of more.

'We'll come back to this conversation when we get back to your place shall we?' Frank looked down pulled up his undies and zipped up.

'You go first,' she slipped her panties on and straightened her hair.

People were still dancing and drinking and there was robust laughter and banter. Someone could be heard giving a plausible impersonation of Stereo Villanova trying to escape custody when Frank walked back into the room laughing with them good-humouredly. Diana collected two glasses of champagne and gave one to Frank who leaned into her, they headed towards their table and the rest of the Legal Aid team.

'Frank!' Brenda exclaimed slapping his bum, 'I can see at a glance I missed my chance to know you better, biblically that is.' Frank grinned.

He was feeling euphoric as the effects of such intense sexual liaison washed over him, heightened by the fear of being caught literally, with his pants down. The couple danced and chatted for the rest of the evening never too far from each other. During one of these intervals, Frank went to the drinks table and found himself standing next to a tall thin man with a dry sense of humour and a forensic legal mind.

'Mal, how are you?' Frank greeted him. Malcolm Geddes had gone through university a couple of years ahead of him though they mixed in Labor circles.

'Frank,' Mal looked at him approvingly, 'good to have you back,' a slight smile played on his lips as he took his drinks.

'Good to be back,' Frank held up two fingers to the waiter indicating he wanted champagnes.

'You're with Brenda's team, I see from the television coverage.'

'All in a day's work, mate.'

'Labor back in the driving seat. Are you going to work with Meredith?'

'She hasn't asked me.'

Vic had joined them in the noisy crowd using sign language to order drinks.

'Hi Mal, is this guy annoying you?' He quizzed and dug Frank in the ribs. Frank almost spilt the champagne.

'He's okay. We were just chatting. See you, Frank.' Malcolm took his drinks.

'See you, Mal.'

Being tall had its advantages as he could see the group of Legal Aid lawyers at a table on the opposite side of the room, he stepped back and waited until Vic joined him. They dodged a few enthusiastic dancers and tacked their way to a couple of tables pushed together on the opposite side of the room where Michelle and Alana, Vic's Sri Lankan wife, were in an animated conversation. Vic put the drinks on the table and sat down while Frank remained on his feet until he caught sight of Diana and held up her drink indicating where to find him.

He pulled out a chair as Vic handed a drink to Alana.

'I feel as though I know you already, Frank,' she teased.

'Frank's been courting our Italian beauty, Diana,' Vic had filled her in on the office romance.

'How is it going, Frank?' Michelle fixed him with tipsy eyes.

'We are having a lovely night,' Frank sounded like a cruise ship Maître-D, smiling and wishing all the guests well.

'Looks as though they have grown very close,' Alana had a Canadian accent.

'Hang on,' Vic looked at Frank, 'you dirty dog!'

Diana emerged from the dance floor somewhat breathless with pink cheeks, she fanned herself with a laminated table of contents for the evening's celebrations.

'I could kill for a drink,' she leant her body against Franks as though to move him over. He offered her his chair leaning across to the neighbouring table and snavelling another, sitting back his knee touching Diana. He felt as though he always wanted to be touching her and marvelled, that they had found each other.

'Let's drink a toast?' Vic proposed enthusiastically. Just then Brenda danced toward the party of lawyers with Marcus in tow and a bottle of champagne under her arm.

'Did I hear the suggestion of a toast?' She waggled the bottle.

'Raise your glasses,' Brenda regaled, 'to justice!'

'To love!' Diana called. All cheered and drank to love.

'To the Legal Aid team!' they charged their glasses again.

'Where is Madeleine?' Diana asked Brenda, 'I haven't seen her for a while.'

'She snuck away early with that French bloke from her Alliance class.'

'Good on her!' Michelle looked blowsy, 'I think I'll just nip off and pick someone up too.'

'That's our cue,' Frank stood and took Diana's hand, 'I shall escort my date home before the Rolls turns into a pumpkin.'

The Rolls Royce and chauffeur, were waiting for them at the appointed time, they climbed inside and held hands all the way home to Diana's place.

Once they were back, Frank loosened his shirt and threw the tie on the padded bench at the base of the bed. She moved in closer, her mouth was on his chest her breath sweet and slightly alcoholic, her eyes misty with lust. Oh boy, he thought and unzipped her dress. It slid to the floor then she threw it over a chair as he scooped her up off the floor in his arms in just her bra and pants and then took her to the bedroom and languorously pulled her shimmering stockings down kissing every part of her tenderly and intimately.

'I am falling for you, Diana' Frank whispered into her neck, 'from the moment we met.'

'I feel the same way, Frank,' she took his face in both hands and kissed him on the mouth slow and full and then firm and hungry until they collapsed, sweaty and sated before falling asleep in each other's arms.

The next morning, he woke and saw the empty space beside him. He could hear the shower running and soon Diana emerged wearing slacks, a black polo neck knit, and her hair caught into a ponytail and very little make-up. Frank felt his heart melt all over again.

'What does Diana Gianiovellis, do on a Sunday morning?' Frank probed, genuinely curious. 'I want to find out all about you.'

'It's a family affair,' she hinted enigmatically sitting on the bed to pull her boots on. He scooped an arm around her waist and nuzzled her neck. She smelt beautiful: a mix of lime and perfume.

'I like those,' Frank let her go, 'am I invited too?'

'Depends,' Diana gave him an appraising look.

'On what exactly.'

'On whether you play bocce.'

'I know how to lawn bowl,' he reassured her.

'That will do. My father and his old friends get together at Petersham Park every Sunday morning. Then we go back home for a big cook-up. Come along .'

'I need to go home and get a change of clothes.'

'Don't let Mum overwhelm you,' Diana warned.

'Alright.'

'Have you got an old rag? Maybe a tea-towel as the balls get awfully dirty after a while.'

They drove to the park and pulled in under a giant Morton Bay Figtree where a bunch of senior Italian men were standing around. There were introductions all around and a comfortable Game with the men who spoke Italian while Diana translated.

'I was going to wait to introduce you to the family. You know, this is it?' They were sitting in the car outside the Gianiovellis family home, a solid brick Italianate house with vegetables in the front yard. 'As far as they are concerned, you are the future father of my children.' She tried to sound humorous and light.

'I hope so,' Frank answered seriously, picking up her hand he kissed her palm. 'Come on, let's go inside.'

A squeal of delight. 'Franco! You came for lunch? Claudia bussed him on both cheeks and talked at him in a stream of English and Italian beaming with the sheer delight of a devoted mother who knows there is love in the air and more babies on the horizon.

He went out to the back porch where Val was grilling lunch. Claudia held Diana's arm. 'Let the men talk a moment. It's important.'

The capsicums, garlic and egg plants on the barbeque smelt beautiful.

'You used to work for Bill Falco, then Frank?' Val questioned.

'In the past. I'm finished with that life now, Mr Gianiovellis,' He knew this was 'the talk' and Val was assessing his suitability to marry his daughter. In a former life, being a member of the Labor Party was the only prerequisite Frank needed.

'Diana, she likes her job, you know. She is a modern woman.'

Val looked up at Frank meaningfully. He wondered just what he was asking. Then he hit on it.

'Well, if she wants to keep working, I will look after our children.' Frank was all in.

'You better get started pretty soon.' Val said.

'Does that mean you approve, Mr Gianiovellis?'

'She loves you. Please, call me Val.'

'I love her, Val.'

'Then, that's that.' Val placed the veggies on a plate with kitchen paper on it.

'Let's eat. We better teach you Italian.'

Over lunch, Claudia doted on Frank chatting about Diana growing up and her community, while Diana and her sister gossiped about the things of life: what the kids were doing at school and how she was joining an exercise group.

Claudia kept gazing at Frank thinking what their babies would look like.

'You are sure that there are no Italians in your heritage?' She asked him when Diana had taken some plates into the kitchen.

'Tell the truth, I have often wondered that myself as I am the only one in the family with black hair and Italian looks. But I don't think so,' he drank some of the short black coffee from his cup. 'My mum died about ten years ago. She said her brother was tall and dark,' he added as an afterthought.

'A lot of things happened during the war, Franco.'

The couple made their farewells to the Gianiovellis family and Claudia gave them a bag of food to put in the freezer. She and Val walked out with them to their car. 'Come back soon.'

'Your place or mine?' Frank looked at the love of his life amorously.

CHAPTER 24

Frank had been on the phone talking to the people involved in Natalie's life from the time he got to work that morning. Calling them back after the findings on Andrea's death may jolt a memory, he calculated. Moreover, he understood there were times when by asking leading questions, people would reveal information or insights, they didn't know they held.

Having already spoken to the woman with whom Natalie shared a house, Camelia had no further information about Natalie. She recounted two cops visiting her to ask similar questions about Natalie.

Waiting while the phone rang for Natalie's employer, AgBlaster, he speculated about the crop dusting and light plane business with their subsidiary, Bolt from the Blue. The businesses While operating out of Lismore airport, had an outpost office in Queensland, doing fly-in, fly-out trips for mining workers.

'Hello, Steve Perry speaking how can I help you?'

'Hi Steve, my name is Frank Phelan and I work for Legal Aid Sydney. We are representing Natalie Mulligans' family who have lodged a missing person report.'

'Mrs Mulligan, did call me a while ago to ask about her,' Steve recalled.

'When was the last time you saw Natalie?'

'February. I can look it up.'

'Do you have any idea where she might be Steve?'

'No idea, as I explained to Mrs Mulligan, our contract pilots take other jobs and if we can't reach them, we allocate another pilot.'

'Is it unusual for Natalie, to just disappear to another job without saying something?'

'Nat is regular and reliable. This is the first time I've known her to drop off the radar,' Steve cleared his throat, 'She always let us know her availability.'

'Was she there at the office for a specific reason Steve?'

'In late January the registration and licensing checks are done for all our pilots. Nat always had her paperwork in order.'

'Was this year different for any reason?'

'This year, C.A.S.S., Civilian Aviation Safety and Security,' he clarified, 'did an audit of our books. You know contracts, payroll, health, and safety. That sort of stuff.'

'Right. Yes, I know what you mean.' Frank looked down at his notes.

'I wonder, who else did Natalie talk to that day?'

'David Arndt, he comes each year and checks the paperwork.'

'Tell me, was anyone else there representing C.A.S.S.?'

'Yeah, a guy called Trevor Cane.'

'Thanks that's useful information. I will give C.A.S.S. a call.'

'Do you want me to put you through to Craig, our boss?' AgBlaster boss, Craig Bellamy, ran both companies, Bolt from the Blue, being the smaller cousin business. Quite literally a family affair.

'In a minute Steve, I'm curious about the other pilots.'

'Craig can give you a list of the pilots flying for us over that time, Mr Phelan.'

'Call me Frank. That could help Steve. Who came in after Natalie?'

'A Māori guy with tats. He flies for mining companies in Queensland and does tourist gigs in Byron. His name is Brendon Papatui.'

'Are you from Lismore Steve? Did you know Natalie's family?' Frank probed.

'Yes, I went to school with her.'

'Did you socialise with her, you know, down at the pub or footy games, that kind of thing?'

'No. I used to play footy with her brother. Me and Nat moved in different circles. I'm younger than her.'

'Do you know if Nat was seeing this Brendon guy?'

'No, I don't think so. She almost fell on the guy as he was coming up the stairs. It happened right in front of me, she didn't even know his name.'

'Thanks again Steve, you've been helpful if you think of anything give me a call. Have you got a pen?' Frank gave his direct work phone number, 'Natalie's mum is worried for her safety.'

'I just hope you find her, Frank.'

'So do I.'

'Anything you think of Steve, doesn't matter how small,' Frank let the question hang in space. He could feel Steve thinking.

'She did speak to Mr Cane,' he recalled.

Frank tried to keep the excitement out of his voice.

'What did they talk about?'

'I don't know. It was odd because mostly he deals with Craig.'

'This time he talked to Nat?'

'Yep. I can switch you through to Craig, hold the line.'

Frank heard the click on the line and a man with a broad Australian accent picked up.

'Craig Bellamy, general manager Agblaster.'

'My name is Frank Phelan, Craig. I'm from Legal Aid, and we are trying to discover the whereabouts of Natalie Mulligan, on behalf of her family. We are hoping you can help.'

'I wish I could, Frank,' Craig said sincerely. 'I spoke to her mum a while ago, but Nat hasn't phoned in like usual,' Craig sounded puzzled. He spoke with a country accent that put Frank in mind of cattle auctions and open fields and slabs of beer.

'Nat's a contractor,' Craig continued, 'one of my best pilots. Sometimes she'll take other jobs but she'll say she won't be around. She is always very professional and keeps good records.'

'How long has she been with you?'

'She took over from her dad. She's been flying for us for a few years.'

'From what you are saying Natalie seems to have checked out for a while without giving any notice?'

'Dusting is seasonal work. Most pilots fly for the mines between crops.'

'What?' Frank pushed.

'Maybe it's women's stuff, Frank. Maybe she has run off with some bloke.'

'Maybe,' Frank concurred.

'The police called me. Took them long enough! I told them the same thing. We hired Nat as a contractor for jobs crop dusting or flying people in and out of the more remote sites like the archaeologists and the miners. Sometimes as far as Broken Hill.'

'Did the police give you their names and numbers?'

'Hang on,' Frank could hear as Craig hunted for the number, 'Here you go, Peter Mangan, a detective, said he was looking into the case. '

'Thanks, mate. Anything else you can think of?'

'Hope she's okay.'

'Did you ask around? Would anyone in your workforce know anything?'

'Unlikely, we're a small rig and I keep across the business. She's always got a job here.' He clearly regretted losing one of his best pilots. They bid goodbye and Frank put the phone down, perturbed by the interest of the Byron Bay detectives, yet again. He caught Vic's eye as he was walking past his office.

'How's the search going?' Vic leaned against the door portal.

'Interesting. Got a minute?'

'Sure. Fire away.' Vic came into the filing cupboard that served as an office for Frank.

'Natalie Mulligan goes missing in Lismore,' he painted the scene. 'Then her cousin Andrea turns up dead on a beach in Sydney. The family reckon the two cousins look alike. What's wrong with this picture?'

'How come you get all the good cases, Phelan?' Vic was dealing with a particularly nasty client charged with domestic violence and dealing drugs.

'Dumb luck, I guess,' he shrugged, 'the last people we know saw Natalie were people at Lismore airport, the auditor, a guy called Trevor Cane, from C.A.S.S. and Steve Perry, who saw her last in February.'

'Remind me. Who's C.A.S.S.?'

'Civil Aviation Safety and Security. Hang on,' Frank recalled, 'Steve reckons one other person saw her the same day. A pilot. They collided on the steps,' Frank looked at his notes, 'Brendon Papatui, Māori guy.'

'Right. Hold that thought. Anyone else?

'Nope.'

'Sounds pretty mundane.'

'Then Andrea Mulligan turns up dead in Sydney, where she lives most of the time. A drug addict who spent time during her childhood with Natalie's family.'

'That's the woman you and Diana were in the Coroner's Court for?'

'Yep. Died in suspicious circumstances. However, some hippy in Nimbin claims he saw Natalie come out of the Post Office and get into a 4-wheel drive.'

'What did the Post Office say?'

'No recollection of seeing Natalie or Andrea.'

'You have doubts?'

'Yes. The two Byron Bay detectives, started sniffing about when Andrea's body is found. They visited her mum and asked questions. They phoned her work and even called in to see her housemate, Camelia.'

'Go on.'

'Our case is the family against the Lismore police, based on Natalie being a Missing Person, and them being dismissive, disinterested, and racist. Why are the Byron detectives sniffing about?'

'Really?'

'We are speculating that Andrea's death may be a case of mistaken identity and she was picked up by sinister forces believing she was Natalie.'

'Which means Natalie is in deadly peril from these people. Explains her disappearing.' Vic absently cracked his knuckles. 'Perhaps they dumped Andrea's body in Sydney, to take the focus off the North Coast, and make the Sydney cops take jurisdictional responsibility?'

Frank and Vic looked intently at one another.

'That is a heavy dimension. Very calculated.'

'Why else would the Byron Bay crew be asking questions? This is outside their bailiwick. Is there any evidence Andrea was up north.'

'No evidence but my guess is the Byron guys are somehow linked to Natalie's disappearance and it ties in with Andrea's death. That's what I've been thinking.'

'I would be going back to the Civil Aviation people, Frank. Ask more detailed questions like how many pilots they have. What about this Brendon guy. Can you interview them to find out how the audit went? Trevor Cane, you need to interview him.'

'Brendon didn't know Natalie apparently.'

'Maybe not until they ran into each other that day.'

'Good on you Vic, you're a champ.'

'You owe me a beer. And the inside story on your romance with our beautiful colleague,' Vic grinned conspiratorially.

'Deal!' Frank reached for the phone and dialled a number.

'Hello,' Elizabeth sounded distant. He supposed she was close to the phone in case of news.

'This is Frank, Elizabeth.'

'Have you heard something, Frank?' The catch in her voice saddened him. He was nearer to the truth now, though not enough to give her hope.

'I was wondering about Rover. Did he have his own plane?'

'Oh yes, the Beechcraft. It was his pride and joy, Frank. He kept it at Tyagarah and would work on it. He taught Natalie how to fly in it,' she said.

'Who else knows about it, Elizabeth?'

'No one. It was Natalie's special place where she felt close to her dad. It was a vintage plane, just their hobby. Natalie took to tinkering on it too, at weekends. I'm not sure it would fly now.' Her voice was warm and reminiscent.

'Elizabeth, until we get to the bottom of where Natalie is at present, Diana and I feel it would be good for you to have someone with you. I think you should call your sons and ask them to take compassionate leave in turns, so you have someone there in the house.'

'Oh Frank,' She clasped the cross hanging around her neck.

He pressed on, 'I don't want to make you alarmed, but we believe Natalie may have unknowingly got in with a bad crowd.'

'Natalie wouldn't break the law, Frank.'

'No, she wouldn't deliberately but what if someone she was seeing did?'

'She's always been so sensible.'

'Even sensible people can be mixed up in events. Just a precaution to keep you secure. Natalie needs to know you are safe. I think that's why you haven't heard from her.' He was going out on a limb. 'Would you like me to phone Jason and ask him to come and stay?'

'Yes, I would dear.' There was hope and acceptance in her tone. 'Just a minute,' She opened her blue spring-loaded address book next to the phone.

'Jason is at Kapooka Army Base in Townsville, his contact number is 07 556643. You'll need to ask to be put through to him. He does phone me each week. So does Nathan. They are good boys,' she added.

'Thanks, is Nathan on the same base?'

'No, he is at Cairs. Nathan is in Logistics.'

'Give me his number too. I can make a call.'

'Just one more thing, Elizabeth. Again, this is a precaution and not meant to alarm you, rather, as extra protection until this is over,' he waits for acknowledgement.

'Yes, go on. I'm listening.'

'You might get a visit from Detectives Condon and Mangan. I don't know why they have involved themselves in this case as it's not their area. Do not let them in unless you have someone with you. They'll say things like 'have you heard from Natalie?' Sound sympathetic, as though they want to find her.'

'Are they corrupt, Frank? 'What have they got to do with Natalie and Andrea for that matter?'

'Honestly, I'm not sure. I don't trust them.'

'Alright,' Elizabeth drew strength from his concern and honesty. The realisation that Natalie couldn't be found because she didn't want to be, and people like the detectives were still looking for her, meant she could be alive.

* * *

Frank then phoned C.A.S.S. headquarters in Canberra and asked to be put through to Trevor Cane. 'Hello Mr Cane. I am Frank Phelan, from Legal Aid, we are representing the Mulligan family in the disappearance of Natalie Mulligan,' he waited for a response.

'Yes.'

'You were one of the last people to speak to Natalie, Mr Cane.'

'I have no idea where Natalie Mulligan is,' Cane's voice clipped, 'I'm sorry I can't be of help.' A finality.

'On the contrary, Mr Cane, I believe we can assist each other. However, I can't disclose information on the phone for security reasons. We should meet in person.' Frank made it obvious he couldn't be brushed off.

'I don't have time for a meeting at the moment.'

'You will have to make time, or I shall bring it up with the of Director, of the Australian Federal Police,' he played his ace, 'we believe C.A.S.S. has knowledge of a drug investigation. Now we have a murder.'

'When do you want to meet?' Cane was defensive and pissed off.

'I'll fly to Canberra in the morning, Mr Cane. I'll see you in your office at eleven o'clock.' Frank hung up the phone. There were currents from this case churning beneath the surface, conflicting trends tugging at the players involved. Getting up late in the day, he shoved everything he could find into his battered leather briefcase before sticking his head around the corner of Brenda's office. She was on the phone, so he mouthed 'going to Canberra' and waved goodnight. Diana had left early to take her mother to the doctor.

* * *

'Welcome to Qantas, Mr Phelan,' a polished air stewardess checked the boarding pass he proffered, and he thanked her as he made his way to his seat where he tried to squish his long legs into the ever shrinking space in economy class. By the time he had read the safety sheet and perused the menu, the captain announced the plane was landing. He alighted and headed for one of the modern, yet nondescript office block attached to the airport precinct with Civil Aviation Safety and Security etched into the glass on the front door. The foyer, reminded Frank of an architectural no man's land, all gleaming white and completely empty. He didn't miss living in Canberra, though it had been his base for some years, he did note that Canberra's roads and highways, even shopping centres were often empty.

Frank caught the lift to the first floor and spoke to the receptionist who showed him a waiting area and asked if he'd like a glass of water. He declined.

'Mr Phelan, I am Trevor Cane, senior manager of aviation security. Come into my office.' Cane was officious and uncooperative in nature. Everything about him was neat and carefully groomed. Frank stood up and shook his hand curtly.

Cane indicated to a chair on the other side of his desk which Frank took as he assumed the upper hand in this transaction with a bureaucrat, a function he was very familiar with from his previous employment. Cane's office looked out at the sheep paddocks surrounding the Canberra airport and the season's changes were etched on the land. It was now April and Canberra was getting colder.

'What I need from you, is a recap of your meeting with Natalie Mulligan, at the offices of AgBlaster, in late January. ' Frank didn't waste time with courtesies. 'Natalie has now been missing for since February and now her cousin has turned up dead. Her death has been ruled suspicious by the Coroner, and you remain one of the last people to see Natalie if she is still alive.' He ploughed on, 'tell me, what did you talk about?'

'Well, I don't appreciate your approach, Mr Phelan. You can't pull rank on an authorised senior manager in the Federal Government.'

'I don't appreciate you stone-walling me, Mr Cane, and jeopardising the life of our client. Now cut the crap and tell me what it was about.' Trevor Cane bridled, his eyes revealing his hatred for Frank's dismissal of his bureaucratic status.

'There have been some breaches of security with contract flyers,' a recalcitrant reply.

'And do those security breaches involve moving large quantities of drugs around?'

'Why would you think that?' Cane retorted.

'Mr Cane, there was mafia surveillance of our office since

taking the Natalie Mulligan case, one person has turned up dead of a heroin overdose Other threats have been going on and this is confidential, the NSW Crime Commission is involved,' Frank allowed a few seconds for that information to be absorbed, 'now, I'll ask again, what did you talk to Natalie about? Was it about drugs?'

'Yes.'

'And...?' Frank waited.

'We, C.A.S.S. that is, asked Natalie Mulligan to keep her ear to the ground and report any illegal drug trafficking by contract planes and pilots. This is top secret, you understand?'

'What did she say?'

'She agreed in a phone call I had with her shortly after. We pay for information leading to a conviction.'

'Right! That wasn't so difficult, was it?' Frank was being patronising, 'Obviously, there is a problem, as your star witness has gone missing. What about Brendon Papatui, the other pilot you spoke to?'

'He is one of the contract pilots we believe is implicated in a conspiracy to move drugs, according to the Federal Police, who instigated the inquiry.'

'Where is he, do you know?'

'They've lost track of him.'

Frank spent hour with Cane and was feeling hungry. He settled on lunch in the nearby suburb of Kingston, one of the original settlements in Canberra, surrounding the Parliamentary circle. He was soon wolfing into an enormous omelette with salad, coffee and water on the side. His flight didn't leave until three o'clock, which meant he could get home before dark. He cabbed back to the airport and bought a newspaper.

Autumn brings a change in the air in Canberra, which sits in an odd geographical configuration to the nearby mountains and experiences freakish outbreaks of bad weather, known to beleaguer regular flights. Today, a fusillade of wind, dust and sleet was barrelling down the highway from Cooma, the small township in Snow Country, towards the airport on the outskirts of Canberra. The wind exhibited a furtive craziness about it. Febrile in effect as it suddenly stopped, switched direction, swirled around on one spot furiously, spat out some leafy debris and gushed off again gathering momentum and a head of steam rushing headlong towards an intersection. It was energised, numinous, harnessed by an addled spirit and trapped by its essence. Cranky with its destiny to finally peter out near Lake George.

'Attention all passengers on QF 455, due to inclement weather conditions this flight will be delayed until it is safe to take off.' Frank gave in. Eventually, another call to all passengers on his flight came over the intercom. It was now dusk; the weather had cleared though still overcast and the wind furies had abandoned the area and left a clinging shroud of clouds damp and penetrating.

'Bloody Canberra weather!' Frank grumped impatiently under his breath as people filed to the departure gates obediently. He looked around and caught a scene on the wall mounted television. A well groomed and earnest announcer stood in front of a damaged building, reporting on the serious situation behind him. One person had sustained an injury, he heard, and it was a bomb. Frank had a shocking realisation: - the bombed building was his workplace! He raced back to the public phone on the wall of the departure lounge and called Mike at home.

"They've bombed our office, Mike!' Emotion cracking his voice, 'Someone was injured. Diana, I think. Can you go and get her. Keep her safe for me. I'm on my way back now.'

'Frank, you still there?'

'Yes. I'm at Canberra airport.'

'I'm on my way. Talk to you later.' The line clicked off.

Frank dropped the phone turned and slumped against the wall beside the telephone. He wiped his face with his hand and heard the second boarding call for his flight back to Sydney. Inside the terminal a smattering of people in suits and workplace attire were walking towards the departure gates Frank re-joined the queue in several long strides clutching his briefcase and a jacket.

CHAPTER 25

The city was buffeted by a windy storm, evoking a sense of strange preternatural forces at work as it had gathered damp leaves that clinging to the pavement into clumps. Then abruptly, it changed direction bounced off the grey-brown walls of high-rise buildings, before scurrying off and squabbling with piles of rubbish aggregated in bins and storm water drains headed into the city's water courses.

It was still light when two men, wearing ordinary grey shirts and trousers, of the type worn by electricians and plumbers, stood on the street outside the Legal Aid office. They put their heads together and conferred for a couple of minutes before walking briskly down the side lane of the building which led to a small, enclosed backyard. A green, metal security gate stood bolted to the wall at the end of the lane separating it from the backyard. A row of metal spikes designed to discourage thieves made the gate look forbidding. The two men walked to a cream metre box attached to the wall beneath a window. Next to it squatted a gas bottle with a pipe leading into the building behind it.

'You sure you got the right stuff?'

'Don't fuckin' worry. The boss said teach 'em a lesson. I got enough.'

The partner remained unconvinced, as neither of them had any experience with explosives, which accounted for their insecurity.

'Go out the front and lookout while I pack the stuff in.' Both carried compact bags over his shoulder. One held the explosives, the other the detonator.

'Check your watch. Act natural.' The Semtex man ordered him.

'Yeah. Yeah, I'll do my job,' his partner spat on the ground, sick of being hassled. 'You plant the gear quick.'

The patchy evening light blurred the silhouettes of commuters hurrying home with their umbrellas being blown inside out. A workforce, clothed primarily in black, created a two-dimensional appearance of the people crossing at the lights and swarming towards train stations and busses. The two bombers completed their assigned task and walked up the street one hundred metres before crossing over to their getaway car, a white van, parked in a loading zone.

'You ready?' Both men clambered into the cabin of the van, with the Semtex guy driving. The other man opened his bag and took out a slim black oblong box that resembled a television remote, with a green button on one side. The Detonator guy waited for them to get further away before he pushed the remote button. The bomb exploded and all hell broke loose.

Diana was feeling vaguely nauseous all day but was determined to finish off writing up her file notes before going home. She ignored the sensation, putting it down to sushi rolls she had for lunch. Everyone in the office was equally busy with their administrative updates, bitching about having to use the outside toilet. According to Madeleine, the plumber was booked for that day-a miracle, as trying to get a plumber in Sydney, was difficult. When she had checked the inside loo earlier in the day, the water was close to the top of the bowl.

'Where's that plumber?' Diana called from the hallway.

Michelle answered from their office.

'Beats me. And I promised him sex if he could come and fix it today! Use the outside dunny.' She went back to her work.

'How could he possibly refuse?'

'Where's Brenda then?' If in doubt bring in the heavy artillery.

'She and Madeleine went out looking for a bigger office to house us in?'

'Thank goodness. I thought we were doomed to a nineteenth-century sardine can with no inside loo.' Diana decided to hang on and went back to her work.

'Got to go,' Michelle stood up slinging her bag over her shoulder, 'after work shopping is calling me. See you.'

'Have fun.' They shared a look as friends which spoke a hundred words.

'Somebody picking you up?' Vic's tone was concerned as he shrugged his jacket on to ward off the rainy weather.

'I'll call a cab at six o'clock when I've done this paperwork, thanks Vic,' she looked up and smiled at her colleague appreciatively.

'If you're sure,' he paused, 'I'm off to the Dojo to kick some arse.'

'Charming Vic, see you tomorrow.'

Vic grabbed his karate kit from under his desk, grinned and raised a hand as he exited the office.

She checked her watch; it was close to six o'clock. Satisfied that all her case notes were up to date, she locked them in the three-drawer filing cabinet. Returning, she stuffed her belongings into her leather briefcase and grabbed her coat, ready to walk out the door and flag a cab. That was when she experienced a wave of vertigo and her stomach churned. She had to throw up! She couldn't stop it. She ran the length of the hall from their office at the street front of the house to the back, where she dropped her bag and coat on the bench next to the door, slid the backdoor bolt and took the stairs into the yard two at a time aiming for the toilet bowl. As it was, Diana made it to the toilet in time, projectile vomiting into the bowl from a standing position. Fortunately, the door was open, and the toilet seat was up, she lurched forward gripping her stomach and heaved once more into the bowl trying not to touch the sides. Her eyes watered as the acrid burning taste of partly digested food and bile coated her mouth. It felt disgusting.

Beside the back steps, a brass tap sat above a large concrete drain in a backyard comprised of old cobblestone bricks, slick with the drizzle. She slipped a little in heels as she took a step toward the tap to wash out her mouth. The tap was tight, and the wind and rain formed a blustery vortex swirling in the cobbled yard behind her. Dismissing the eery feeling passing through her peripheral vision, she wrestled the stiff tap with both hands then washed her mouth and hands and took a drink. Moving back to mount the stairs she gripped the handrail to steady herself and placed her foot on the bottom step.

A massive WHOOMP from an explosion, sucked all the air out of the world leaving it suspended in silence for an eternity before it blew the side wall to smithereens smashing a jagged hole in the fabric of the building. The explosion was deafening, and shock waves of energy rolled from it's epicentre and knocked her sideways. Her whole body shook, and her heart pounded in her ears as she clutched the railing listening for the unearthly silence before a landslide of shattered shards of mortar, bricks, broken glass, splintered wood, and masonry fell in perpendicular sheets of pulverised material.

Another hailstorm of slate tiles from the building rained down on the tin roofs of surrounding sheds and outhouses of the neighbours. Time and space were disjointed for those moments and, although the blast shook the building and the earth, another sound punctuated the scene as the explosion itself subsided. The sound of wailing sirens haunted the air around her, while lights swished above the roof of the building.

It was at this moment that she thought this was indeed a bomb intended for them, the Legal Aid office and not an accident involving a gas bottle. Tentatively, Diana pulled herself to her feet and crept around the corner of the house to gauge the damage. The impact was visceral and deeply compelling, she witnessed the raw destruction and felt powerless and frightened. Was this revenge? The fear gripped her as she looked at the gaping hole in the wall facing the alley at the side of the building through the dust and debris. Everywhere dust was settling. From the side of wall, a cavity gaped where the gas bottle was missing and confetti from hundreds of files fell in streams from the skies above the building.

She turned and ran up the stairs to the back office striving to make it to a phone in the staff administration area. She was shaking as she grabbed the phone and dialled triple zero.

'This is Kim, where are you calling from?' A calm female voice asked.

'A bomb exploded at my work!' Words rushed out.

'Are you okay?

Yes, I am alright.'

'Where are you?'

'The address is Legal Aid NSW, at 93 Smith Street in Surrey Hills.'

'What is your name?'

'Diana Gianiovellis, tell the bomb squad. Please hurry.' She sucked in air.

'Diana, are you still there?

'Yes.'

'Where are you now?

'I'm out the back. I can't get past the gate as it's locked.'

'Is there anyone else there with you.' Kim's voice matter of fact. She sounded so mundane like asking, what you want on a sandwich.

'No, I am alone working back.'

'Diana, the fire brigade, and police are there now. I'm putting Oscar on the line, he supervises bomb disposal.'

'What did you see, Diana?' The man's voice echoed in her ears.

'Not much, I was in the back toilet. Then the bomb went off.'

'Can you go back into the outhouse? We've got all the services on the ground or on their way now. My colleagues will make contact and take you to safety when we secure the area. Okay?

'Don't be too long.' Diana struggled to retain her grip on the emotions she was experiencing.

'We won't. Anything else you can think of Diana?'

'This could be the mafia, ask the Crime Commission.'

'Thanks.' Oscar's voice terse. He disconnected.

This information added a complex dimension to the disaster that the emergency services were dealing with. Oscar began giving short sharp orders.

'Will, call the Crime Commissioner.'

'Yes. On it.'

'Tell him we have a situation. A bomb has gone off. I don't care how you do it but get her on the phone. Go round to the Commissioner's place if you must.'

'Carmen, get on the phones and tell the chiefs of fire and police this may be a mafia hit.'

'Okay.' Carmen began working the emergency line that gave direct access to the chiefs of police, fire and emergency services.

'Relay to them a witness to the bombing has flagged the mafia. Right now, we don't know who was responsible.

Thought it was either a terrorist attack or a disgruntled client exacting revenge.'

'Then find the Director of Legal Aid.'

'She's already called in. She's on her way. Brenda Schwartz.' Carmen reading her screen confirmed.

'Make sure the witness is kept safe and out of sight of the press.' Oscar was gone. Once on the road he put the siren on the roof of his black Ford Mondeo, and sped into the city while giving orders to the team at the disaster site.

'Theo, are you receiving?' The line crackled and then cleared. 'What's the status?'

'We've cleared the house and the area for bombs. The firies are dousing the last flames and Terry and Fred are suited up ready to go in and pick up the witness.'

'Okay, good.' Oscar swerved to avoid a pedestrian. 'Keep the witness under a coat we don't want her on television.'

'Carmen already called. We have it covered.'

'Speak to the Police and Rescue coordinators and make sure they interview everyone. Put a call out to commuters using the street to get to the train station or buses at central.'

'Got that. They're going to ask if it's a terrorist attack.'

'We think it could be a mafia hit. Tell them the chiefs and the Crime Commissioner are involved. I'm only five minutes away coming down Oxford Street now.'

He cut Theo off and picked up a call.

'We have to call the Minister, Oscar.'

'Five minutes, call the Minister when we have it locked down. Phil,' Oscar's eyes focussed ahead watching the road while talking with Phil Summerhayes, Executive Commander of the Combined Emergency Services and First

Responders, (established after the Hilton Bombings in 1978) an overarching body set up to deal with organised threats to state or national security internally.

'Okay, I'll notify his office. Tell me, what have you got.'

'A bomb has gone off decimating the Legal Aid office. No one was dead or injured however a lawyer was working back. She called it a bomb. Said it could be a mafia hit.'

'Jesus, sounds bad,' Phil qualified, 'fortunately no one was killed.'

'We have my bomb disposal squad on the ground along with the police and firies. This lawyer pointed the finger at the mafia. Told me to ask the Crime Commission. We have gone to get the Commissioner.'

'How did the witness reach that conclusion?'

Don't know. Guess we will find out.'

'The Commission is like the secret squirrels,' Phil said.

'Yeah right. They are tight-lipped lot.'

'Hang on I'm pulling into the crime scene now.'

Phil waited on the line a moment.

'It's a clusterfuck mate,' Oscar summed up bluntly.

The fire trucks from Pitt Street fire station, had responded to the explosion independently of the bomb threat, their sirens wailing in a raucous clamour. Squad cars and Police Rescue vans converged on the street, as well as two ambulances. The cordoning off and coordination was flawless, crime scene tape circumnavigated the scene. The streams of dazed and confused residents were picked up and conveyed to waiting areas while dozens of police cars combed the streets for the perpetrators, others watched the crowds gathering. The Bomb Squad and Police Rescue, conferred with the firemen who were quenching the flames with three long white canvas hoses screwed into street hydrants with men wrestling the power of water coursing through them.

Diana, sitting on the toilet lid hugging herself, was contemplating an escape route as the pressure to preserve her own life grew stronger. Scared that she would be engulfed by flames, she stepped out and cast about the backyard trying to work out how she could escape. If she hitched her skirt up, she could scramble onto the toilet roof which backed onto the house next door. She ran up the stairs, peeped in the door and leaning in, grabbed her bag and coat. Descending the steps, she could hear the crackle of a walkie-talkie and a man giving rapid-fire orders. The relief overwhelmed her. Tears began welling up as adrenaline raced through her body.

'Don't fall apart, Diana!' She admonished herself sternly.

The lights shone and a barrage of shouted orders as a grinding motor hoisted a ladder over the building. The place was on fire, but it hadn't spread through the whole building, just the filing room where Frank was with boxes of archived files. It only took a short while for two bulky shadows to appear at the laneway in full bomb protection gear with monitors and machinery, shielded by masks. One man lifted his visor and called out her name. They had got her message about a bomb, she thought, and this was the bomb squad. Thank God!

The voices approached her stepping into the hazy light framed by the metal gate at the end of the laneway, a strong spotlight illuminated the bomb crater. Unable to contain herself she ran into the light and was silhouetted waving both arms over her head.

'I'm down here!' She shouted at the top of her lungs hoping

the people didn't mistake her for the bomber. The bomb squad operations team spoke into their radio transmitters on their shoulders and the clearance team gave the go-ahead. One man walked toward her signalling with his hands to move back away from the gate. The other person was communicating with the fire brigade on the street. The man slid his visor back from his face.

'Are you alright? Did you phone this into triple zero?'

'Yes, and yes. I am Diana Gianiovellis. I work here.'

'We can't bring you back through the house in case there are more explosives laid.' He spoke calmly.' Move back as far as possible. Okay.'

She went to wait in the toilet while they swept for more bombs before they came back with a wire rope pulley attached to a truck and pulled the gate off.

The two men appeared in the gap where the gate had been and moved toward her.

'We got to move quickly. The wall and the roof are unstable. We are going to cover your head with your coat.'

'I need to carry you out. Are you fine with that?'

'Yes,' Diana lifted her arms ready to be carried to safety by a Michelin man. It felt like a bizarre science fiction film set. The man picked her up and carried her out at a run delivered to an open doored ambulance on the other side of the street where two paramedics were waiting with the boxes of supplies under a whirling light. By now there were dozens of bystanders staring in disbelief at the crater the bomb had carved in the building. Mike Purcell, stood beside the open doors at the back of the ambulance looking grim. He saw the bomb squad approaching carrying a person under a coat and made way for them positioning his body so he could block off the crowd or a ravenous press pack packed behind the cordoning tape.

'Hi, I'm Mike Purcell, I'm a friend of Frank.' He could see how much Diana was absorbing before continuing. 'He phoned me when he saw the explosion on television and asked me to make sure you were safe.'

Diana bit her lip trying to contain the shock. Her muscles ached and she gave him a wan acknowledgement, more of a grimace.

'Here sit down, let's have a look at you.' A female paramedic, her straw blond ponytail pulled back off her face, took Diana's arm and guided her past Mike. Her no-nonsense demeanour was calming. Beside her stood her partner, a younger man with a crewcut. They were all standing at the back of the ambulance with both doors open to protect Diana from the press and onlookers.

'My name is Lorraine, this is Harris, my partner.' Harris put a fancy silver space blanket around Diana's shoulders and poured a cup of tea from a thermos that was milky and hot.

She held the cup with both hands feeling the warmth as Harris inspected her for bruises and cuts then dabbed antiseptic on her legs.

Mike's body faced her shielding her from the street. He had dispatched police officers to the perimeters of the crime scene and had people walking among the crowd gathered hoping to find a bomber gloating over their work.

'Good to see you, Mike.' Diana's voice quavered. 'Frank has talked about you.' It was only then that she realised there were television channels busy filming and talking into microphones at the borders of the cordoned area.

'Thank goodness you alerted the bomb squad. That was very brave of you.' He waited while the paramedics did their job before saying.

'For now, I want to take you into the hospital Diana, to check everything.' Lorraine agreed she was in shock and needed to be observed overnight. 'Is that okay by you?'

'Yes,' Diana nodded her head. 'We can phone your mum and let her know you are safe and will be staying in overnight,' Mike added.

'Alright,' she got to her feet a little wobbly. A face appeared at the open ambulance doors. Mike recognised a colleague in law enforcement and they two shook hands.

The other face was Oscar Carabine, head of the bomb squad.

'It's alright, this is Oscar, they will want to interview you as you are the only witness thus far.'

'Hi Diana, we spoke on the phone. Thank you for your bravery.' Diana felt nonplussed. Wouldn't anybody do what she had done in the circumstances?

Oscar spoke into his collar. 'Got to go, mate the Minister is here. Take care you're in good hands, Diana.' Oscar departed.

'How is Frank?' Diana asked Mike.

'Completely freaked out. He's flying back now,' Mike took her arm to steady her. He connected with Lorraine, 'We right to go?'

Lorraine helped her forward, lifting the blanket over her head, 'I'll walk with you to the car.' The press and bystanders were casting about for a centre of attention and found it, in the Minister of Police, a tall block of a man with slicked back greying hair and a lumpy doughy face on top of a charcoal grey suit. Lights, people holding microphones cameras hoisted on shoulders, tripods and reporters speaking into cameras all buzzing at once.

The firies, police and the bomb squad were going through the house sealing off the wall to protect the files and the information stored in there. The blast had imploded the whole side of the building and taken out Frank's office, creating a pile of debris and the ticker tape confetti from the files store in the room.

'We're going over to St Vincent's Hospital emergency. There are people with malicious intent.' He let the sentence trail off not bringing it to the natural conclusion.

'We were going to put a guard on you.'

'Thanks, Mike,' She wondered whether the bomber was from the same gang who tossed her flat over. The processing went quickly, facilitated by Mike, who took the Head Nurse, aside showed his identification and shared information. The bomb blast was getting wall-to-wall coverage on television in the waiting rooms and wards. They showed Diana to her own room in the maternity ward and asked whether she had eaten anything.

'How do you want to handle your parents, Diana?' Mike, a skilled communicator, figured her family would be distraught.

'Can you say I'm a bit shocked but helping with your inquiries?' She suggested, 'Say I wasn't in the building. Strictly true. Oh, and let her know Frank is on his way to take me home. Everything is alright.' He waited as she constructed the story.

'They worry about you a lot?'

'Mum, yes over the top.' Dianna allowed herself a moment of tired warmth.

Mike went out to phone the Gianiovellis family and returned a few minutes later.

'Spoke to your dad, and explained they couldn't see you until you gave a witness statement. He asked you to call them in the morning.'

'Thanks, Mike. After the robbery they are protective.'

'The robbery?' His brows shot up.

'Yes, my place was searched. We think the mafia may be after our client.'

'That's for tomorrow,' he glanced at his watch and sat down in a chair next to the bed.

'I'm just going to stay until the police guard arrives, okay?'

'Shock is a natural thing but it's tricky as you can change your impressions or question what you've seen.'

Her mouth felt and tasted awful.

'I need a shower.' A nurse came in with a clean change of hospital clothes.

Standing under the hot cleansing torrent Diana experienced a shattered sensation as though the bomb separated all her cells and body systems.

The nurse brought her a sandwich and a cup of tea which she gobbled down while Mike who waited outside, he re-entered with a notepad, 'This won't take long. How did you get involved with this case?'

'We were asked by the Mulligan family to represent them over their daughter Natalie, who had disappeared. Then her cousin was found floating in the bay in Sydney.'

'Why would the mafia be interested?'

'I honestly don't know. Andrea was a drug addict and Natalie is a crop duster pilot. Frank talked to the civil aviation people in Canberra.'

'Could it be mistaken identity?'

'We have no proof. The Crime Commission people were watching the mafia watching us. Maybe go through the CCTV footage.'

'What did you notice and see?'

'I felt nauseous and threw up. I was just focussed on the toilet bowl'. She recounted thinly. 'The inside toilet is blocked so I had to run outside. Lucky, I did.'

'Go on.'

'I washed my mouth and hands. When I was coming back up the stairs the wind and drizzle swirled, and I listened for a few moments. The bombers may have known people were inside the office as the lights were on and the radio as well.'

'What time was that?'

'Must have been about six o'clock, as the others had only been gone a short while.'

'What were your first thoughts, Diana?'

'I thought there was a gas bottle explosion and so I went and looked down the lane. That's when I saw the hole in the wall.' He wrote this down, 'Then I thought it was a bomb. Nothing else would make a hole like that. Whatever happened, it threw the gas bottle out into the street or somewhere.'

He stopped taking notes and then posed another more open-ended question.

'Anything else you can remember about the scene no matter how silly?'

'I don't know. I think the shock was setting in and I knew I had to call in the bomb squad in case there was another one. I had a weird feeling while I was outside as though something bad was about to happen.'

'What did you do then?'

'When the explosion went off, I ran up the back stairs and I phoned Triple 000 and gave them the address.'

'Smart woman,' he grimaced.

There was a tap on the door and Mike got up and pulled the roller curtain around the bed in front of Diana then walked to the door and opened it.

A young police officer was at the door and Mike stepped out for a quiet conversation with her explaining that Diana was on the pointy end of a bomb blast. Mike and Constable Mellors entered the room together.

'This is Diana Gianiovellis.' Mike said by way of introduction. 'She witnessed the bomb blast at the Legal Aid office.' He turned to Grace, ' Don't let anyone in, unless you see their ID. I don't care if they have a white coat on, stay in the room and have your gun handy. This could be a mob hit.'

'Diana, this is Constable Grace Mellors,' Grace leaned forward to Diana and held her left hand with a warm, firm grip.

'You've been very brave, Diana, not many people have the presence of mind to phone in a bomb, while in shock. I shall be here to keep you safe,' she gave her a protective smile.

Mike checked his pager for any messages from his team then raised his eyes.

'We're expecting Frank Phelan, Diana's partner, to arrive from Canberra,' he addressed Grace, 'he's a tall dark-haired guy. A bit distraught.'

'I'm going to go now. Constable Mellors is on the door she'll guard you.'

'Frank will be relieved to know you're alright.' Mike moved off, his hand on the door handle, 'I can see he must care for you very much.'

Diana reddened and he raised both hands apologetically. 'Look, I'm sorry, I've known Frank Phelan for almost a decade, and I've never known him to be so upset. I will be back soon.'

Frank rushed to catch a cab to the hospital as soon as he landed in Sydney, fighting back tears. Later that night, Diana awoke to find Frank, asleep in the chair beside her, she asked him to call the nurse as she had a heavy period and needed some pads. When she returned from the bathroom, he helped her back to bed and put his arms around her shoulders as she cuddled up closer.

CHAPTER 26

Olaf picked up one of the other books he had found in the Bond University Co-operative Bookshop written by an academic, Dr Suzanne Riordan, who studied various forms of new ageism and the occult. After scanning the back cover blurb, Olaf ran his finger down the contents list before reading the forward. New Age literature, Olaf discovered, was awash with the statements, forecasts, clairvoyance and prognostications of channelled wisdom that was delivered to often unsuspecting people, by characters from the spirit world. Some new-age gurus, such as the insouciant Seth, claimed to have received visions and instructions from the spirit of Hermes. These ventriloquised pearls of wisdom and age-old occult knowledge typically, gave the recipient legitimacy. An oldy, but a goody, Olaf read on. New agers believed in the existence of 'guardian angels', personal guides, indigenous shamans, and masters-teachers in the form of voices that spoke to them. New Age followers call on the assistance of these various guides to assist them in navigating the embodied world of every day such as 'easing the traffic flow on their way to work.'

New Ageism had its genesis in the alternative revolution of the 1960s and 1970s which provided the perfect backdrop for many people to reinvent themselves, drawing from a wide range of spiritual movements and ideas about magic and magical thinking. There were faeries and elves, nature spirits, witches and warlocks who wielded power over ordinary unawakened people. Many of these people relied on plant-based psychotropic drugs to transcend their everyday lives. Some went on to form a 'Grass Cult Embassy' and over time, felt persecuted for being rejected by society not to mention having their cars pulled over by the cops for driving under the influence of drugs. It became something of a game for the police.

* * *

Olaf slipped on a pair of black chinos and a loose white linen shirt before grabbing the handset of his portable phone and dialling a number in Denmark, he knew by heart. The phone rang and rang before clicking over to the voicemail of Dr Berthe Berthelsen his friend, mentor and counsellor. Olaf was disappointed she hadn't picked up the call though he conceded it was mid-morning in Copenhagen, and she would be at work. He left a message for her and was about to hang up when she answered.

'Hi, Olaf. Hang on.' Berthe spoke to someone else in the room.

'I'll pick up in the study. Okay?'

Ja, Berthe,' Olaf waited. There was a click and a warm familiar voice.

'I'm here now. How are you, Olaf? Still in Australia?'

He'd lost sight of the nuanced comfort of one's culture as it enfolded them both in their native tongue and gave a voice to their long and close relationship. He knew Berthe when she worked as a counsellor. She helped the police with the impact of trauma on their professional and personal lives. Later, she was called upon as a trauma specialist for populations impacted by people smuggling, child abuse rackets and other horrific human crimes.

Now Berthe worked as an academic, she took on several postgraduate students as a mentor, including Olaf. In her seventies, she was still working for the University of Copenhagen 'my life's work' she called it.

'I'm here in Surfers Paradise, Berthe, looking out at the ocean.' He studied the broad horizon, 'I am on a smuggling case involving a new age cult. I wanted to talk with you about cults.'

'Sure. I don't have a lot on right now. How are you?'

'I'm good. Apart from the pesky acid reflux,' he said. 'But that's not why I rang you.'

'How can I help?'

'What can you tell me about New Age cults?'

'What can I say Olaf?' Berthe was clearly engaged with the topic. 'The New Age belief system divides human history into a series of specific ages typified, by certain characteristics innate to humanity. There was, as with many mythologies, a Golden Age, where people lived in a civilisation of great technological advances and spiritual wisdom. War, cruelty, and selfishness not to mention sexual profligacy were rejected. Pictorially and metaphorical, New Agers define this glorious era, as predominantly white.'

'What do you mean by that?'

'On the whole, it is the white middle and upper middle classes that embraced New Ageism, as they had the resources and education to launch counter movement against the existing order and then go and seek an alternative lifestyle. Are you with me so far?'

'Uh huh,' he affirmed. 'Go on.'

'According to the New Age literature, the world had spiritually degenerated, an Age of Aquarius, was not only imminent, they claimed, but would restore the global balance. My research shows that most new agers believe that divinity is integral to humanity and their universalistic approach accepts all approaches as equally valid.'

'So, it is a spiritual rather than a political movement?'

'I believe so. Their creation story and the language centres on the idea of holism, for example, an ocean of oneness, the infinite spirit of the universe and so on, with which humanity connects via intelligence and consciousness to release a divine life force.'

'A very attractive proposition for people seeking happiness or feeling powerless,' Olaf surmised, 'people who would be easy to manipulate and exploit.'

'Oh yes, you have nailed it, Olaf!' Berthe chuckled again. 'There are big profits and fame for gurus. Imagine being told you have a higher self that is connected to the essence of the universe? That your soul lives in a divine place? That's a powerful story!'

'Irresistible.' Olaf was enjoying himself too. 'We are dealing with a cult that conforms with those concepts calling themselves the Seraphic Throng of Heavenly Light, their guru is Seth Lord High Alchemist.'

Berthe erupted in laughter again, caught her breath and

sighed.

'Oh, Olaf that is so funny! It has everything including the Christian mystical trappings of angelism. New agers are nothing if not eclectic and they'll adopt anything mythological or spiritual and weave it into their theology. Which divine entity does their guru channel?'

'I believe it's Hermes Trismegistus, the ancient Egyptian alchemist.'

'He has quite a following including the Theosophists at the turn of the century. What does the guru promise the followers? Eternal life perhaps?'

'Weightlessness,' Olaf answered.

'They must be charging quite a lot of money for the ability to defy gravity, I would guess?'

'Thousands, in addition to the smuggling kickbacks with plastic goods they import.'

'That's where you come in, chasing international drug smugglers using a seemingly harmless cult?'

'Not so harmless, Berthe. Pretty exploitative, including unpaid workers and innocent young women.'

'It was ever thus Olaf, nor will it change. Where there is God, sex, money and mythology, there will be crime and cults.'

'Thanks, Berthe. The human condition then?'

'Your work in policing these fraudsters and criminals is invaluable, Olaf. Just don't think you can save the world.'

'I don't think I can save the world. I'll let you go. Let's talk again soon my friend and thank you.' He felt a wave of affection for her.

'Anytime, Olaf,' Berthe responded, 'lovely to talk and hear your voice again. Goodbye and take care.'

Olaf picked up the brochure from the Movement. Sir Raj, he read, received a visitation from the spirit of Hermes himself. No matter how popular he was with his following ultimately,

Sir Raj lost his bid for immortality on earth and died of cancer.

Staring out from his veranda, Olaf succumbed to the yearning of homesickness for his native land. Australia was a striking and remarkable place, but he wanted to go home. The doorbell rang and he crossed the room putting his longneck beer on the coffee table. Opening the door, he took in a luscious, olive-skinned woman wearing a trench coat and high spiky heels with a large tote bag slung over her shoulder.

'Olaf?' Her voice husky, the coat fell open revealing voluptuous breasts and a thick mat of black public hair.

'Come in. Would you like a drink?'

CHAPTER 27

Greg and Olaf were pondering over the masses of paperwork the case against the Movement and the smugglers generated. The whole team were gathered in the training room, having collected their research, receipts and orders for plastic paraphernalia, dating back several years to Sir Raj, the previous guru who authorised them. They documented everything from Seth, in addition to taping all the interviews with the Elders and key members of the cult. Their evidence revealed a pattern by the smugglers of larger and smaller lots of drugs, relative to the amounts of money being logged as paid. In the second accounts book, records were kept scrupulously up to date by Ruth Zelwag. At least, Olaf calculated, that seemed logical to him, the smugglers paid the Movement more money for more drugs imported, and less for smaller batches.

'How many other businesses do you reckon the smugglers

are operating with?' Nick was curious to know.

'Customs would have a database of companies importing and exporting so we could match names against the Rising Sun Imports Company. Plus, we've matched those shipping numbers and the bar codes with the boxes of drugs and the wrapping.' Olaf confirmed.

'We had better work fast while we have the culprits in custody,' Damien observed.

'They have to take the drugs somewhere for the next stage of the distribution, but they will have dozens of company names and dispensable workers who have false passports and, who move between countries.' Olaf liked working with the Australian team moreover, he clicked with Greg and took him into his confidence.

'I'm waiting for a call from a colleague in the Asian Crime Gang Unit, in Singapore,' Olaf continued. 'Busting Triads and military juntas is their daily bread, and she will have excellent intel on the drug routes through secondary countries into Australia.'

They were sitting in the debriefing room surrounded by files, boxes of loose sheets, interview notes and tapes tracking them on a whiteboard. A diagram that looked like spaghetti and meatballs. Sue's epithet for it. Additionally, they had deposit slips and bank records for sums of cash that didn't match up.

'What do we know about the cult?' Greg had expanded their crime mapping to white sheets of butcher's paper on tripods around the office. The door was open and from time to time a member of the research team would duck out to collect a piece of research for the two senior detectives.

'Always follow the money. Because the Elders ran the whole show and knowingly got involved with the smugglers, they are easy to trace. The cult business is firstly a money-making scheme because, unless you have a big population and can grow your donations and sales, you run out of money.'

'Like a pyramid scheme, you mean?' Donna piped up.

'Yes, just like a pyramid scheme.' Olaf confirmed. 'They are selling enlightenment through memberships and plastic stuff and saving costs through indentured labour, but their products must be super expensive. The cult members and wannabes, must be persuaded that, by spending ridiculous amounts of money on plastic, 'blessed' things, they will find God, love, weightlessness or whatever.'

'The cult followers are supporting the existence of the organisation by working and paying rent. It costs to house and feed twenty or so people, so either they keep recruiting more people or fund activities through illicit means,' Greg explicated as he drew dollar signs next to the cult circle.

'John Owens or Seth, is the talent. He's the good-looking, charismatic one who love bombs the girls and makes the guys feel like cool spiritual warriors,' Olaf expanded.

The session went on for another two hours before someone mentioned pizzas and coffee.

By the time they had finished the drawing of the interconnections between the cult and the drug smugglers, they had filled in significant amounts of information. They drilled down to how much each seeker was costing the Movement and how much profit, if any, was derived from their work and donations.

From the seized documents and receipts, they were able to calculate what went through the books of the Movement, which was a registered charity, through its outreach work and tax exemptions.

'Costs go up and seekers lose interest and leave. Perhaps there is pressure on the 'high value' seekers to stay and recruit others,' Greg could see that it was a business of diminishing returns unless the Movement had rich benefactors or another source of income.

'We've got the Elders on receiving contraband, laundering proceeds of drug money, tax evasion. We've got Seth where we want him however, he will bolt if he sees an opportunity and, we have terrified the throng of young people enough to keep them quiet for a couple of days.'

After lunch, the team sorted and curated all the documentary evidence and logged their first-hand accounts of the bust into the computer system. Greg called everyone to sit around the main table. He could feel the energised buzz in the air. They were doing challenging, intelligent police work. Meaningful, not just chasing down lazy stoned bums and petty criminals.

Olaf asked for their attention. 'Greg is going to run us through where we are up to and outline our thinking on the bust. Then we'll fill in the gaps together. If you geta thought, hang on to it until Greg's finished. Okay?' Everyone murmured yes. The frisson was palpable. Olaf stepped back giving the floor to Greg.

'Well done everyone! Great work.' Olaf congratulated his team.

'Over to you Greg.' Greg had picked up a plastic ruler as a pointer and systematically moved through the diagram talking to all the points they thrashed out.

'Now we've shared your research and conclusions. Nick, Sam, Sue, Donna and Vanessa, we'll go around the room then brainstorm.'

Vanessa pushed her auburn hair off her face and looked at the paperwork she had in front of her. She had been the point person at Tweed Heads station, who coordinated the raids on the warehouse and the ashram, as well as maintained contact with the Brisbane team. She trained as a forensic accountant, before changing careers to be a police officer. Her astute head for figures hadn't been recognised, until Olaf went through the personnel files to find his team. When they were done with this job, he and Greg advised all of them in individual debriefs, to update their resumes and they agreed to be referees. Olaf commanded authority and respect, because he shared the recognition and accolades for the successful busts. He had worked with many teams over his career, and realised that the less envy and the more trust one had, the better the outcome.

'We are assuming the smuggling ring is moving drugs that are easily hidden and sold. Perhaps the kickbacks change or the types of drugs change. For this shipment the Elders received a hundred grand in cash however others have been less,' Vanessa cast her eyes over the ruled book of payments received and recorded by the Elders.

Unexpectedly, Olaf smiled when he looked at everyone, 'This is gold. Criminals don't always document their crimes so thoroughly.' His team relaxed and bantered with each other a little.

'Reviewing the interviews of those members staying at the ashram aside from the Elders, the team concluded they weren't aware they were handling contraband,' Greg had learnt more from working with Olaf than all his years at the academy and in policing, and he appreciated that Olaf explained his thinking. 'Does everyone agree? Sue, Nick any comments?'

Olaf stepped back while Greg unthreaded aspects of the case and gathered the perceptions and observations from the team.

'John Owens is the only outlier, I'd say,' Sue spoke up and looked around.

'My sense of the guy is that he is lazy, greedy and self-interested,' Nick contributed. Two of the others agreed. 'And, if there was more money to be had through kickbacks, he would have demanded it.'

'You're right, I think,' Greg confirmed, 'there's no evidence Owens was getting more money than his regular retainer for being the guru.'

'Thoughts, Donna and Sam?' Sam had been tasked with watching the ashram, noting the comings and goings and then meeting up with Greg and Sue, to bust Ruth Zelwag, and interview the seekers. He and Greg briefed the rest of the team on the operation there.

'Sam and I interviewed ten of the seekers present at the ashram. We asked them whether there were any other members not living at the ashram,' Sam picked up the account.

'Yeah, there are some other members who don't live at the ashram but have shared houses nearby. They come to the ashram for praying and meals. Sort of group bonding.'

'Did you get addresses or names?' Greg asked.

'Yes, we have the names and addresses of all the seekers both resident and non-resident including a house near Tyagarah airstrip where three people are living at present. Gilgamesh was there and said most of the group didn't know each other's birth names only their spiritual ones.' Donna highlighted.

'Surely, Gilgamesh knows what name he was born with?' Sue raised her voice.

Everyone laughed. It was good to break the tension and put things into perspective.

'The other group were itinerants staying at a backpacker place at Byron Beach, not the dedicated cult members.' Sam chipped in.

'Yeah, we found that too, there was a central group of dedicated members and a floating group that moved in and out.'

'That's good. Now let's look at the whole field of activity,' Olaf said. 'Don't just look at it as crime and wrongdoing by individuals. It's a business. A business network that is international. The cults are running their own businesses too. Their products are the same really and the smugglers are just out-sourcing the importing and warehousing while the cult is sell-ing weightlessness and God.'

Greg, following the theme, 'You are saying that they are at-tracted to each other because of their business model and lack of ethics?'

'That's exactly right, Greg. International smugglers need to have outlets to receive and disperse their products. Asian import and export companies, naturally attract unwanted at-tention from Customs and the cops. Thus, it is a symbiotic re-lationship. They need each other.' Olaf took a sip of his coffee and made a face before continuing. 'The smugglers form part of a worldwide ring because the import-export company is Malaysian, and the goods are made in China. The cult buys crappy plastic paraphernalia that they peddle as magic arti-facts and a repository of super secret powers, from the pro-ducers and importers.'

Greg and the others thoroughly enjoyed this master class in the logic of international smuggling and the team threw the ideas around freely.

'With a little research, we found the Asian network iden-tified small businesses in Australia with whom they can do business and they offered them more money.' Vanessa and Sue had been researching the importing business, The Rising Sun, and others, they talked to Customs officers and govern-ment regulators and gathered background information.

'What else have you got?' Greg sat on the edge of the desk giving the space over to Vanessa and Sue.

'The company and its customers registered as bringing goods into the country appear to be legitimate importing and exporting business.' She looked at the notes organised into a spreadsheet.

'Each company we are dealing with, and we uncovered five,

does have genuine business dealing and transactions.' She described in detail the Rising Sun's activities and Greg drew on another whiteboard set up the diagram of the linkages.

'Sue spoke to Customs officers about the Rising Sun imports business. She asked how drugs got through Customs. They were a bit defensive at first,' Vanessa looked at Sue.

'Because only a small percentage of containers get scanned and taken apart,' Sue qualified. 'There is less attention paid if they have been operating for years and years as Customs focusses on different types of business for a set period. The import companies also need to have people on the docks and on their payroll so that in the event they do get spot-checked by Customs, they get advance warning.'

'Other businesses may be more intricately involved in the smuggling. For example, Vanessa found a couple of Chinese medicine companies importing bulk herbs and components of medicine that are compounded here in Australia. The Rising Sun company is a subsidiary of a larger company based in China, which is connected to these two Australian companies.'

'They are business planning?' Vanessa queried.

'Certainly,' affirmed Olaf, 'money is what motivates them and binds them together. For the Movement, the import smuggling company looked at the goods being ordered and figured out what sort of turnover they show, then offered them lots of cash to look the other way. The other outlets are connected in other ways.'

'It is a worldwide network!' Greg put the picture together.

'Yep. You got it, Greg. Some of it is legit and some of it is illegal. We can shut down parts of the network but never all of it.'

'Right,' Olaf stepped in, 'where are we up to with the two smugglers and the Tommy Tortoise Truck?'

'We have a cover story for the truck being delayed that allowed the Brisbane team time to sweep the shops and warehouses they targeted.' Greg and Nick had organised a minor accident and taken some photos of the truck apparently tipped over the shoulder of a road leading to Brisbane.

'They have problems with truck breakdowns. We are putting it on the news tonight.'

'Nick?' Greg indicated to go on with the account.

'Mr Van Cong and Mr Van Nguyen are both in custody for smuggling drugs but as they have very little English, we've put a call out for a Vietnamese interpreter so we can charge them and read them their rights. Until that person arrives, they haven't had access to a phone or a lawyer. The clock is ticking.'

Everyone began talking at once. Greg caught Olaf's eye.

'I know it's great stuff everyone will be heard.' Greg used his hands waving them palms down. 'As soon as Brisbane calls, we can charge the smugglers. We have the Elders, and all the evidence to charge them and put them away. We are going to a bail hearing and arguing not to give them bail as they are a flight risk. We have cautioned Seth or John Owens, for a small amount of cannabis and told him not to leave town, however, he is still in custody and cooperating.'

'No doubt he wants to,' Donna quipped.

'Let's wrap up the paperwork And let the bad guys and women stew overnight. We'll release the truck story to the press, and we will pressure Owens before releasing him.'

The relief erupted in the room with the team talking and laughing all at once.

'Thank you everyone!' Olaf raised his voice again before they dispersed, 'You were all fantastic. The drinks are on me. We'll meet at the pub in an hour, ring your families.'

The door opened as the team was packing up, talking animatedly and getting ready to lock up the evidence and go to the pub. The duty sergeant responsible for the day-to-day business of the station popped her head around the corner, 'Greg, the desk received a notification from Crime Stoppers. A young woman rang, wouldn't give her name, but reported seeing a dope deal late one night on the Tyagarah airstrip. She said thinks she saw a woman who looked like the dead woman washed up in Sydney.'

'Thanks, Bev, have we got the tape of the call?' Greg queried.

'Yes,' she answered.

'Be with you shortly.'

'This gets more and more interesting,' Greg cut his eyes to Olaf, 'sure you don't want to stay?'

Later that evening, the local Television Channel WIN ran a minor traffic incident story, on their News at Six program, *'A small truck has rolled off a local road in slippery conditions.'* Pictures of the mist, the truck and ambulance and the police. *'The police would like to speak to the driver who left the scene. The van, which was towed away, and traffic was held up while debris was cleared off the road.'* A nothing story attracting no interest other than those smugglers waiting for the boxes to arrive.

CHAPTER 28

Darryl Chess was a nondescript guy with long mousey hair and a sallow pimply complexion, who grew up on his parent's cattle farm near the rural town of Lismore. Having left school, he got a job working for Australia Post, delivering the mail by motorbike. Like many young people he went to see bands and drank a lot though unfortunately, never scored chicks. He became a fan of Thelonius Manshaven and the Thigh Masters, a hideously loud, post punk rock band often billed at the Lismore Workers Club. The change in him was incremental but he felt a yearning for something. Something more exciting than his monotonous day to day life. He began hanging around the band after their shows and they let him help with loading the band's gear.

It had been a big weekend of music and drinking and Darryl, barely remembered making it home to the bedsit he rented or crawling into the unwashed and stained sheets. He had to get up at five on Monday. When the alarm inevitably went off, he threw one arm over his eyes and reached out flapping his other hand around trying to feel the clock. Amazingly, he had the presence of mind to put the clock on the kitchen bench the night before. Grumpily, he got out of bed stomped over to the kitchen and hit the stop button before staggering into the shower alcove. He arrived at work late and was groused on by his boss.

Once out on the run astride his motor bike the day improved. To relieve the boredom, Darryl played the latest single by the Thigh Masters, Rip Out My Tongue, blasting from his Walkman as he drove along the footpaths of Lismore. Occasionally, he'd stop his motor scooter to deliver a spectacular piece of air guitar imitation.

A fantasy began formulating in his brain. 'What if I chucked in my job and went to work for the band?' The tantalising thought tugged at him, persuasively. The weather was warming up when Darryl turned his motor bike into Schrodinger Street, a very steep street that crested the hill above Lismore then dove into the back of the university campus where a stand of gums skirted the Engineering Faculty buildings. Usually, it was his slowest street because it was so steep and didn't have footpaths, meaning he would have to drive into each resident's driveway to deliver the mail. That day, Darryl stopped the bike, keeping the motor purring while he peeled off the mail from the bundle on his lap held together by a large elastic band.

At each mailbox on that steep climb, he tarried longer, listening to the beat of his own inner drum. A voice was saying again and again 'dump the mail, dump the mail man'.

By the time he had reached the top of the hill he was fully committed to his new path.

Gunning the motorbike down a rough trail used by cross country bike riders, he entered a thicket of the trees and shrubs, and cut the motor. It was two o'clock in the afternoon, about half an hour before he was due to finish his round. He climbed off his bike, stealthily looking for somewhere to conceal the rest of the mail bundles. A fallen gum lay like a lifeless skeleton just to his left beyond the trail, so he clambered through the lantana and kicked around underneath it, trying to dislodge anything reptilian hiding there. Having cleared a space, he stashed the bundles of mail into it and shoved leaves and branches over them, then stepping back, he spotted a padded envelope peeking out. He carried some more leaf litter to cover it up and satisfied with the camouflage effort, he remounted his bike and cruised slowly back to the depot along a few streets on his beat in case some little old lady was waiting for the Cross Stitch Monthly, to be delivered and reported him missing in action.

He experienced an exhilarating sense of elation as though a weight had been lifted from his shoulders, even his hang over had dissipated. He caught sight of himself in the side mirror of his motorbike and jutted his chin. When he finished the run, he returned to the depot, acting noncommittal as he bundied off for the day. His supervisor barely registered as Darryl disappeared out the door. Everything was normal.

The following day, Darryl improvised when he rang into work to say that he had to go to Brisbane, for 'tests' and would be gone for a week. He was obscure about the nature of the tests leaving to his supervisor to conjure up a spectre of fast metastasising cancers. His supervisor, Don Goodman, gave him the benefit of the doubt until he began getting calls from the residents of Lismore, asking where their mail was and why it was late. It was not the first time a postie had dumped the mail and gone missing.

'John, can I see you?'

John, was a postie all his working life with a leather bum and matching face.

'No way boss! I'm not doing any more of Darryl's run, give it to Spud,' he called out over the sorting booths.

'Take Spud and do a search in the bushes behind the university will you? I reckon Darryl has done a runner. No mail is going missing on my watch!' It was the most obvious place to hide the mail bags.

'Yeah, alright, but you owe us,' The mail was divided up between the posties doing extra shifts until Don could get a casual a week later.

* * *

Elizabeth looked out her windows waiting for the postie to bring a Spring bulbs catalogue, when she noticed a dark coloured car pull up on the opposite side of the street. Two men in suits got out of the car and began walking towards her house. Ever since Rover had died, she always kept the flyscreen doors locked, more so now she was conscious of what Frank had said about strange visitors looking for Natalie. He had cautioned her not to let anyone in the house she didn't know. There was a knock on the door, she opened it and saw two suited men, clean shaven with bland faces and white shirts.

'Mrs Mulligan, my name is Detective Sergeant Paul Condon, and my colleague is Detective Sergeant Peter Mangan.' Elizabeth stood waiting without saying anything.

'We are following up on the disappearance of your daughter, Natalie.' Condon spoke first.

'After the sad death of Andrea Mulligan. How close were they?' Mangan feigned sincerity.

'May I see your identification please?' She was politely holding back until they showed their badges, which showed they were from Byron Bay, not Lismore. Here were two detectives asking about Natalie and Andy. Why were they coming to her house, she wondered, when the crime had occurred in Sydney? Both Julie and Noel and her had given statements saying they didn't know Andy's whereabouts prior to being picked up and killed.

The two men, lanky and insolent, reminded Elizabeth of people sculpted by their prejudices after twenty years in the job. They believed in power, a law which they wielded and bent as they required.

'Can we come in and talk?' Condon a smarmy smile that made him look even more untrustworthy. Elizabeth felt chilled by his weasel words.

'No. I'm not comfortable with letting you in, detectives,' she said firmly, 'I am a grieving widow who has just lost two family members. My lawyer is arriving here shortly, please leave your card and we can arrange to come down to the station to answer any more questions you might have'. Her chin higher as she maintained her ground. It was not the first time she had stood up to the authorities on behalf of her relatives and family.

Reluctantly they agreed. 'If you hear from Natalie at all, please call us.'

'Yes, of course.' She hadn't heard anything from her daughter.

Just then the phone rang in the hall.

'Goodbye detectives. I must go now.' She closed the door on them.

'Hello Frank, it's nice to hear your voice, the police have just left'. She knew they were at the bottom step. 'You are on your way now? Oh good.'

'What did the police want?' He was curious.

'Oh, they said they were following up Natalie's disappearance. They mentioned Andrea's death and wanted to know if the girls were close. I didn't let them in.'

'I am glad to hear that,' Frank relaxed, 'did you ask for identification too?'

'Both Detective Condon and Detective Mangan were from Byron Bay police station. They asked if I had heard anything from Natalie.' There was a catch in her voice as anxiety seeped though.

'I think you are safe, they were fishing for clues and perhaps thought you knew something that would help them solve both mysteries,' reassuring her he went on, 'however you were right to not let them in.'

Her voice trembled, 'Do you think that Natalie's disappearance has anything to do with Andy's death, Frank?' He did think that, however he decided not to say so.

'You know, Elizabeth,' his tone comforting, 'I tend to think

Andy may have got into trouble with some bad people, not necessarily anything to do with Natalie.'

The next day, Elizabeth collected the mail from her letterbox and took it back inside locking the flyscreen door behind her. She put the padded envelope on the hall table then picked it up again and looked at the postage stamp. It read Alice Springs. She let a wave of emotion wash over her. Natalie is in Alice Springs with Uncle Fred she thought, no, she knew! The certainty settled on her as she opened the padded envelope and took out the contents turning it over. Freddie Mercury! Puzzled, she regarded the DVD, with the photo of a garish, young man with short hair and buck teeth. There wasn't a note, just one word written in black Texta on the front 'Rover.' She slipped the DVD back into the padded envelope and resealed it with sticky tape wrapping it around several times. Natalie was alive! She drew strength and resolve from knowing her beloved girl was safe for now. She called Frank back at the office.

'You'll need to keep acting as though nothing has changed. Have you got a pen and paper?' He gave her the Legal Aid post office box number. 'Take the package to the local post office and put it in another envelope, don't give it to the person behind the desk. Put the stamps on and address the envelope and put it in the mailbox to send it to us.'

'What will happen, Frank?'

'Don't try to contact Natalie. We'll be in touch as soon as we know what's in the envelope. It might be nothing just a way of saying to you she's still alright.'

'I will wait for you to call. Thank you and thank Diana,' She hung up, leant against the hall wall and broke into tears.

Both her boys had stayed over for a week on leave from the Army, which made her feel safer and was lovely company.

Every day she missed her husband Rover, his infectious sense of humour, his tenderness, and his curiosity. The bookshelves were lined with every type of book which was testament to his eclectic reading tastes. There were novels, histories, political analysis and autobiographies interspersed with a range of DVDs like Nelson Mandela, The Man from Snowy River and George Benson and, of course Aretha Franklin. Rover loved soul music. He also revered Gough Whitlam.

'He was the only political leader that recognised and respected Aboriginal people and their connection to their land back then,' Rover would say sagely.

She would wistfully run her hand across the books, it had been almost two years since she had held her husband and stroked his forehead. Saying goodbye was heart wrenching for her but a release from his suffering. Rover had smiled weakly, his eyes on her, then he looked up at all the family around him.

'See you mob in the dreaming.' He was gone.

Natalie was inconsolable.

CHAPTER 29

t only took a week for Legal Aid to be rehomed in an immaculate new office block with a clean functional kitchen and toilets that worked. Brenda swanned about feeling both satisfied with the change and anxious about making her staff feel secure. At least they were now on the third floor of a beautiful terracotta and green glass office building on Elizabeth Street within easy walking distance of the Central Station. Their clientele hadn't changed however the security arrangements had been strengthened with all clients and visitors having to register at the building concierge downstairs and be signed in.

Diana had taken a conscious step away from the intensity and inevitability of her romance with Frank however, she came back to work and a week later, they were sitting in a window seat of Enzo's cafe talking idly about their new workplace and what they would eat for lunch.

'Thank you, for looking after me.' She rested her hand on top of his across the table.

He gazed at her lovingly. They could hear Enzo grinding coffee.

Frank felt torn and uncertain as the ground had shifted although he was always ready to listen.

'Talk to me Diana,' they looked directly at each other.

'I am feeling mixed up,' she admitted. 'Being objective about the circumstances explains the why but not the actual effects. It's been a whirlwind of crime and misdemeanours. I've fallen for you.' His face flushed with happiness.

'But...?' He waited for her to say something more. Something. Anything.

'But I need some time to process everything. I told Dad I might go to Italy with him.'

'Diana, these past months have been the most unexpected and tumultuous of my whole life.' The food arrived. Enzo was hovering over them to get the gossip on the bombing and the love relationship.

'Enzo I'm not going to tell you about an ongoing case, and we can't jeopardise the chances of catching whoever did this.' Frank dismissed Enzo.

'Take all the time you need.' Then as an afterthought. 'Go to Italy, we can split up your caseload. Or I can get another job out of criminal law.' His words rushed out before he could bring them back.

'And do what?' Diana arranged her focaccia on her plate.

'A desk job. Be a house husband. Do some consulting when the kids go to school.' There it was, he wanted kids!

Much to his surprise, Diana burst out laughing putting her

hand up to her mouth in genuine surprise and mirth.

'Hold that thought, Frank Phelan. She urged, 'it has potential.'

At this point he reflected briefly on the right time to propose to her. He would wait until he had a ring. Instead, he changed the subject.

'There is a card saying there is a package waiting at the Post Office it may be evidence of what has happened to Natalie Mulligan.'

'I'm with you Frank, what do you want to do?'

'The package is at the Haymarket post office. Elizabeth forwarded it to us. Usually, Madeleine or whoever is going to the Downing Centre will pick up the mail from the locked box,' he held up a key and waggled it, 'I put up my hand as I suspect this is something important related to the case.'

'The bombing was to scare us off the case, I believe, and Natalie's disappearance is related to Andy's death, though I don't know how.'

'My thoughts exactly!' They paid for their meals and said goodbye to Enzo.

'We can't take it back to Legal Aid.' She stressed.

'We could leave it right where it is for now?' Frank chewed his lip.

'No, we have a responsibility to those girls to act.'

'Yes, you're right.'

'How about we jump in a cab and go to see Mike? Then at least it will be out of our hands and with a law enforcer we trust.'

'Good thinking.'

The two lawyers set off and crossed Elizabeth Street at the

lights walking down Eddy Avenue until they reached the imposing brutalist office block on Pitt Street that housed a food court, a Post Office and the Department of Education.

'Let's come back through the food court and ask security to help out – show them our identity?'

'Give me the key, Frank and stand guard.' They reached the post office boxes which were tucked into the side alcove next to the customer service area. She opened the box and casually stuffed the contents of the Legal Aid locked box into her handbag included a padded package addressed to Frank, the size of a slim paperback novel. Frank stood behind her facing out.

'Okay, let's go.' Diana moved off having locked the box.

They wound their way through the novelty shops and the food outlets holding hands and looking casual. The security facility for the whole building took up a corner of the ground floor and looked out on the lifts through two wall-length plate glass windows.

The two lawyers approached the office, extracted their identity cards and walked into the office and up to a bench where a man in his forties wearing a security uniform was watching monitors behind the screen. Diana explained they were Legal Aid lawyers, whose office had been bombed and they were expected at the Major Crime Gang office.'

The guard watched her, keenly interested.

'What can I do for you Miss Gianiovellis. That was a frightening event we saw it on the telly.'

'It was indeed,' she agreed.

Frank spoke up, 'We would appreciate an escort to hail a

cab as we have papers to deliver, we don't want them falling into the wrong hands.'

'Too easy.'

'I'm flagging these people a cab. Back in a minute,' the man addressed his partner in the Security Office. The three of them made their way through the revolving doors onto Pitt Street and hailed a passing cab.

'Will you be right now?' He held the door open for Diana who sat sideways and swivelled her legs around.

'Yes. Thanks, mate.' Frank got in the opposite side leaned forward and said to the driver, 'Take us to Yurong Street please. I'll direct you.'

'Over here driver thanks,' Frank pulled out his wallet and peeled off twenty bucks.

For the second time, Frank found himself back at Mike's office, the invisible building blending into the top end of Yurong Street, opposite the Jewish School. Only this time, it was him and Diana waiting downstairs for Mike to sign them in. Frank looked at the DVD before returning it to Diana.

'Let's hope it is what we think it is,' Diana put it back in her bag.

'The package is postmarked Alice Springs.'

'Frank, Diana,' Mike briefly shook their hands, 'A bit unexpected. Let's go upstairs to the meeting room, it has electronics.'

Mike signed the visitors in, and they entered the lift together without saying much until the doors closed.

'We have a DVD sent by Natalie Mulligan to her mother, Elizabeth. None of us has seen it yet however it could explain why Natalie disappeared and why the mafia have been busy looking for her.' They filed out of the lift when it got to the third floor. Mike led the way and zipped his security card in the slot for the meeting room.

Diana handed Mike the package.

'Freddy Mercury?' Mike frowned questioningly at Frank, then back at Diana.

Taking the disc out of its case Mike slipped it into a DVD player sitting below a television screen and pressed 'Play'.

After the opening lines of Stairway to Heaven, there was a scooting noise followed by a piece of blank tape which segued into the film that captured five men discussing drug dealing inside the hangar at the Tyagarah airfield. The sound of the conversation was clear, moreover the intention of the meeting was unambiguous. They watched the first few minutes saying nothing absorbed by the conversation.

Mike whistled. 'Holy shit! No wonder the mob are after you. That's Luigi Grollo, a mob kingpin from around Griffith and Stanthorpe. That other guy, is Con Grollo his son.'

'We think the Māori guy is Brendon Papatui, might be the last person to see Natalie,' Frank added, 'see those two guys? They are DS Condon and DS Mangan from Byron Bay Drugs Squad.'

'Natalie obviously did a drug run with them and saw their faces.' Diana said.

Mike reached for the phone and dialled a secure line out. 'This is dynamite. Sorry Diana no pun intended.'

'Andrew Fullilove,' he covered the mouthpiece. 'You remember him, Frank?'

'Andrew, we have an evidence tape that will nail Luigi Grollo on the missing woman and maybe link them to the recent bombing of Legal Aid.' Mike listened.

'Yeah, believe me, it's kosher. I wish we always had evidence like this. Andrew, there's a couple of bent detectives involved.' Frank was writing names on a post-it he handed to Mike. 'Hang on, DS Paul Condon and DS Peter Mangan, both in Byron Bay Drug Squad.' He nodded thanks to Frank, his face serious. 'The DVD was posted to the lawyers for the missing woman, Natalie Mulligan. Hang on I'll check.'

Frank and Diana looked at Mike expectantly, 'It was sent to Natalie's mother?'

'Yes,' Frank responded, 'I asked her to forward anything. It's got an Alice Springs postmark.'

'Where is Mrs Mulligan?'

'I told her to stay close to home and make sure her family was with her.'

'Hi Andrew, the tape comes via Mrs Mulligan. My advice is put a cop on the Mulligan place first before you act on the bent cops.' He listened. 'No, we don't know about the dead woman other than she was Natalie Mulligan's cousin,' he confirmed. 'Okay, we'll see you soon.' He hung up the phone and dialled an internal number, 'Xenophon, come into Room 202, will you? Bring the evidence registration kit.'

'That will get the ball rolling,' Mike's voice was charged and determined. A tap on the door and a young officer enters with a camera.

'Xenophon, I need to remind you that you have signed the Federal Secrets Act, a warranty and that anything you see or hear in this room must be held as totally secret by you or you will be prosecuted and jailed. Do you understand?'

The young man, who wore glasses and a blue uniform,

paled, visibly taken aback.

'Yes, sir.'

'Okay then, this evidence is top secret, we need a record of having receipted it and have it recorded and registered that only the people in this room know its contents, that we know.'

Then to Frank and Diana. 'Sorry for the delay, we just have some insurance bureaucracy to do before Andrew gets here to view the tape.' Once completed, Mike signed the documents which were filed into the top-secret file.

'Who else knows about the existence of this tape?' Mike addressed them.

'I'm not sure,' Diana pondered, 'we figured the mob were after something when they broke into my flat. Perhaps they were trying to get an address for Natalie? We didn't know about the tape.'

'I would say only Elizabeth, the mum.' Frank calculated the repercussions of this explosive evidence. 'I told her not to open it but to forward it to us discreetly. We came here as soon as we collected it.'

'You did the right thing. If they find Natalie, they will kill her.'

'We now know Natalie was working undercover for C.A.S.S. tracking pilots who were transporting drugs and that she got involved with Papatui, doing a drug run.'

'I'd like you to stay here until Andrew arrives so you can brief him on everything you know. I'll get my team onto the warrants and the Rapid Response team to pick up the Grollo clan. Do you want a cuppa or something?'

'Yes please,' Diana said.

Over the next hour a major operation began. Mike briefed

his team, got warrants for the mob, for the bent cops' homes and bank accounts. He organised a large team to move in and pick up the henchmen and impound the vehicles and any crops in the barns. He notified customs to watch for and pick up Brendon Papatui. He ordered them to hold everyone without bail until they had consolidated the evidence.

Once things were in motion he came back into the room with cups of tea and biscuits and sat down with Frank and Diana. They were joined by Commander Andrew Fullilove, now head of policing for the State of New South Wales, a thin, hawkish-looking man in his late fifties, his beard kept short was shot through with grey, modified his hooked nose, even his shoes shone with military precision.

'Commander, you remember, Frank Phelan?' Mike made the introductions, 'and this is Diana Gianiovellis his colleague. You met Diana briefly when the office for Legal Aid was bombed.' Fullilove stepped forward and formally shook hands.

'Good to see you again. I am surprised Legal Aid was mixed up in mob reprisals,' he observed dryly. 'I shall be briefing the Commissioner and the Minister. First, I'd like to get the story from you as you are closest to the coalface.' He sat down at one of the tables ready to listen. Someone brought him a cup of tea. He nodded thanks.'

Fullilove had seen the tape before talking to Frank and Diana.

Over the next hour they went through the story of Natalie Mulligan disappearing. How they took the case for the Mulligan family, the discovery of Andrea's body, the robbery and all the events leading up to the bombing and collecting the tape. They were sure the DVD tape was from Natalie because it had been sent to her mother. A police stenographer recorded everything, including impressions and intuitions the lawyers expressed.

'I wonder if Natalie made a copy of this tape?' Diana speculated aloud. They had all watched the casual conversation about killing Natalie and moving the drugs.

'Extra insurance. It's been filmed from above the men talking,' she observed 'You saw how the angle has been tilted and they are in an aircraft hangar?'

'The camera looks like it is set up in a plane's wingtips. She may have a copy made in case parts of it get obliterated.' Mike suggested. Mike walked him outside, 'I'll get someone to drop you back at your office.'

CHAPTER 30

‘You don't have a very good track record with women. The first one died, the second one nearly drowned then left you for a war zone and now, the third one got robbed and bombed by the mafia.’

‘That's harsh, Mike.’

‘Well, it's true! Objectively speaking.’

‘In my defence, I was not directly responsible for any of those events. I think I am a steady kind of guy.’ Frank rebutted his friend, despite feeling it may be true.

‘It doesn't look good, mate.’

‘What do you mean by ‘not good’?’

‘I mean, irrespective of your commitment and intentions, Diana is weighing up whether you are a safe enough guy to marry and have kids.’

‘You think so?’ Frank was taken aback.

The two friends were sitting on stools at a window table

in the Admiral Hotel in Woolloomooloo, looking out at the wharves as the squally wind chopped the surface of the ocean beyond their window. It was a chilly, overcast afternoon in Sydney, and Frank felt a sinking sensation that maybe, he was losing Diana.

On one level he understood. It had been a rocky ride. He hardly swept her off her feet with romance and flowers. Except for the Law Ball, when she initiated transcendental sex and the earth moved. Probably the rollers on the leather armchair. Afterwards though? Later that night in her bed? When they made love. That was exquisite, he sighed, reliving the feeling.

Mike was looking at him measuring the amount of ego damage versus the need to tell his friend what he was doing wrong. He opted for the latter.

'Listen, Frank, typically women are the ones making decisions about having kids and wanting a stable family life. Diana needs to know that you want a safe loving environment too. That's why I am on a desk job. Ally and I had a conversation, and I chose her. I chose us and our life together over being out on the edge and bringing the druggies and scumbags to justice.'

Frank agreed. Surely Diana knew he wanted a safe life for her?

They both drank their beers and were quiet for a few moments.

Even after the criminals were caught and the mafia and the cult members were facing trials and jail, Diana seemed a little distant, he acknowledged.

'Another beer?' Mike indicated to Frank's glass with his own empty one.

'One more, light,' Frank agreed.

Mike walked over to the busy bar where a gaggle of young bucks in suits with long tan, shoes were making a noise. He carried the glasses back to the table. When he put the beers down Frank looked up at him with an expression of, 'What should I do?' How could he resolve this? Mike responded.

'Look, Diana loves you and you love her. You need to talk to her about marriage and the future and then ask her what she needs to make that work.'

'Good advice, mate.' Frank took another sip of his drink and repressed the desire to run out of the building, jump in his car and drive over to Diana's, armed with this information.

'Marriage is about negotiating a way to have a fulfilling life together. Loving the person is not enough. It's where you begin however, it's more about the commitment and willingness to make it work for all of you.'

'And the sex?'

'Always. You know what they say?'

'Guess I've been married to the job, Mike. I don't have a lot of experience in successful long-term relationships.'

'Maybe you should get another job, Frank. One with better pay and more job security. You'll need it when you have kids. Labor just got into New South Wales, so that's helpful for a place at Attorney General's somewhere the mafia has no influence.' Mike took a sip of his beer.

'Didn't your sister just get elected to Canada Bay?'

'Yeah, but I can't ask Genie for a job. It's called nepotism.'

'Never been a problem for the Labor Party before.' Mike said with a wry look.

They finished their drinks. Mike slid off his seat and checked his watch.

'Gotta go, I'm picking up the kids from after-school sports.' It was a bit after five o'clock and the weather hadn't improved.

He leaned in and gave Mike a hug, patting his back. The friends walked together along the street pulling their jackets up against the damp wind.

'Look forward to the next catch-up. Come and have dinner soon, Ally would love to see you. And Diana.'

'Thanks, mate. I will.' Frank opened his car door and climbed in.

Later, when he got home to his spacious industrial apartment, he walked in and turned the lights, heating, and news on. It still felt empty. Diana had been staying with her parents whilst she was on leave after the bombing. He called her and asked her to lunch with him tomorrow, which was a Saturday.

'That would be lovely. Want to meet somewhere or will you pick me up?'

'I'll pick you up how about half past twelve at your mum's?'

'See you then. I must go, I'm cooking tonight.'

Warmed up from contact, he considered this thing called love, when you can't bear to spend a night alone. Mike's words resonated. What a hell of a ride from the time in Nimbin with April, and the murder of Andrea by the mafia. The bombing of Legal Aid and Diana being injured. It was the first time in months he'd been able to sit outside their situation. He got it. Looking up his Filofax he found Meredith Mason, now the Attorney General of New South Wales. He'd kept her home phone number.

'Frank! Great to hear from you,' she was genuinely pleased.

'Congratulations on the job, Meredith.' He felt remiss, but she quickly dispelled his misgivings.

'What about you? Murder, mayhem, and mafia?' She commented, 'I've been in the party too long, keep thinking in three-word slogans. God how exciting!'

'I'm good, Meredith, though I have done my time with crooks. They are too dangerous.'

'Are you single Frank?' That came out of nowhere thought Frank.

'No, I am seeing someone.' He leaned over and turned Miles Davis down.

'We could use someone here, Frank. Would you consider working for the State?'

'Sounds like a good plan at this stage of my life, Meredith,' he could hear rustling papers. Someone in the background, presumably one of her kids, was asking when dinner was ready.

'Good. Here we go, we're sitting this week and I've got time on Tuesday afternoon. Meet me in the Traveller's café in Macquarie Street, around three, I'll shout you a coffee and I want to hear all the dirt on the mafia too.'

'I'll be there. It's good to catch up. Been awhile.'

'See you, Frank.'

'Bye Meredith.' Frank hung up. He had a light sensation. 'That went well.' He announced aloud, pleased with himself.

* * *

Sydney has a truly magnificent climate and true to form, the day shone beautifully across the city. Frank picked up Diana from her parents' house and took her to Bar Italia, on Norton Street in Leichhardt, where they ordered fettuccini porcini and after walked up the street for a coffee and dessert, stopping to talk to people Diana knew from her childhood. It seemed she knew everyone they passed. The older ones would kiss her and send love to her parents giving the eagle eye to Frank. Diana introduced them and, given that she linked her arm in his, and they were comfortably intimate, denying their relationship would be silly.

'This is Frank Phelan, my beau. We met at work.' Diana was moved by the happiness expressed by people in the community who launched into Italian assuming he was, of course, Italian.

'Frank is embracing his inner Italian. Give him time.' Her dark eyes shone. They strolled on further until they reached another coffee shop.

'It's been quite a while since connecting to the people we used to know,' she reminisced, 'Dad had a practice on Marion Street.' They slowed and Frank stood in front of her.

'Diana, I love you! Will you marry me? I want to hold you close every night. I'll even go to church again.' He had practised his speech and now they were face to face, he wanted to express all his love and commitment to her.

'You know that marrying me is marrying my whole noisy, effusive family? I have spent years backing my mum out of my life. Dad is different he is naturally shy.'

'I like that sort of family life. I haven't had enough of it and being with Genie and Dan reminded me how much I miss family life. I want that life with you.'

They walked arm in arm. He felt the need for further declarative statements.

'Honestly, darling,' he said emphatically, 'I am a steady-state sort of guy. My past girlfriends found me boring.' Self-deprecatory and earnest, he looked into her eyes.

'Not a hero then, Mr Phelan?' she quipped.

'Only by accident. I just did the decent thing when an injustice was presented to me,' he gazed at her, pleased at having found a narrative that made sense to both.

'I don't want any more danger,' he reiterated.

'I guess, having only met you in January, I wanted to work out what a normal relationship might look like.'

'Does this mean you do want to marry me?'

'Did you seriously doubt that?' She pulled back looking directly up at him.

'I love you, Frank Phelan. I have never loved anyone this way and it terrifies me. I cannot imagine living a day without you. What if something were to happen to you?'

The words came tumbling out. Words Diana hadn't articulated, even to herself. After a few months of being targeted, robbed, and bombed, she was scared she would lose him. Just as he was afraid, he would lose her.

'You've been reserved,' he stumbled. It sounded obvious and clumsy.

'I will do anything to make you feel happy and safe. Anything.' He pulled her closer and hugged her to his chest rubbing his face in her hair, which smelt heavenly. His heart burst as they kissed each other passionately on the mouth right there on Norton Street. And that was that.

CHAPTER 31

Frank Phelan liked being a married man and concluded that he wasn't a commitment phobe after all, and hadn't delayed matrimony. He just hadn't met the right woman. He married the Labor Party and remained committed for two decades. He and Diana were married in a suburban brick church built in 1880. It snuggled into the fabric of the street and was covered with flowering camellias and variegated ivy. Directly opposite, sat a corner pub of the same vintage, God and grog thought Frank, when they went to inspect the premises for the nuptials. It's the Australian way. Claudia and Val were over the moon, and Val beamed as he walked Diana down the aisle. She wore a knee-length ivory satin dress with an embroidered fitted bodice. Simple and utterly elegant. A string of pearls with earrings matched a piece of lace pinned with cream roses on her head. Her sister Izzy, had spent two hours on her hair. Frank Senior, couldn't have been happier for his son as he sat upright on the Phelan side of the aisle with sister Genie, Dan and their kids. The reception was held in the Italian Club in Ashfield, with family and friends including Brenda, with Marcus Guthrie in tow. Having left his wife in Mosman, Judge Guthrie swore his undying love to Brenda, whose desk still hid a handgun.

Once the case against the smugglers and the cult leaders was cemented, Detective Chief Inspector Olaf Petersen, returned to Melbourne where he grew restless and felt ungrounded. Australia, he concluded, had no borders with other countries with different customs and cultures. Unlike Europe. He yearned for the deep history of European life. Even the big cities in Australia seemed to hover above the earth, rather than being embedded within it. Like a mirage in the desert. He rang Greg Foreman and the team in Tweed Heads on a conference call to say goodbye and pass on his contact details in Rome, where he relocated, with the Carabinieri Nationale Contra Mafioso. Once there, he settled into an apartment on the side of one of Rome's seven hills and met an Italian divorcee, who taught adult education classes run by the American University of Rome. She took Ancient Roman History, including weekly field trips to historic sites. Confident and sensual, Maria Lombardo, flirted with everyone. Or was it his imagination? He fantasised about her while trying to read the life of Cicero. One class excursion to the Capitoline Hill in late August, he and two other students turned up. A warm summer shower began to fall. The weather got worse, and the two young students abandoned the class, leaving Olaf and Maria to run into a two-thousand-year-old atrium, dripping with water. He opened his raincoat and pulled her inside smelling her damp musky warmth as she pressed against him. He felt totally alive, right in the moment, his skin and senses tingling as he folded her into his body.

The spiritual carpetbagging business took a bit of practice for Kevin Bogan. He managed a few runs at different religious sects looking for a fit. Some of them wanted the sort of zeal he was unable to give, while others were less prescriptive.

'The fuck!' he muttered as he left the Church of Christ's Passion, one evening. 'Who wants to sit around holding hands and reciting crap. It's not an AA meeting.'

The Evangelicals were more expansive and individualistic. They stressed the authenticity of a personal experience of God, or the holy spirit or whoever floated their boat. Kevin plumbed human nature categorising the different types of people involved in sects and cults with stereotypes. For example, the True Believers, the Talent, the Sheep, the Earnest, the Sinners, the Seekers, the Con Artists and the Needy. To boil it down, the barriers he confronted, relative to his initial motivation of finding 'a nice little earner', were many. Firstly, the social aspect. It meant hanging out with a bunch of flaky people he didn't like and pretending he believed the bullshit they were into. Secondly, there were organisational barriers. He had to join an organisation and stick it out until he was in control. Then there was a personal dimension. Kevin wasn't a con man by nature. What you saw was what you got, he liked to say. Instead, he picked up some work cleaning pools in the suburbs, rather than going out west to the mines. Sitting at a bar one afternoon, cradling a beer and reading the Telegraph newspaper, his eyes fell on a report of the trial that occupied a single column on page two. According to the reporter, the Movement was disbanded and classified as a cult, while the Elders or Zelwags, were all sentenced to prison time. The Asian smugglers, also part of an extensive people smuggling racket, were imprisoned for years, before they would be extradited home to Malaysia to face the music there. Life moved on for the seekers: they grew up or found another cause or joined a Pentecostal church, regardless, none of them were found guilty of breaking the law. There was no mention of Seth in the article. Excellent, thought Kevin! No mention either of police looking for another party (him) to help them with their inquiries. As it happened, Seth was released from police custody with a warning, once he had given them all the information he had on the Zelwags. He never divulged anything on Kevin Bogan and his role as a minder. The whole event was a close encounter with a prison cell. Seth toyed with giving up dope until the air cleared but rejected the idea and got a job in a surf shop in the centre of Byron Bay instead. He could remain stoned and content with doing as little work as possible.

Natalie called her mum once she had negotiated with the police to return and give evidence, which was corroborated by Trevor Cane of C.A.S.S. In a surprise move, she applied to be a pilot with the Flying Doctors Service based in Alice Springs, which she got at the phone interview hands down.

Having been granted immunity for her evidence she gave back the money for the drug run out of Tyagarah. She bid farewell to her mum and brothers and lifted the Beechcraft and her dog into the azure skies. Uncle Fred was waiting for her as she flew into his camp late one afternoon.

Lucy Lush Box ditched her phony spiritual name, the one Seth had found in the furniture catalogue while waiting for a Thai takeaway, and joined a cult-busting organisation. Her evidence against the mob was damming, as was Natalie's, meaning the cops arrested the whole network including, the big boss Luigi Grollo and his son, Con. Andy had torn a nail struggling to get free of the thug who killed her, so the forensics team found blood between the back seat of the four-wheel drive used to kidnap her. The mobsters overlooked the evidence, and police were able to piece together her fate concluding, it was a case of stupidity, mistaking her for Natalie. The man at the Post Office was taken into custody and subsequently tried and jailed for being an accessory to murder.

April Moreland was feeling beaten up by her first posting as a war correspondent. The injuries from the car bomb she would recover from, the emotional and mental trauma of watching her friend die, and the terror she experienced, would take longer. Maybe forever. Jake Abraham, from the Globe, called her when he saw the news of the bombing. Later, she accepted his offer and flew to Boston for a visit. He was standing at the Arrivals Gate as she walked off the plane with a limp in one leg from the knee reconstruction. On seeing his face above all the passengers and visitors, she gave him a shy wave. He looked just as she had imagined, wearing a faded pair of Levi jeans with a loose red college sweatshirt as a layer against a cool evening breeze. His face was creased, his grey hair needed a cut and rimless glasses completed the effect of a distracted professor that belied his sharp incisive mind.

"Hi, you,' he greeted her taking her luggage, guiding her by the elbow.

'Howdy stranger,' she leaned on him for support.

'Want to go for a drink?'

'Sure. Love to.'

Notoriety preceded Stereo 'Elvis' Villanova, taking up residence at Long Bay's minimum-security wing. Everyone had seen the television footage of his daring escape attempt at the Downing Centre. It was played again and again on television, as witness to his flamboyant chutzpah. By the time he was sentenced, he was a bit of a legend with the inmates. Hell! The collective summation went, in the exercise yard and at the dining table: if that skinny, coked up, Elvis wanna-be, punk arse could get to the door of freedom – then so could anyone of them. Moreover, Elvis the artist, being very popular in jails all over the Western World, made Stereo's sojourn in custody bearable. Rather than being some biker's 'wog bitch', he became a celebrity performer and before long was putting on concerts in Elvis drag after dinner, every Friday night including, renditions of Johnny Cash, Tom Jones, and other crooners of the genre. Stereo's passion for all things Elvis, was a positive effect on morale, especially for the lifers. He organised an Elvis fan club, lobbied for Elvis's movies to be a regular feature on Sundays and traded singing lessons for other favours. His piece de resistance, however, was to organise an Elvis Festival every year at the same time as the event on the outside in Parkes, Western New South Wales. The Channel 9 television, obligingly did an annual follow-up story on the event featuring Stereo in full Elvis regalia singing Jailhouse Rock accompanied by all the other Elvis fans in jail.

Many months had passed by the time Frank and Mike, his best man at the wedding, caught up for a beer at the Admiral Hotel on the Woolloomooloo Wharf.

'You're looking good mate,' Mike noticed, 'wet nose, glossy coat.'

'Thanks. Attorney General's Department suits me,' Frank's eyes shone as he took a sip of cold beer, 'so does marriage. I love it!'

'How many weeks has Diana got to go?'

'She's on mat leave now. Baby is due any day.'

'Exciting,' Mike enthused.

'Got any advice for me? You've done this three times now.'

'Yep. Some things should remain a mystery.'

'What do you mean?'

'Stay next to Diana's head and hold her hand and avoid checking out how a small watermelon can pass through the birth canal.'

'Right. Anything else?'

'Don't take anything she says as a personal rejection during labour. It's not about you.'

'That's sound advice mate. I'm a bit nervous. The gyno suggested I was a 'geriatric first-time father,' Frank confessed sheepishly. Mike chortled, highly amused.

'Welcome to forty. You'll be fine Frank Phelan. Call me. Let us know she's arrived.'

'You can count on it.'

Frank and Diana gave birth to a baby girl with black hair and blue eyes, weighing eight pounds and three ounces. They named her Giuliana Claudia Gianiovellis Phelan. Frank thought he would melt into a puddle with love.

THE END

ACKNOWLEDGEMENTS

This book is dedicated to my beloved brother Roger for his humour and generosity of spirit and to his wife, Susan for her kindness and support. Thank you both from the bottom of my heart. Always, my boundless love and appreciation goes to my children Alex and Sarah who have barracked for me throughout this writing life. They made many wonderful and thoughtful contributions and are invaluably honest. To my wider family and friends who declared it 'a good story', a big thank you.

My thanks and appreciation to Luke Harris of Working Type for his professional work, brilliant skills, his patience, creativity, artwork and knowledge of our industry, I literally couldn't have done it without him.

I would like to acknowledge and thank my editorial sleuths Bryce de l'Epine and Felicity Holmes for their fastidious attention to detail and good faith. The red pen rules! To my readers Linda Bottari, Jaleen Caples and Libby Summerfield thank you for your insights, time and suggestions as you make me a better author.

Thankfully I have the wisdom and experience of the eminent Mr Richard Potter SC and am so glad to have him in my corner recommending I kill off some of 'my darlings' rather than be sued. I have loved chatting about the evolution of the law and war movies with him over coffee. I acknowledge the Bunjalung people and pay respects to them and their ancestors past and present as custodians of the lands on which much of this story occurred.

Like many books, mine began with a short story about a bunch of corrupt officials, a mafia scion, a grand plan for an airstrip situated on a glorious hinterland and a cult. Perfect for a crime really. However, this book was some time in its realisation as it was bookended (no pun intended) by massive global events involving climate change and flooding and the soul crushing emptiness of Covid in a regional setting. In short it was a battle. Now I am back home in Sydney, my relief is visceral as I catch myself staring at the city horizons with warm affection. This feeling of coming home inspired my third book which is about a local murder and a love letter to Sydney. As other writers can attest, we write into an archetypal future of possibility. For those friends and readers that embrace Frank Phelan, a decent bloke at a career crossroads, and wondered what he would do with his life after politics, I hope you're satisfied with the outcome.

The last acknowledgement goes to the storytellers that came before me. To all the women, and Indigenous women are overrepresented in this group, who have gone missing and not been found, who have been dismissed or written off and erased and disappeared from history. I want to acknowledge you and your lives. And finally, to my readers you are what drives me to tell stories and improve. It is humbling when people enjoy them and lose themselves. If that's you then don't hesitate to tell your friends, give the book to someone for Christmas or ask for it at your local bookshop and library. Personal engagement and word of mouth is the human in the humanity of storytelling.

The crime fiction ecosystem in Australia is vibrant and growing thanks to all those writers, readers and the book industry who sustain and nurture its diversity. I am proud to join my Sisters in Crime in this endeavour and welcome the surge of women writers. Thank you to all those crime writers you are truly inspirational!

www.ingramcontent.com/pod-product-compliance
Lightning Source LLC
Chambersburg PA
CBHW070846260626
47170CB00007B/2518